'AFTER~DARK'
TALES

By the same author

Tales, Weird And Whimsical   ISBN   0 9527388 1 3
Encounters With Plain Ghosts   ISBN   0 9527388 0 5
Tales From The Dark Side   ISBN   0 9527388 2 1
An Invitation To The Curious   ISBN   0 9527388 3 X

Frontispiece   The Tower and Spire, Ormskirk Parish Church

'AFTER~DARK'
TALES

T. M. LALLY

HOMESTEAD

BOOKS
ORMSKIRK LANCASHIRE

Homestead Books,
32 Heathey Lane, Shirdley Hill,
Ormskirk, Lancashire, L39 8SH

Although inspired by actual locations and real events, past and present, these stories are entirely fictional. Any similarity to persons living or dead is purely coincidental.

British Library Cataloguing in Publication Data:
A CIP record of this book will be available from the British Library.

ISBN   0 9527388 4 8

Cover Design/Composite Illustrations/Situation Plans & 'Plain Ghost Trail' Sources Map: by the author.

Printed and bound in Great Britain by
Independent Reprographics,
Unit B23 The Malthouse Business Centre,
48, Southport Road, Ormskirk,
Lancashire, L39 1QR..

CONTENTS

To my wife and to all those loyal readers who have found pleasure in these ghostly tales.

ILLUSTRATIONS

SITUATION GUIDES

THE PLAIN GHOST TRAIL

TALES, WEIRD AND WHIMSICAL
(1) PIKE'S LANTERN
(2) THE BARN
(3) PEPPER-POT COTTAGE
(4) CANAL BRIDGE 14
(5) THE RAFFLE PRIZE
(6) A LIGHT ACROSS THE MOSS
(7) THE FIREPLACE
(8) BOLTON'S STONE
(9) JUMBLE
(10) PUSH AND PULL PADDY

ENCOUNTERS-PLAIN GHOSTS
(11) THE BRIAR PIPE
(12) VARIATION ON A CIRCLE
(13) KEEPER'S COTTAGE
(14) STAINED GLASS
(15) LADY MARGARET'S ECHO
(16) NOCTURNE
(17) SOME WAY OR OTHER
(18) BRIC-a-BRAC
(19) POACHER'S MOON
(20) UNCLE CHARLIE'S CLUB

NOT TO SCALE

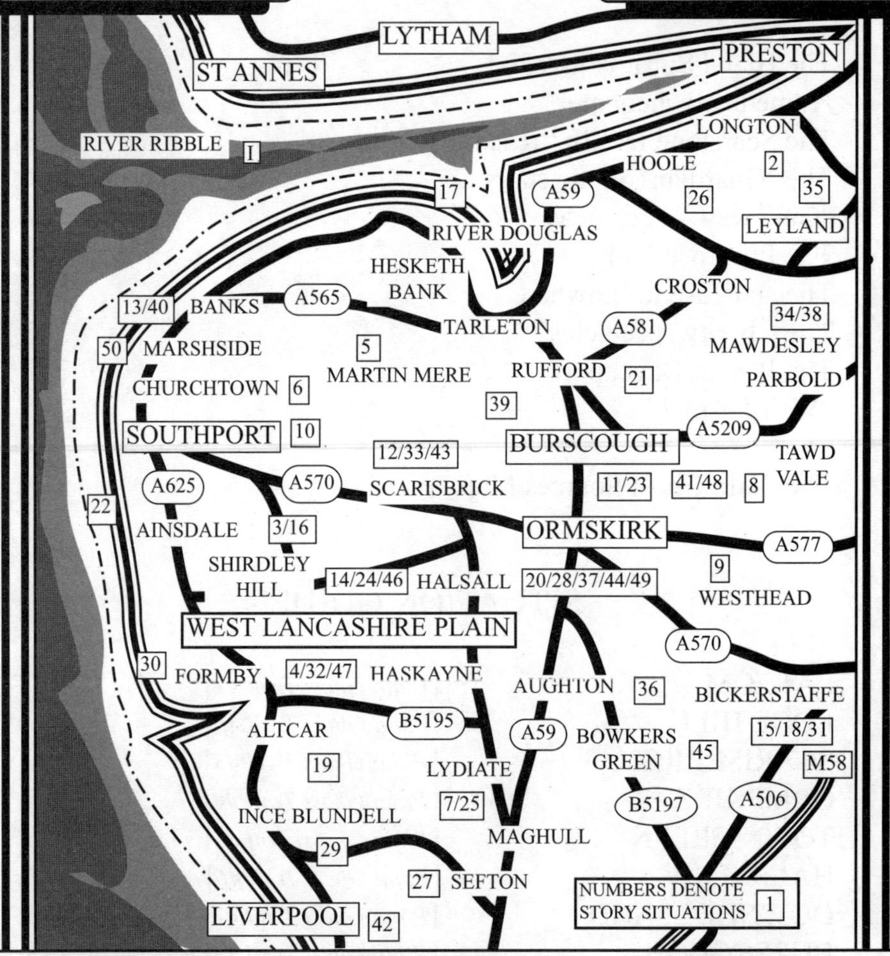

TALES FROM THE DARK SIDE
(21) AN INVITATION TO DINE
(22) STORM WARNING
(23) FOOTSTEPS
(24) PART EXCHANGE
(25) THE POTATO CUP
(26) THE MARVELLOUS PROOF
(27) I AM NOT THERE
(28) A WALL WITH A VIEW
(29) RITES AND CEREMONIES
(30) A FAMILY VISIT

INVITATION TO THE CURIOUS
(31) WHEN THE NORTH WIND
(32) THE REGENCY CLOCK
(33) THE STAIN
(34) ON HARROCK HILL
(35) NO DAY WITHOUT ITS LINE
(36) PADDY'S PATCH
(37) THE GOODS THEREIN
(38) THE MURDSLEY STEPS
(39) MERTON HALL
(40) RALPH'S WIFE

AFTER-DARK TALES
(41) THE BLAND SPIRIT
(42) THE FIFTH JOURNAL
(43) THE SACRED CROWN
(44) INHERITED PECULIARITY
(45) DUST
(46) DO NOT DISTURB
(47) THINGS THAT GO BUMP
(48) OH, YES THERE IS!
(49) THE POCKET DAVENPORT
(50) THE GHOST WALK

Map locations and labels:

LYTHAM
ST ANNES
PRESTON
RIVER RIBBLE [1]
LONGTON
HOOLE [2] [35]
A59 [26] LEYLAND
RIVER DOUGLAS [17]
HESKETH BANK
CROSTON
BANKS [13/40] A565
MARSHSIDE [50]
TARLETON
A581
MAWDESLEY [34/38]
MARTIN MERE [5]
RUFFORD [21]
PARBOLD
CHURCHTOWN [6]
[39]
SOUTHPORT [10]
BURSCOUGH
A5209
A625 A570 [12/33/43]
SCARISBRICK
TAWD VALE
AINSDALE [22]
[11/23] [41/48] [8]
[3/16]
ORMSKIRK
A577
SHIRDLEY HILL
[14/24/46] HALSALL [20/28/37/44/49]
[9]
WEST LANCASHIRE PLAIN
WESTHEAD
A570
[30] FORMBY [4/32/47] HASKAYNE
AUGHTON [36]
BICKERSTAFFE
ALTCAR B5195
A59 BOWKERS GREEN
[15/18/31]
[19] LYDIATE
[45] M58
INCE BLUNDELL
[7/25]
B5197 A506
[29]
MAGHULL
[27] SEFTON
LIVERPOOL [42]

NUMBERS DENOTE STORY SITUATIONS [1]

AUTHOR'S NOTE

as to the inspirational sources from which the following tales are derived.

After-dark Tales is the fifth volume in the '*Tales*' series of ghost stories set in and around the West Lancashire Plain, and follows the same pattern as the first, second, third and fourth books (*Tales weird and whimsical, Encounters with Plain Ghosts, Tales from the Dark Side* and *An Invitation to the Curious*) respectively. Once again the supernatural stories in *After-dark Tales* have been inspired by local architectural and geographical features, historical events and folklore.

The Bland Spirit is set in Blythe Hall, Lathom, where Ivor Novello, Noel Coward, Gertrude Lawrence and other famous guests came from London to spend theatrical weekends with the Earl of Lathom in the 1920's, and is the focus of an unwelcome 'spirit' in a family seance. A part of Neville Street covered by the Promenade in Southport, and Joseph Williamson, the Mole of Edge Hill, and his 'lost' tunnels, recently discovered beneath the City of Liverpool, are the inspiration for *The Fifth Journal*. A Victorian Hall (designed by Pugin, the famous architect) with its truncated tower and secluded position in the woods in Scarisbrick, was once owned by one of the richest 'commoners' in the country and is now a private school. It is home to a valuable medieval collection of paintings and wood carvings, one of which inspired *The Sacred Crown*.

In *An Inherited Peculiarity*, a mock-gothic house in Ormskirk hosts the protective and vengeful wooden 'angel', one of several replaced by stone carvings in the chancel of a local church, and a cuff link found in the grounds of Mosscroft Hall, demolished to make way for a golf course, is the inspiration for *Dust*. Old sandstone posts, now devoid of their gates and with no apparent use, can be seen in the country lanes around Ormskirk, standing at the edge

11

of open fields. A very unusual gatepost of this kind is the basis for *Do Not Disturb*. The modern replacement of an ancient stone cross during the millennium celebrations, coupled with the peculiar staircase in Downholland Hall, gave rise to *Things That Go Bump In The Night*. A much loved pantomime performed on the stage of a village hall is the scene of strange happenings in the story *"Oh Yes There Is"*, when a pair of spectacles from the Lathom Charity, founded over three hundred years ago, invite the ghostly attentions of an unauthorized member of the cast.

An unusual antique with a secret religious purpose and a macabre secret, linked to a Civil War tragedy and an ancient family vault in Ormskirk Parish Church, are the principal ingredients in *The Pocket Davenport*. A derelict weather station, with its fog bell (installed in 1896 after a tragic drowning incident) and treacherous salt marshes and bird sanctuary on the Ribble estuary near the village of Marshside, is the setting for *The Ghost Walk*. It is the place where a fund-raising event ends. However, for one little girl in the party it is the start of a daunting experience and a 'ghost walk' into the past.

It will come as no surprise to readers of other books in the series to find the same haunting mixture in these ghostly tales. A light-hearted seance that goes badly wrong, an indoor game of bowls using a gruesome jack, or a unique writing desk with its grisly secret — such are the constituents of an unsettling, not to say unnerving, collection of uncanny stories.

This scary concoction of supernatural ingredients in *After-dark Tales* should appeal to those with a taste for the eerie and macabre, although it has to be said that such a disquieting brew might upset the finest of palettes if over-indulged after the midnight hour.

T. M. Lally
Shirdley Hill
2004.

LATHOM

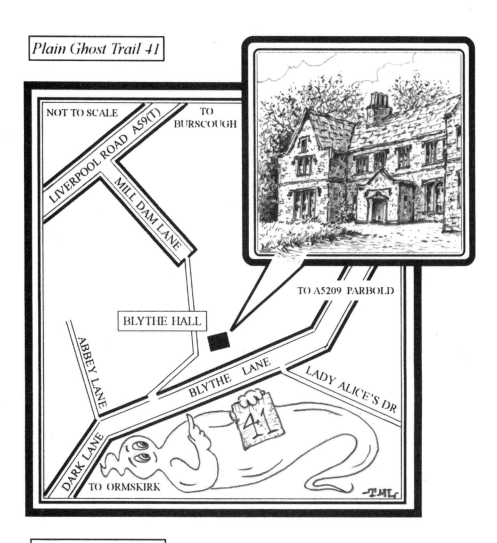

Plain Ghost Trail 41

NOT TO SCALE

LIVERPOOL ROAD A59(T)

TO BURSCOUGH

MILL DAM LANE

TO A5209 PARBOLD

BLYTHE HALL

ABBEY LANE

BLYTHE LANE

LADY ALICE'S DR

DARK LANE

41

TO ORMSKIRK

INSET Blythe Hall

THE BLAND SPIRIT

"Is — is there anybody there . . . .?"

Silence.

"Is there anybody there . . . .?"

The silence was broken by the sound of a suppressed giggle, a series of scuffles and a sharp slap.

"Oh, for goodness sake, you two!" Glenda Wilbrahem snapped in exasperation, causing the candle in the centre of the table to waver and splutter. "Do try and take it seriously — and that goes for both of you!"

"But he tried to grab my . . . .!"

"No I didn't!" declared a young man sitting opposite Glenda.

"Oh yes you did!" retorted a pretty blonde girl, giving the young man a sharp poke with her elbow.

"Come and sit next to me, Shirley my love," suggested an older man sitting next to Glenda.

"No way," Shirley replied. "You're worse than Roger!"

"I say — that's not fair!" Roger, the young man quipped. "Uncle Toby is every inch the gentleman."

"That's not what I've heard," Shirley smirked.

"Well, I'm sure I don't know what you mean . . . ." spluttered Toby, the offended uncle, to the great amusement of the other party guests seated around the table.

"On stop bickering, all of you!" interrupted Glenda in a vexed tone. "Please do settle down and concentrate."

The room gradually fell silent as the guests replaced their hands, palms down, on the table and gazed into the depths of the flickering candle. The pale yellow flame cast its soft light upon these intent figures, their faces now serious and alert, while, in the wavering glow from the burning coals in the ornate fireplace, their elongated shadows cavorted on the drawing room walls in a merry dance.

"Right," breathed Glenda, "— let's try again." She paused and then in a low voice repeated her question.

"Is anybody there . . . .?"

Silence.

"If there is a spirit present here tonight, please give us a sign . . . ."

Silence — followed by a faint knock. It came from the table.

"Is that you, Roger — messing about again!"

"No, it wasn't me — I swear it," answered the young man indignantly.

"No, I'm certain it wasn't him," Shirley added. "It came from the table . . . ." She hesitated for a moment, obviously unnerved by this sudden development in the party game. "I really don't think it is a good idea to be doing this," she continued apprehensively. "Isn't it supposed to dangerous — trying to communicate with the other world?"

"Nonsense, my dear," chuckled Uncle Toby. "It's only a bit of fun. You can always come and sit next to me if you're frightened."

"I'd rather not be sitting here at all," the young girl answered nervously.

"Go on, Mrs. Wilbrahem — give it one last try," urged Roger, still puzzled by that faint sound, "and then we can pack it in if nothing happens."

Silence descended once more, accompanied by a general sense of wary anticipation.

"Is there anybody there . . . .? I call on you, invisible spirit, to give us a sign . . . ."

The candle began to waver and the fire roared and crackled.

It was followed by a resounding knock, which reverberated

round the drawing room.

The table began to vibrate and rock from side to side — and then rose from the floor.

In that instant a cold blast of air swept into the room, extinguishing the candle and swirling around the dismayed party. The heavy oak table crashed to the ground and the guests leaped back, overturning their chairs in panic.

"Switch the light on," screamed a terrified Shirley. "Switch it on!"

The light revealed a most unusual sight.

In the centre of the table a pool of brackish water slowly spread out to the edge and drip rhythmically onto the plush carpet below. A line of glistening water drips led away from the table and out of the room.

It would seem that Glenda's summons had been answered and the unseen visitor had come and gone — and left a sign.

* * *

Some weeks earlier the Wilbrahems had received complimentary tickets for a much-loved play by a celebrated 19th century London dramatist to be performed by members of the Laythom Dramatic Society in the village hall. They attended the final performance, and as the cast lined up to take their bows the curtain descended to enthusiastic applause from relatives and friends in the audience. After the second curtain call the chairman of the society (who took the part of the unfortunate husband in the play) stepped forward to deliver the obligatory speech for such occasions, thanking the cast for their hard work over the previous months ("the best production by this society in recent years"), the scenery and properties department for their stage sets ("better furnished than my own drawing room") and finally the audience for their generous support ("full houses for every performance") during the week. However, one particular "thank you" greatly intrigued Glenda Wilbrahem.

"We mustn't neglect to thank the playwright himself, for had he not stayed at the Hall it's possible that this wonderful comedy might never have been conceived."

Glenda remained behind after the audience had departed and took the opportunity to introduce herself to the chairman.

"Oh, really — the new owner of Bland Hall," he beamed, obviously impressed by her status and delighted by her presence at this local function. "I did hear the Hall had been sold. I'm so glad you took the trouble to come and see our production, considering the problems of settling into a new home. I do hope you liked the play."

"Yes, I did — very much so," replied Glenda warmly. "I was fascinated by one of your comments about the play — or, more to the point, about the playwright and a Hall. Were you referring to Bland Hall?"

"Yes, indeed," the chairman nodded. "It is a widely held view that he got the idea for this particular play while staying at Bland Hall with the London set."

"The London set . . . .?"

"That's right — friends of the Earl of Laythom, a previous owner of Bland Hall," the chairman answered. "He was passionate about theatricals, you know — owned a theatre in London, so I believe. And he was also renowned for his theatrical parties as well. A number of famous guests came up from London — celebrities and socialites — many of the big names in the theatre at the time."

"Really — and they all stayed at Bland Hall?"

"Yes," he replied. "They used to write one act plays and sketches for their own amusement. In fact, this very hall was made into a private theatre for their performances."

"On this tiny little stage?" Glenda laughed. "It doesn't really live up to West End standards."

"Well, I agree — but you have to remember that it is a converted building which originally belonged to old Laythom Hall. That Hall was demolished after the First World War, and the family moved to nearby Bland Hall, spending a huge amount of money on the place in the process."

"I suppose they had to keep up expensive 'London' standards," Glenda surmised, "considering the quality of the guest list."

"Yes — theatrical get-togethers could be very costly, no doubt," the chairman agreed, "but thanks to the Earl's passion for the theatre and generous party spirit we now have a much-loved and universally celebrated play."

"So you really think there is some foundation to the story?"

"Well, you never can tell," replied the chairman. "The play's title and Bland — the names are quite similar, aren't they? It does makes you think . . . ." He paused, pondering the matter. "As to the idea behind the play — a seance invoking the return of a ghost," he continued, "whether that happened at the Hall, I couldn't really say."

"It's an interesting idea, I suppose," answered Glenda, turning to her husband. "Don't you think so, Henry?" Her husband, a reluctant and somewhat bored theatre-goer, muttered something on the lines of "stuff and nonsense" and "time for a nightcap" and turned to go.

Glenda thanked the chairman and followed her husband out, leaving the village hall as a patron of the Laythom Dramatic Society and an admirer of the famous London playwright.

Glenda revealed this admiration some weeks later during a house warming party for a select gathering of friends. In the course of general conversation she mentioned her trip to the theatre, recounting the plot of the play and the chairman's story. This descriptive account was further augmented by "bloody stuff and nonsense" from a slightly intoxicated Henry. She couldn't recall which guest actually suggested a replay of the seance in the story, but it was taken up by Roger, one of the younger people at the party, who thought "it would be good for a laugh". Glenda thought so too.

Off she went to the kitchen to find a candle while the others seated themselves around the oak table in the drawing room. Some minutes later a candle, flickering and spluttering in the darkened room, illuminated the faces of the 'players'. The palms of their hands were spread out, side by side, on the wooden surface, and an air of frivolity and mock suspense pervaded the light-hearted group.

Glenda called them to order, and began the session.

It quickly dissolved into hilarious confusion.

The hostess called again for order and began the ceremony again.

"Is there anybody there . . . .? I call on you, invisible spirit, to give us a sign . . . ." The invisible *spirit* dutifully obliged.

The candle began to waver.

It was followed by a resounding knock, which reverberated round the drawing room.

The table began to vibrate and rock from side to side — and then rose from the floor.

A cold blast of air swept into the room, extinguishing the candle and swirling around the dismayed company. The heavy oak table crashed to the ground and the guests leaped back, overturning their chairs in panic.

"Switch the light on," screamed a terrified Shirley. "Switch it on!" *The light revealed a most unusual sight.*

In the centre of the table a pool of brackish water slowly spread out to the edge and drip rhythmically onto the plush carpet below.

It would seem that the unseen visitor had left a sign after all.

This development certainly hadn't been in the original play — and unfortunately for Glenda she would soon find that this newly-invoked spirit bore no relation to the flirtatious and silly ghost in the celebrated domestic comedy.

And furthermore, on this occasion there was no medium to turn to for help.

* * *

The storyline of the play is very well-known. The second wife of leading man decides to hold a seance at a dinner party, inviting a eccentric medium who lives nearby, to come and take charge of the proceedings. Unfortunately for the husband the seance succeeds in spectacular fashion when the spirit of his first wife immediately appears after the seance, gliding through the french windows into the drawing room. The only problem is that the flirtatious ghost can only be seen by her husband. This of course leads to all manner of domestic problems with his new wife and the frivolous spirit, much to the husband's frustration when trying to hold a conversation with both of them at the same time.

However, in Glenda's case it wasn't so much a feeling of frustration as one a growing unease over the coming days. The calm ambience within the Hall had been displaced by a troubled, even threatening, influence which now, it seemed, pervaded the house.

Something had changed.

There was, as yet, no appearance of a ghost in the house — but there was a sign. The building had been remodelled at the beginning of the previous century incorporating a gallery at one end of the main hall, and it was here, late one evening, that she first glimpsed something very unsettling. That night, after switching off the main chandelier and making her way across the hall floor to retire for the night, Glenda happened to glance up — and saw the vague shape. This shape seemed to hover at the end of the gallery before disappearing into the shadows. She hesitated for a second before calling out.

"Henry . . . . Is that you up there?"

There was no reply.

She switched on the chandelier. The main hall was bathed in light.

To her relief she saw no-one there — the gallery was empty.

'My imagination playing me up again,' shivered Glenda. 'It hasn't been the same since that seance.'

What she saw next definitely wasn't her overwrought imagination. Something fell from the gallery, hitting the ground with a soft plop. She crossed the hall and looked down at the floor — and saw a spot

21

of water, glistening in the light.

Something hit the back of her neck.

It was freezing cold and wet — it was water.

She sprang back and looked up.

The next drip fell from the gallery above, to be followed by another — and then another. Soon there was a small puddle at her feet. Glenda raced up the stairs and along the gallery. At the far wall she came upon the 'sign'. A pool of brackish water lay on wooden boards, slowly spreading over the surface of the floor and dripping over the edge to the main hall below.

"Henry . . . !" Glenda called to her husband. "Henry — come here and look at this." Henry came out of the master bedroom.

"What's the matter, darling — and what are you doing in the gallery?"

"There's something very strange here — by the wall," she replied. "Come and see for yourself."

He joined her and gazed down at the pool of water.

"Oh, dear — I think we've got a leak in the roof," he declared unhappily. He examined the ceiling above the gallery. "No — I may be wrong," he concluded with some relief, "but there isn't any sign of a drip or damp patch up there. You're right, Glenda — it is very strange."

"So where has the water come from?"

"No idea," Henry pondered, deeply puzzled by this strange manifestation. "It's a bit of a mystery. Perhaps Beryl, the maid, has been cleaning up here . . . ." He paused, recalling the seance, and then added in a humorous tone. "Or may be that spirit of yours — creeping round the Hall."

"Don't joke about it, Henry," Glenda retorted. "No — there has got to be a rational explanation for it all."

"Well, Bill Jones, the head steward at the golf club, used to be plumber, so I've been told. I'll get him to come round and look at the piping — check if there's a leak somewhere in the heating system."

22

"Tell him the water is coming from the wall," Glenda said thoughtfully. "There's probably a leaking pipe behind it."

"Well, take my advice," chuckled her husband. "Don't, on any account, mention a mischievous water spirit when he turns up. You never know — Bill might have come across one or two of them in his old line of work."

"One or two malicious golfers full of spirits and soda water, more likely," snorted Glenda. "He must have nerves of steel to deal with that unruly crowd on a Saturday night."

Unfortunately the resident head steward at the Abbey Golf Club, the ex-plumber with "nerves of steel", didn't quite live up to expectations — in either department.

* * *

"I . . . . I can't find anything, Mrs. Wilbrahem — there isn't any sign of a leak, as far as I can see."

"Are you sure, Mr. Jones?"

"Yes, I . . . . I am," the ex-plumber stammered rather nervously. He seemed very ill at ease.

"Did you check the wall at the end of the gallery?"

The mention of the gallery further exacerbated his anxious state.

"Er — yes . . . ." He paused. "Yes I did."

"And there is definitely no sign of a broken water pipe in the wall?"

"A broken pipe — no, there isn't," Bill Jones answered. "It's the wall — I'm sure there's . . . ." He halted, somewhat sheepishly.

"There's what . . . .?" Glenda asked rather impatiently. The ex-plumber hadn't quite lived up to her expectations, considering her husband's recommendation. 'The fellow's a bit of a dope, like most of the men at the club,' she thought to herself. "Well — what about the wall?" Glenda continued, trying to hide her annoyance.

"I . . . . I can assure you that there isn't a broken pipe there," Bill

23

Jones heatedly answered, stung by her tone of voice. "There are no water pipes in that particular part of the Hall — and the roof above is as sound as a bell."

"So there is nothing there?"

"Oh I wouldn't say that, Mrs. Wilbrahem," he replied shaking his head. "Oh no, I definitely wouldn't say that."

"What are you talking about — what do you mean?"

The ex-plumber hesitated and mopped his brow.

"There's no pipe in that wall — but there's definitely something else . . . ."

"Something else?"

"Yes. Something else — and it grabbed at me — tried to pull me into the wall!" He halted and gave a shudder.

"What nonsense!" Glenda declared. "Have you been drinking?"

"No, I haven't — but I'm going to, you can be sure of that." He picked up his bag of tools and hurried out of the house, driving away in a cloud of dust.

Some minutes later the phone rang. It was her husband — and he sounded very vexed.

"What have you been saying to Bill Jones," Henry began heatedly. "I've just had him on the phone. He's very upset."

"I can't understand why. I didn't upset him, I can assure you, darling," replied Glenda in amazement. "He scampered out of the house in a most peculiar state of mind — and he left one of his electronic gadgets behind in the gallery."

"Well, the head steward at a Golf Club is the wrong person to upset, I can tell you," Henry declared, obviously thinking of his own position and bar bills. "I'll call in at the club on the way home — see if I can sort it out."

Later that evening Henry Wilbrahem returned home and greeted his wife. She expected an immediate row, knowing her husband's temperament when things went wrong. However, Glenda saw from the worried expression on his face that it was far more serious.

"I'm afraid Bill Jones is very upset," he said in a grave tone of voice, "and you're not going to believe what caused it."

Henry went on to relate his conversation with Bill, and the ex-plumber's experience in the gallery of Bland Hall.

On arriving at Bland Hall Bill carried out a preliminary check of the radiator piping on the ground floor and found everything in order. He then went up to the gallery to check the ceiling for signs of water damage.

That also had a clean bill of health.

He felt that there was no need to check the far wall for water leaks because the piping in the Hall did not extend to that part of the building. However, Glenda Wilbrahem had been very insistent on a thorough inspection of that part of the gallery, and so he bent down to make a visual check of the wall.

There was no sign of dampness or mildew on the plaster surface.

Nevertheless Glenda had been quite adamant about it, so the ex-plumber decided to try the damp meter, just in case.

He reached into his bag for the meter, a device with two sharp electric prongs which, when pushed into a surface, would register the smallest amount of dampness. Switching on the power, he pushed the two sharp prongs into the surface plaster.

He gasped with surprise at the immediate effect.

The needle in the dial reacted violently, shot off the scale and vibrated madly — and at that precise moment a hand, putrefying and blackened with decay, slowly emerged from the surface of the gallery wall. He gasped in astonishment and instinctively drew back as claw-like fingers reached out, narrowly missing his throat by inches. The gruesome fingers unclenched themselves and drew back for a second attempt to grab him.

Bill was transfixed, unable to move.

He couldn't breathe or cry for help, overwhelmed by a powerful unseen force within the wall itself. The blackened hand came closer and closer, slowly casting about in front of his face, decaying fingers remorselessly searching for their quarry.

The hand suddenly halted right in front of his nose.

It had found him.

At this crucial moment Bill somehow found the will to move, and, uttering a scream of terror, struck out blindly with the damp meter. More by luck than intent, the electronic prongs passed right through the phantom hand and the effect was immediate. A blue flash arced between the prongs and a myriad of sparkling electrical charges danced along the ghastly arm and into the wall. This electric shock broke the spell, and Bill Jones was released from the deathly influence of the hidden assailant and fell back onto the floor, just in time to see the spectral hand and arm swiftly withdraw into the wall. He scrambled away in relief.

"Bill told me that he thought the horrible arm was covered in the tattered remains of a sort of quilted leather garment," Henry went on, " and on one of the fingers he saw a huge ring — the sort used to seal old-fashioned documents with wax. He described the design as one of those gargoyle things you see in churches."

"I can't believe it," uttered Glenda in disbelief. "A hand in the wall . . . .?"

"I thought so too," Henry nodded. "But there is one thing he is certain of . . . ."

"What was that?"

"The hand and arm were dripping with water — and Bill had a very damp collar to prove it."

"No wonder he dropped his damp meter in the gallery and left the house in such a hurry," remarked a rather disturbed Glenda.

"I think you can definitely cross Bill Jones off your Christmas invitation list," said Henry in an attempt to lighten the atmosphere.

His wife was not amused. Her thoughts were on other matters.

Glenda Wilbrahem began to realize that it would be more difficult to cross the *other one* off any kind of list. Thanks to her seance an invitation had already been given — and accepted.

Unfortunately it would seem that this malevolent *guest* was now part of the fabric of Bland Hall.

* * *

"Excuse me, Mrs. Wilbrahem," Beryl, the live-in domestic, inquired nervously. "Can you spare a minute . . . .?"

"Yes, Beryl," answered the mistress of the Hall. "What is it?"

"It's the water, ma'am . . . ."

"Water . . . .!" Glenda gasped.

"Yes, ma'am. It has wet all the carpet at the bottom of the staircase leading to the bedrooms."

"Stairs — water on the carpet?!"

"Yes — it's soaked through. I think someone has carried a bowl of water across the hall and spilled it there," the maid replied, anticipating a torrent of blame. "But it wasn't me, I can assure you, ma'am," the woman hastily added.

"There — there," Glenda calmed the maid who was clearly upset by this unusual incident. "Don't worry, I believe you, Beryl. But how do you know someone came across the hall?"

"It was the trail of drips on the floor, Mrs. Wilbrahem. They came from the gallery. I went up to have a look — and followed them up to the gallery and right back to the far wall."

Glenda was speechless — and utterly confounded by the facts.

"Perhaps there's a leak in the roof, ma'am," the maid suggested timidly. "May be you should call some one to come and look at it."

"Thank you, Beryl," answered Glenda, trying to conceal a feeling of rising panic. She already knew one person with experience with water leaks, and he wouldn't be seen dead in the Hall. "I'll have a word with Mr. Wilbrahem about the problem."

When Henry arrived home he also had some news for Glenda. It concerned the gallery, or, more to the point, the wall at the end of the gallery.

27

"I called in at the club to have a word with Bill Jones again and bumped into that chairman chappie," he declared. "The one in that play we saw in Laythom."

"Ah, the man who played the unfortunate husband — I didn't know he was a golf club member."

"Yes, and a long-standing one at that," her husband replied. "He certainly knows a lot about this area, and we got on to the subject of old buildings. He told me one or two interesting things about Bland Hall — facts not mentioned in the deeds of the Hall."

"Damp walls, I suppose," replied Glenda sarcastically. "They weren't mentioned in the deeds when we bought the place."

"As a matter of fact he did mention the walls," answered her husband. "He told me that part of the fabric is very old indeed — especially the area around the main hall and gallery — goes back as far as the thirteenth century, so he believes."

"But I thought the Hall was early seventeenth century," pondered Glenda. "It is in the deeds of the property."

"That's right — but he told me the origins of Bland Hall go back much further — to the Middle Ages and the Abbey."

"You mean that old ruin at the back of the Hall?"

"Yes — and he said the original Hall could have been the Infirmary for the monks — or Black Canons, as he called them."

"Well, it did say in the deeds that Bland Hall had been a Catholic seminary."

"But only in recent times, my dear," declared Henry, "— nothing to do with the ruined Abbey."

"Well, I remember reading that the stables used to be a chapel."

"So do I, now you mention it," Henry nodded. "I think I'll have another look at the deeds."

"I'm going into town tomorrow," Glenda offered. "I'll call in and collect them, if you like."

A phone call to the family solicitor completed the arrangements, and the next evening the couple sat down to read the bundle of

28

papers which comprised the deeds of Bland Hall. Some were typed on modern paper, some were handwritten in old fashioned copperplate style, and some were in Latin script, on parchment now dog-eared and faded by age and long confinement.

However, certain sections did make interesting reading, and the details are condensed below.

The Hall, a large country house, is probably late 16c or possibly early 17c in origin with alterations in the early 19c. It was radically remodelled and enlarged in c.1920 by the Earl of Laythom, and partially reduced in c.1975 by some demolition of earlier building work. The ground plan comprises the 'H' design of the original building with extensive wings attached to the rear corner of the right hand wing. The building includes two storeys and attics on the older portion with a wide single storey stone porch in the centre. A skittle alley (made out of specially imported pine) was constructed in one of the wings by the Earl, who indulged a passion for all things American. On the demise of the Laythom family line the Hall remained empty for 8 years until 1932, when it was acquired by the Catholic Passionist Order. It became a junior seminary under the name of St. Gabriel's Retreat, and the skittle alley was removed and replaced with an ornate private chapel.

"You were right, my dear," Henry Wilbrahem remarked. "There was a chapel in the Hall."

"And the next owner replaced it with the present stables," answered Glenda, turning over a page. "Ah — this might explain the dampness."

In 1974 the Order ran out of funds and the Hall was sold on to the owner of a supermarket chain for a substantial sum. The Hall was once again remodelled with a swimming pool in the rear wing and 7 en suite bathrooms with mosaic walls on the upper floor.

"That would need a substantial amount of water pipes, don't you think, Henry?"

"I suppose it would, my dear," he agreed. "But Bill Jones was quite sure the pipes didn't extend to that part of the gallery."

"And do you notice there isn't any mention of an earlier building," declared Glenda, "unless it is somewhere in these old Latin documents, and I can't make head or tail of them."

However, she did find a very interesting reference in the bundle of papers.

Bland Hall was remodelled at great expense by the 3rd Earl of Laythom as a residence to replace the family home in Laythom Park (demolished shortly after the 1st World War) and converted an outbuilding on the estate into a small theatre to entertain his theatrical friends, including dramatists and celebrated actors, with impromptu plays and sketches. It is thought that one acclaimed playwright conceived the idea for his famous 'spirit' comedy at the Hall during this period.

"Oh, look — it does mention the play after all," Glenda observed, but added with a hint of disappointment, "— but nothing about a spirit haunting the place."

"Well, you can't ask the playwright about it now, my dear," her husband chuckled. "He's long gone, I'm afraid."

"More's the pity," answered Glenda. "Let's hope the spirit has too."

This hope was soon to be dashed and replaced by fervent prayer.

* * *

A disquieting surprise awaited Glenda when she returned from her weekend in London. A letter, with the words "*Mrs. Wilbrahem — confidential*" scrawled across the front, lay propped up on the vestibule table.

It was from Beryl the maid.

Dear Mrs. Wilbrahem
I am sorry to have to tell you this, but I just cannot work at Bland Hall any longer, especially after what happened last night while you were away in London. I know that I should give some notice and I am sorry to leave you this way, but I could not stay in that house a moment longer.
Thank you for your past kindness.
Fond regards
Beryl.

'What on earth could have happened,' thought Glenda, completely mystified by the strange letter. She decided there and then to give Beryl a call.

"Hello . . . . Beryl?" Glenda began. "I've just found your letter. What's it all about?"

Beryl once again apologized for her sudden resignation. "But I just couldn't stay a moment longer," she continued. "Do you know Mrs. Wilbrahem, for some time now — since the night of your party when I think about it — I've thought there was something funny about the house — that it had somehow changed."

"Changed . . . .?"

"Yes — that's the only way I can describe it. It all started when I was cleaning the main hall. I felt some sort of presence there, as if someone was watching me from the gallery — watching and waiting. And now I am quite sure that the house is haunted."

"Haunted — how can you be sure?"

'Because I actually saw the ghost last night . . . ."

31

"You saw a ghost," declared Glenda with astonishment. "You must have imagined it?"

"I wish I had," returned the depressed maid, still unsettled by her experience. "I think something must have woken me up in the early hours and I could not get back to sleep. So I went down to the kitchen for a glass of hot milk. I was returning to bed when I literally bumped into *him* — coming out of your room!"

"You saw a man coming out of my room!" Glenda gasped.

"Yes — and I can tell you it was the most frightening thing that has ever happened to me, seeing that thing in the doorway — I almost died of shock on the spot."

"Was he a burglar?"

"I wish he had been — then I could have made some sense of it all. No, he definitely wasn't a burglar — but he was a horrible sight all the same, covered in thick dust and cobwebs, with his fancy clothes all rotten-like and falling to bits. He carried a sort of bucket in one hand, and there was an odd shaped thing sticking out of it."

"You poor dear — it must have been absolutely terrifying for you," Glenda replied sympathetically.

"It was — especially when he turned his head and saw me standing in the darkened corridor . . . ." Beryl paused, and Glenda sensed her disquiet at the other end of the line.

"That's awful, Beryl dear," she consoled her, "— really awful."

"It got worse," replied Beryl. "Without uttering a sound he began to move forward, slowly raising his other nasty hand — reaching out to grab me."

She went on to describe the next moments. That hand was a dreadful sight, all bone with bits of loose blackened skin hanging from it. The terrified woman panicked and threw the glass of milk at the spectre — but it went right through him. A devilish smile crossed his festering countenance and he moved silently towards her. Beryl was absolutely demoralized and looked for some place to hide, so she ran back along the corridor to the alcove at the top of

32

the stairs, and managed to squeeze behind the pedestal and flowers. The next minute the ghost passed by, his eyes enraged and mouth in a fixed snarl. He paused briefly at the top of the stairs, surveying the hall below — and then to Beryl's surprise and relief he carried on down the stairs, across the main hall and up to the gallery.

"What a terrible experience, my dear," said Glenda in a shocked voice. "But if you're right — and there is a ghost in the Hall . . . ."

"Take my word for it, Mrs. Wilbrahem — there is! What I saw next convinced me that *he* was a real ghost. I actually saw him disappear into the wall at the far end of the gallery . . . ."

"It's so hard to believe such a thing."

"Well, I can assure you I saw it. And I also know where those drops of water on the floor came from — that horrible thing left a trail of them dripping out of his leaking bucket."

"Did you know Mr. Wilbrahem called in a plumber to solve that problem several days ago."

"Ha — you'll need more than your average plumber to sort this out, believe me," retorted Beryl. "After that I ran down the stairs as fast as I could and spent the rest of the night locked in the pantry. I decided there and then that I would not spend another night in Bland Hall and when I went upstairs in the morning to pack my stuff I found another weird thing."

"What was that?"

"I looked into your bedroom and saw your bed was ringing wet," declared the maid, "— pillows and duvet absolutely soaked through."

"What can I say," answered a thoroughly alarmed Glenda. "There must be something we can do about it all."

"Didn't you tell me something about a play you recently went to see in the village hall," prompted Beryl.

Glenda nodded and recalled the title.

"That's the one — and there was something about ghost in it?"

"Yes, there was . . . ."

"Well, what did they do about the ghost in the play?"

"Ah, yes," replied Glenda, recalling the last act of the comedy. "All the guests met together for another party."

It gave her an idea.

She too would have another seance — to try and undo the ghostly damage inflicted on the fabric and domestic harmony of Bland Hall.

However, unlike the development of the play, matters were to take a turn for the worse.

* * *

Glenda awoke with a start, and raised her head from the pillow, listening intently.

A faint noise reached her ears — and she immediately recognized the sound. It was the drip — drip — drip of water, falling in a steady rhythmic pattern — and it came from somewhere within the darkened bedroom. There was, however, something very peculiar about this disconcerting sound.

Each drip was followed by a soft gurgle and rustling of cloth.

She sat up and called to her husband in a low voice.

"Henry . . . . Henry, wake up . . . ."

Another drip was followed by a gurgle and rustling cloth.

"Henry, please wake up. I think we've got a leak in the ceiling . . . ." She reached over to the small table which separated the twin beds, switched on the light — and saw a vision straight out of a horror film.

Henry was wide awake, his eyes bulging in their sockets, his face swollen, and his hair standing on end — and he was unable to speak

He could only gurgle.

This was on account of a grisly misshapen and battered object jammed between his purple lips.

It was a leather funnel.

This gruesome device was held firmly in place by a bony hand, decomposed and claw-like, which protruded from a tattered leather sleeve. This in turn belonged to a tall figure. His fine attire, once rich in design and of the highest quality, was now in the last stages of decay, tattered and covered in dust and cobwebs. This ghastly apparition sat astride her husband, pinning his arms to his side and his body to the bed, thus preventing any escape. He crouched over Henry like an animal who had finally got its prey.

The source of the dripping water was immediately apparent in the lamp light.

Above the funnel this malignant creature held a leather bucket, from which a regular drip of discoloured water fell, each drop causing the unfortunate prisoner to gurgle, and convulse his feet in an involuntary response, rustling the bed clothes with the only free part of his body. The creature glared down upon the unfortunate owner of Bland Hall, his lips parted in a cruel sadistic grimace of pleasure, relishing the pain and terror of his victim. Glenda realized that Henry, her poor husband, was slowly drowning and she uttered a scream of despair.

The fiend turned and fixed her with a terrible stare.

Judging by the expression in his black eyes when he caught sight of her flimsy nightdress and partly uncovered body, and the way he licked his lips and grinned lasciviously as those black eyes roved over her shape, it was clear what he had in mind. It was plainly obvious that he was capable of other vicious acts and had indulged them on many occasions. The creature couldn't resist such a tempting prize — and decided to have his pleasure there and then. He withdrew the funnel, and the remains of the water spilled out of Henry's mouth, running down his chin, soaking the pillow and bedclothes and leaving him retching, choking and gasping for air.

The spectre dropped the funnel into the bucket, climbed from the half-drowned victim and soaked torture bed, and began his advance on the terrified woman, his intentions clearly evident.

Glenda had to lure him away from her husband and in that perilous instant she recalled the words of her maid, Beryl, who had recently faced the same dire problem. *"So I ran back along the corridor to the alcove at the top of the stairs, and managed to squeeze behind the pedestal and flowers"*. Glenda reacted with the same urgency and alacrity, and dashed from the bedroom, narrowly avoiding the creature's grasp and thwarting the *amorous* intentions of her villainous assailant.

Beryl's words saved the day.

Thanks to her slender figure Glenda too was able to squeeze into the alcove, and once again the spirit of Bland Hall was deprived of his quarry. He passed by the alcove and stood for some moments at the top of the stairs gazing down upon the main hall bathed in the moonlight which streamed through the fanlight window in the ceiling. His black eyes cast about, searching for his latest obsession, the mistress of the Bland Hall.

Defeated, he continued on his way, across the floor and up the stairs to the gallery — to finally disappear into the far wall.

A line of drips, flimsy beads of sparkling jewellery glistening in the moonlight, marked the way of the ghost's passing, the last visible evidence of his dreadful presence and timely departure.

* * *

Glenda wasted no time. Something had to be done — and quickly.

First of all the date of the seance was brought forward, and then Henry, not yet fully recovered from his ordeal, had to be persuaded to take part. The horrible experience left its mark physically and mentally, and was plainly noticeable to the guests assembled around a roaring fire in the drawing room that evening.

"You don't seem your usual self, Henry old chap," Uncle Toby remarked. Shirley and Roger nodded in agreement.

"All that stale air in the golf club bar, I shouldn't wonder," joked

Roger.

"You could do with some fresh air, the amount you spout," whispered Shirley, giving her companion a sharp nudge with her elbow. "Can't you see he's not very well."

"Come along, you two," interrupted Glenda. "Settle down — and do try to be more sensible this time."

"I really didn't want to come after what happened last time," declared Shirley. "I don't mind admitting I was very scared. Anyway, why are you holding another seance?"

"Because they held another one in that play," Roger broke in, "— to undo the effect of the previous seance. Isn't that right, Glenda?"

"Yes, that's correct," answered Glenda rather nervously.

"Why, old boy," said Toby, turning to Henry, "— you haven't had any problems in the Hall, have you?" Henry trembled and turned pale. He began to rise from the table, but Glenda gently restrained him.

"Of course not," she replied. "It's just as Roger told you. They held another seance in the play, and so I thought we would do the same."

Shirley wasn't convinced by this reply. She sensed something was wrong and whispered to her companion. "What do you mean — undo the effect?"

"They inadvertently brought the ghost of the first wife back into the house," Roger whispered in reply. "She caused a lot of trouble and so they met again to get rid of her — send her packing back to where she came from."

This titbit of information only served to make Shirley more unsettled and anxious. She all too clearly remembered the rocking table, extinguished candle and pool of water.

"Palms on the table, everyone," Glenda spoke in a low voice, trying to control her trembling hand as she lit the candle in the centre of the table.

"Then let's begin . . . . Is there anybody there?"

She already knew the answer to the question — but would *he* join them again and give a sign?

The drawing room remained silent.

"I say again — is anybody there?" she repeated, but there was no change.

"No luck tonight, Glenda," Toby chuckled.

"I can't understand it," muttered Glenda. "We are all here — in the same places round the table."

"Ah, but aren't you forgetting what happened in the play?" Roger spoke quietly.

"There was a maid — came into the room sleepwalking, I recall," declared Glenda, remembering the scene. "But it wasn't the maid that caused the problem — it was the bandage."

"The bandage . . . .?" Shirley gasped.

"Yes — the maid had banged her head, and the bandage was the link with the spirit of the first wife," Glenda exclaimed. "They took the bandage away and expelled the spirit."

"Well, let's bring Beryl in with a bandage on her head," suggested Roger, "— and see if anything happens."

"That wouldn't do any use," replied Glenda. "Beryl wasn't in the house during the last seance. It was her night off."

"Well, we could still try it out," Roger said enthusiastically, "and see what happens."

"Too late, I'm afraid," Henry replied. "She's gone — for good."

"Anyway, I don't think she could help us," Glenda interrupted. "I can't understand it. Nothing has changed."

"Oh yes there has," Roger declared.

"What do you mean," Shirley cried. "We're all in the same places as before. Everything is the same, as far as I can see."

"No it isn't," answered her companion humorously. "And you're staring right at it."

"What . . . ." answered the perplexed girl. "Oh, you mean the candle . . . .?"

"Not the candle — the candle holder, silly. It's a different one!" And so it was.

"Yes — you're quite right." Glenda explained. "It is a different candlestick. The other one was an old battered thing. I found it on a shelf in the pantry and Beryl told me later that she thought it came from the attic in the old wing. But I didn't think it looked right and spoiled the setting — so I bought a nice silver one in town."

"So where's the other one?"

"Oh, I'm not sure," replied Glenda. "I gave it back to Beryl."

"Well that could be our 'bandage' — if we had it," Roger surmised.

"I'll ring Beryl this minute," Glenda decided. "Let's hope she didn't throw it away."

Glenda returned moments later.

"We're in luck," she smiled. "Beryl took it back to the pantry. She told me that she put the candlestick on a shelf behind the door."

The old candlestick was quickly retrieved and set in the middle of the table. The seance began once more.

"Is there anybody there . . . .?"

Silence — followed by the violent wavering of the candle flame.

"It's working, old girl," Toby hissed.

"Shhh . . . ." The atmosphere had changed — become colder, in spite of the roaring fire in the grate. Glenda could feel *his* presence. She had experienced that same feeling some nights previously. Her husband Henry felt it too, for she was aware of his trembling hand next to hers. She spoke again, her voice high-pitched and anxious.

"I say again . . . . Is there anybody there?"

The table began to move, ever so slightly at first — but then more violently as did the candle flame.

Glenda sensed the time was approaching — that crucial period where action was needed to overcome this hidden force gathering in the room.

The table rose from the floor, the candlestick began to rock backwards and forwards — and a gust of wind swirled round the people at the table.

At that precise moment Glenda sprang forward and grabbed the candlestick before the flame was extinguished. Raising it high above her head, she hurled it straight into the burning coals of the crackling fire.

An almighty scream, a cry which struck terror in everyone's heart, pierced the darkness, resounding through Bland Hall. The table toppled with a mighty crash and the swirling cold wind swept around the room, beating against the guests, scattering books, papers and cushions in confusion before bursting through the curtains and the window — out into the still night air.

The guest picked themselves up and scampered from the haunted drawing room into the main hall. There they saw a trail of drips leading across the floor from gallery stairs, drips which gradually evaporated into curling wisps of steam floating away in the warm air.

The *spirit* of Bland Hall had departed.

* * *

"It certainly is a battered old thing," observed Shirley, as she pulled the scorched candlestick from the ashes of the fire with the fire tongs and placed it on a sheet of newspaper. She examined it, turning it over slowly. "That's interesting — there's a design on the bottom of it."

"Never mind that — just get rid of the horrible thing," retorted Glenda. "Throw it in the dustbin."

"No, hold on," Roger broke in. "If it's that old, it might also be very valuable. Bring it into the kitchen, Shirley. We'll have a go at cleaning it."

The recent stay in the fire had not helped matters and the severe scorch marks only added to the dilapidated and misshapen appearance of the candlestick. Roger guessed that it was made from soft metal, possibly pewter, and, judging from the deep scoring and chipped edges, it had been very roughly used in its life. However, Shirley was right about the design on the base.

"It looks like one of those weird carvings you often see in churches," she declared.

"Gargoyles, you mean . . . .?"

At the mention of this word Glenda gave a start and suppressed a startled cry. She recalled the ex-plumber's description of the ring on the hand in the wall "*the design was like one of those gargoyle things you see in churches*" and she had a horrible thought.

'Could this candlestick have belonged to that malignant spirit?'

Beryl thought it came from the attic and, if its appearance was anything to go by, it could have lain there for years, possibly centuries.

"Yes — gargoyles," answered Shirley. "— mythological beasts — or maybe demons, if you believe all that stuff about Satan and Devil worship. If the person who originally owned the candlestick was into that sort of thing — then no wonder we had all that trouble in the seance."

"Well Bland Hall is the right sort of place for 'that sort of thing', as you put it," quipped Roger, winking at Toby who had just entered the kitchen. "The place is older than you, Toby — bound to have loads of spooky demons in its closets."

Shirley turned to Glenda. "See what I mean about Roger," she snorted. "He can never be serious about anything. I told him that I didn't like what we were doing the first time, but he ignored me as usual."

"Roger might be joking," Uncle Toby replied, "but he has a point, all the same. Someone told Henry that Bland Hall goes way back, possibly to the Middle Ages, and that's an awful lot of history. This old candlestick is part of it, and could be valuable."

"I don't care how much it is worth," Glenda retorted angrily. "I just want it out of the house."

"I'd snap it up if I were you , Toby," laughed Roger. "It could be more valuable than you think — that is if you found the other one."

"What do you mean," Glenda gasped. "— the other one?"

"Well — it is often the case with candlesticks," Roger smiled. "They come in pairs — so there's probably another one of these knocking around somewhere in the Hall."

The thought of another devilish candlestick lying concealed in the house was too much for Glenda Wilbrahem. If Roger's hunch proved correct and it was true about the candlestick — then there still remained a fatal link with the supposedly departed spirit.

Later that day the party guests prepared to leave, and Glenda and her husband saw them off at the imposing entrance of the Hall.

"By the way, Glenda," laughed Roger as he started the car. "Don't forget the ending of the play. After the seance the poor guy ends up worse off than before — his second wife comes back to haunt him as well."

Glenda recalled the final moments of the play, when the paintings fell from the walls and the objects flew off the mantelpiece.

'Who else might *he* bring back with *him* — if *he* does decide to return . . . .?'

She couldn't face the thought, not to mention all that extra water, and decided there and then to sell up and leave. Henry was in full agreement and days later the 'For Sale' sign went up in the garden, "any reasonable offer considered".

* * *

"Thank you for coming to see me so soon," the solicitor greeted the new owner of Bland Hall.

"Don't mention it," replied Mr. Burton-Smith, warmly shaking the solicitor's hand. "Fortunately I was in town on other business, and found I could spare a few minutes."

"Well, please take a seat," indicated the solicitor, pointing to an old well-worn leather armchair by the fire. "The matter won't take too much of your time, I can assure you." He produced a faded foolscap envelope from a large metal box and placed it on his desk. "I tell you in confidence that our practice has recently been engaged by a development company," he continued, opening the envelope and withdrawing a sheet of paper, "— and retained to deal with matters concerning the Laythom Estate which, as you already know, adjoins your own property, Bland Hall."

"Yes, I have heard rumours about the sale of the estate for building purposes," nodded Mr. Burton-Smith. "Is this why you wanted to see me?"

"No — no, not at all," declared the solicitor quickly, "— although the matter is related to the Laythom estate — or to be more specific, the deeds of old Laythom House. I came across this in some estate documents and thought a copy of it should be given to you, since there is a reference to Bland Hall in it." He passed the faded sheet of paper to Mr. Burton-Smith. "It's an extract from the papers of a Dr. Robert Wilson, Antiquary and founder member of the Victorian Heraldry Society. It seems he was engaged to translate some early land deeds concerning 'Mastfall', the products of trees and dead wood. It was a vital part of the economic system of those times, you know, together with the ownership of a water course which ran through the Laythom Estate."

"I can't see the relevance to my property," answered the new owner of Bland Hall. "Is there a connection?"

"Yes, there is — as the late Doctor discovered."

Mr. Burton-Smith read the paper by the late Victorian academic with growing interest.

Document 6 (translation catalogued as 12-de Bland)
I found that the translation itself (from the Latin and early French) revealed nothing out of the ordinary. The main point of interest was the transfer by Geoffrey de Bland of his claim

of mastfall in Tarlesworth, Greetly and Burscoff to Prior Benedict of Laythom Abbey. The date of this transaction was 1206. However I did discover another document within its sheaves, possibly placed there by accident (or for some unknown reason) because it was dated some two hundred years later. The translation of this brief document did, to my surprise, reveal something quite out of the ordinary.

It was an account of a criminal proceeding taken against Robert de Bland at the Lancaster Sessions. The main charge stated that "He did, by felonious means break into the house of John of Lyardale, Parson of South Mells, accompanied by others unknown with intent to steal both monies and various possessions of the aforesaid cleric".

The charge went on to describe the circumstances of this unusual case.

"The Parson he did tie to his bed, and did place a device in his mouth, and did put water into his mouth, and did cause so much torment as to force the poor Parson to divulge his treasure." In this it seems Robert de Bland was successful in his diabolical method of torture for the charge went on to state that "the Parson was robbed of his jewels worth one hundred shillings and a Pyx, a precious jewel stone (I have since discovered that this gem stone had a special Medieval religious significance in that it was supposed to encapsulate the body of Christ) from the church altar."

A brief note in French, by another hand, was added in the right hand margin. It translates as "Tried this month of January, found not guilty of all charges and acquitted. The Pyx has been lost to us for all time. Unfortunately the Lord of Bland Hall has not."

I have concluded from this note that the Lord of Bland Hall had great influence in high places, and that his wicked escapades were not solely confined to this one incident.

An additional note was written on the rear of this unusual document.

I have found the seal of Robert de Bland on one of the deeds of tenure, and it bears comparison with the personal seals of those from the closed Monastic Orders of the early Middle Ages. It is of great interest and truly in keeping with his dark nature. The design is that of a head of an imaginary mythological beast, a cross between a wyvern and devilish gargoyle, a design no doubt conjured up from the depths of a depraved mind.

"I see what you mean," nodded Mr. Burton-Smith, revising his opinion of the matter. "A very unsavoury character, by the look of it — although it still remains a mystery as to why Doctor Wilson's paper ended up in those earlier deeds."

"Who knows," the solicitor smiled. "I suppose you could say Robert de Bland was a troublesome neighbour — probably disputed some earlier family transaction with Laythom Hall."

"Well, I hope there won't be a dispute over these latest developments," said Mr. Burton-Smith. "My wife is very concerned about it — can't abide the thought of awful neighbours and a noisy housing estate springing up by the Hall and spoiling her view. She has got this idea into her head that the previous tenants, the Wilbrahems, sold up and left in a hurry because they had got wind of something like that."

"Oh, I can assure you that the Wilbrahems had other reasons for selling the Hall so quickly," the solicitor replied. "Water leaks and severe nervous health problems, so I believe."

* * *

Mrs. Burton-Smith got her way as usual.

She wanted an oval window, even though it was out of keeping with rest of the facade, and, in the opinion of the architect engaged on the project, "it would upset the delicate symmetrical balance of a fine architectural line".

"I really have set my heart on it, Georgie darling," Mrs. Burton-Smith appealed to her doting and over-indulgent husband. 'I want it,' she thought to herself, 'and I'm going to have it.'

Yes, it had to be said that Mrs. Burton-Smith always got her way in all things. The marriage itself was an ideal example of this. She was much younger than her husband, extremely attractive and vivacious: and she was also a snob of the first order. Extremely selfish by nature and overbearing in character, her overriding ambition was the acquisition of wealth and social status, and no doubt "Georgie darling" would eventually be discarded when the time came to move on to richer pickings. She was also his second wife, having lured him away from a perfectly happy marriage, causing great upset and misery in the process.

Unfortunately, in the case of the oval window she got much more than she bargained for.

This window was to be situated at the end of the gallery above the main hall. Her reason for this architectural blunder was the light — or lack of it.

"It is much too dark up there, Georgie," she complained. "We need a window in the end wall."

"Do you think so, darling," her husband sighed. "It seems perfectly fine to me."

"No — my mind is made up. An oval window it shall be."

Work commenced the following week, and during the preliminary stage the builders unearthed something which was to "upset the delicate symmetrical balance" of the Burton-Smith household.

The initial inspection of the wall, once the outer facing of plaster had been chipped away, disclosed that the stonework was part of the fabric of a much earlier building, possibly thirteenth century in the opinion of the foreman.

"It is very old," he told Mr. Burton-Smith.

"Why do you say that?"

"I've seen its like in some of the old churches around here," the foreman explained. "Its the way they built them — two walls with an infilling of rubble and no damp-proof coursing. There was probably a wing on the other side of this wall and the gallery ran through to it. So, when the Hall was remodelled and the older wing knocked down, this became an outside wall and dead end."

The next day Bert, the labourer, found more evidence which backed up the foreman's theory. This evidence was found at the base of the wall at the end of the gallery. The man raced out of the Hall, white as a sheet, and came galloping across the courtyard, calling to the foreman.

"You'd better come an' 'ave a look at this, 'arry," Bert yelled.

"Hold on, mate," replied Harry, busily engaged in measuring some lengths of timber. "Can't you see I'm busy checking this delivery."

"Well, I ain't goin' back wivout you, 'arry," the agitated work-man retorted, "— that's for sure. It 'as given me a right old turn, and I ain't kiddin', either."

The pair returned to the Hall and climbed the stairs to the gallery. The workman refused to go first, and followed with some trepidation at a discrete distance.

" It's there — at the bottom of that wall," he muttered, pointing along the gallery, "an I ain't goin' any further, mate."

"For heaven's sake," the foreman declared in exasperation, "what's the problem?" He reached the far wall and looked down at a jagged hole in the stonework. "Well, is this it?"

"Aye, it is," replied Bert nervously, "— and when I made it a . . . ." He paused. "Somethin' came out and tried to grab me!"

"Don't be daft — you're having me on, you rascal . . . ."

"I ain't, I tell you — it wus a ruddy great arm, all 'orrible like!"

The foreman laughed and bent down to examine the cavity.

"Well, you're right about one thing," he said in a more serious tone of voice. "There is something in there — in a secret compartment, by the look of it."

He began to chip away with his hammer and chisel, and after some moments carefully withdrew a large block of stone from the wall. The light of day fell upon the contents of a long-hidden secret.

The contents were very unusual and extremely damp. The rotten and decaying articles, which crumbled to the touch, were, in Harry's opinion, the remains of a leather bucket and funnel. Beneath these mysterious articles he found something else — something which had stood the test of time and was in as good a condition as when it was first placed in this secret compartment centuries earlier. This object was a pewter candlestick with an unusual design upon its base, one so often seen in church architecture. This discovery was followed by another — a ring with a similar design.

"No ruddy great arm in there," chuckled the foreman, as Bert mustered his courage and joined Harry to look over his shoulder, peering into the secret cavity.

"Right, mate — an' I'm glad to 'ear it . . . ." He stopped and gazed intently into the far recesses. "Hold on a bit, 'arry," he muttered. "You've missed somethin' — right at the back."

And so it turned out, for his sharp eyes had spotted another object in the dark recess. The foreman reached in and pulled a small leather pouch which crumbled away to reveal a glittering stone within. He polished it with his sleeve, and it sparkled all the more. It had a reddish hue and was obviously a gem stone.

"I bet it's worth a bit, mate," the workman declared in astonishment. At that precise moment Mrs. Burton stole up behind them. This habit of constantly monitoring the progress of the window and checking up on the men annoyed the foreman intensely.

"Don't let me catch you two wasting time — or we'll find some-one else to do the work," she would admonish them at regular intervals, and Harry had to restrain himself from giving the offensive woman a piece of his mind. However on this occasion, when she caught sight of this splendid jewel, glittering and sparkling in the light, she immediately claimed possession with "that belongs to me, since it was found in my house. It's mine — so hand it over." The ring, with its weird design, and the candlestick were a different matter. Mrs. Burton-Smith took an immediate dislike to them. "And get rid of that load of old rubbish while you're about it," she ordered. The workmen, clearly annoyed by this high-handed attitude, threw the fragments of leather, ring and candlestick back into the cavity.

"She might as well keep this lot as well," muttered Harry under his breath. "I ain't carting it down to the skip for her benefit."

"Good idea, mate," Bert agreed. "I didn't like the look of the stuff anyway." The block of stone was replaced and the wall replastered later that day.

Meanwhile, Mrs. Burton-Smith had the jewel mounted in the form of a gold pendant and chain and it did look exceedingly attractive when placed round her swan-like neck. She was highly delighted with the glittering gem.

However she certainly was not pleased with the thoroughly soaked carpet outside her bedroom door next morning — and the trail of water drips which led back down the corridor to the stairs. She followed them across the main hall and up and along the gallery to a damp patch on the wall below the newly inserted oval window.

"Georgie — Georgie!" Mrs. Burton-Smith shrilled angrily. "Just come and look at this . . . .!"

"Oh dear," sighed her husband, contemplating the watery scene. "I wonder what has caused it?"

"Those horrid workmen. I told you they needed watching," she declared. "Now look what they have done — caused a leak in the wall."

"Oh, they seemed very professional to me, my dear," Mr. Burton-Smith replied. "It certainly is a mystery . . . ."

"Never mind that — call a plumber . . . . Now!"

* * *

Epilogue.

Mrs. Burton-Smith, the attractive and amoral second wife of the owner of Bland Hall, is faced with a dilemma (although the vain creature is presently not aware of it) which will require firm and resolute action if it is to be resolved in time.

Unless she takes certain measures, there will shortly be a violent encounter when she will not get her own way — *ever again.*

These preventive measures ought to include an opinion from the previous lady of the house regarding the invasion of dampness, water drips and their consequences, and the advisability of wearing a precious stone (stolen in such horrible circumstances in the Middle Ages and known as a Pyx) around her pretty swan-like neck.

However, she could always take a second opinion, seeing that there is one to be had, unknown to her, close at hand.

Indeed, the Bland Spirit would relish the pleasure (in more ways than one), should *he* be consulted.

But, of course, by then it will be much too late.

Either way Robert de Bland will have his way.

LIVERPOOL

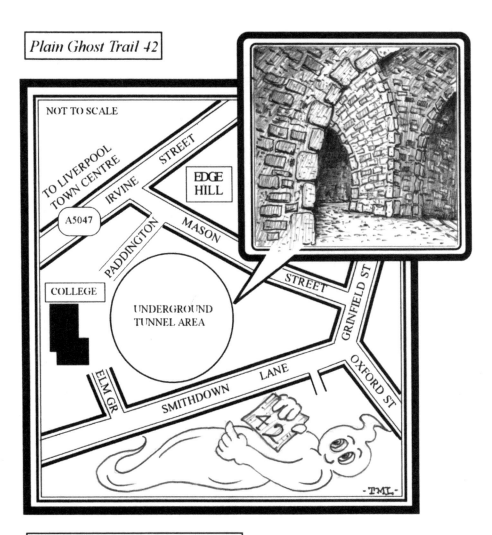

Plain Ghost Trail 42

NOT TO SCALE

TO LIVERPOOL TOWN CENTRE

IRVINE STREET

A5047

EDGE HILL

PADDINGTON

MASON STREET

COLLEGE

UNDERGROUND TUNNEL AREA

GRINFIELD ST

OXFORD ST

ELM GR

SMITHDOWN LANE

42

- TML -

INSET *The Williamson Tunnels*

THE FIFTH JOURNAL

On reflection I am tempted to conclude that the brief article in the Southbeach Visiter, the town's long-established newspaper, was the root cause of Trevor Foster's present dilemma.

STUDENTS TRY TO UNEARTH URBAN MYTHS

A group of Southbeach College students have contacted the editor in the hope of gaining some help from our readers.

The Design and Multimedia students are researching a college project for a 'fly-on-the-wall' documentary and they are trying to find out about any underground tunnels in the Southbeach area.

They are also keen to hear from anyone with interesting or unusual urban myths of this area, so, if you can help, please contact the editor who will be happy to forward any item to Trevor Foster, the student project co-ordinator.

By sheer coincidence I was acquainted with Trevor Foster, or I should say his parents, and just happened to bump into them in the supermarket some days after the article appeared in the newspaper. I inquired about the response to the article.

"Oh yes, he has had some replies," Mrs. Foster answered, "— but he is rather disappointed with them, I'm afraid."

"Really . . . . Why is that?"

"Most of the letters mentioned a tunnel under Southbeach Promenade, and it all sounded very promising," replied Mrs. Foster.

"Trevor was very excited about it — until he got the bad news."

"Bad news . . . .?"

"Yes — a newspaper cutting in one of the letters," her husband joined in. "Unfortunately the tunnel has been filled in." At that moment Trevor arrived. "We were just talking about your disappointment, Trevor," his father continued, "— the newspaper cutting about the tunnel."

"Oh, yes — I'm a bit miffed about it," Trevor sniffed. "It was just the sort of thing we had in mind for the project."

"Bad luck," I commiserated with him. "No tunnel then?"

"No," Trevor replied. "I was really keyed up — until I received this." He reached into his coat pocket and produced an envelope. Inside was the revealing newspaper article, which he handed to me. On reading it I could see why he was so disappointed.

SOUTHBEACH LEGACY LOST.

Many townspeople are probably unaware that a tunnel, complete with shops and arcades lay hidden under Victoria Street for many years. This tunnel was once a roadway which used to lead to what was the original seafront by Queen Victoria's statue and now the Promenade. On either side of this roadway were shops selling souvenirs and refreshments, and in those early days of the resort's growth, when the tide came up to the Promenade Gardens, day trippers would walk from the railway station to Victoria Street to make their way to the beach via this roadway. In later years, when the tide line receded, this roadway became obsolete and was covered over to form the new Promenade, leaving these Victorian shops and arcades hidden away underground for many years.

Unfortunately the volume and weight of modern traffic has significantly increased in recent years and major road-works have been carried out to strengthen this section of the

Promenade. Alas the tunnel has been filled in, thus losing an important legacy of life in those Victorian days, and no longer exists.

"What a shame," I concluded. "It would have made a super tourist attraction." The disappointed student nodded.

"Yes, it would," he agreed. "I don't think we will find another tunnel as interesting as this in Southbeach."

I recalled part of his earlier article "*And they are also keen to hear from anyone with interesting or unusual urban myths of the area*", and drew his attention to it.

"I seem to remember that your project also included the area around Southbeach," I reminded him. "How far does it cover?"

"The coast between Prestley in the north and Liverhead in the south, and inland to Ormsley."

"Ah . . . . Liverhead," I mused. "Would you be interested in something unusual from that area?"

"Well — yes, I suppose so," replied Trevor cautiously, "although our College lecturer might disagree. It might be too far from Southbeach — out of the area. Anyway, what is it?"

"A sort of journal, I suppose," I explained, "handwritten — in an old school exercise book."

"You mean a diary?"

"Not exactly — more a weekly account than a daily entry," I told him. "I found it in a bundle of old sheet music in a charity shop — came from a house clearance, so they told me. The journal was written just before the First World War, but unfortunately part of the front cover had been torn off, so I don't know who actually wrote it — except for the Christian name "Jack". That is still legible."

"It sounds interesting," Trevor declared with growing enthusiasm. "When can I see it?"

"I'll drop it in at your house and you can decide if it's suitable for your project."

It was — except that it also paved the way for Trevor's current predicament.

* * *

The journal was old, faded and misused. Most of the front had been torn away, leaving a jagged edge which ran the length of the cover. However, the Christian name of the owner, "Jack", and the date "1910", were still legible on the remaining brown strip. The leaves were dog-eared and yellowed with age and the handwriting was in that style known as 'copper-plate', neatly laid out and well spaced. The words "NUMBER FIVE", printed in the top left hand corner of the first page and underlined twice in faded red ink, led Trevor to deduce that this faded exercise book was probably the fifth in a series of journals.

The first entry began in the middle of August.

15th. August

We have moved in at last. It was a tiring business all the same, what with the lateness of the baggage cart, the laxity of the carter and narrow passages which made unloading most difficult. For some reason Number 38 has been unoccupied for some years. The house agent seemed reluctant to dwell on the subject, and I had the impression that the house had been difficult to let. He told mama that the previous occupant was very old and the last of that particular family line. The rooms are of ample proportions but in need of a thorough spring clean and decoration. However I am very pleased with my bedroom, a spacious room with a splendid view across to the city. From our situation I can clearly see a train emerging from a railway tunnel in clouds of steam and black smoke, the engine belching fire like some man-made iron dragon dragging its line of captive carriages back to its lair.

'Mmmm . . . . I don't think those tunnels are what our lecturer had in mind,' mused Trevor, rather disappointed at this reference to railways. "The College has enough information on the local railway network as it is."

He put the journal to one side with the intention of returning it at the earliest opportunity. Later that evening he picked it up again and decided to read a few pages more before putting it away in his brief case.

22nd. August

I have settled into my position of assistant clerk at the Mersea Harbour Board Office, and the days pass tolerably well, helped in great measure by the never ending to'ing and fro'ing of the busy river traffic. Ships of all shapes and sizes and of all nationalities pass by my small window, and I often think of my dear father in the Company Office in Bombay and wonder if he will return to England on one of these ships when his leave is due. Mama tells me it will be next year.

29th. August

I heard the noise again last evening. It seems to come from the chimney breast. At first I thought it was my imagination and then I put it down to rats behind the walls of the house, which is very old.

It was in the early hours, well after midnight, when I awoke to hear it again, a persistent scratching sort of sound, rather like the chalk scraping on a blackboard. I was quite vexed at this constant disruption to my sleep and I decided to trace the origin of this very unpleasant noise. By a process of elimination, quietly checking the rooms one by one, I have found the source. It comes from the bottom of the house — from the cellar. I think this sound is carried up the chimney flues and into each room. It is having a rather unsettling effect on my nerves. I do not think it is caused by rats. I am astonished to find that Mama is unaware of the sound.

At this point Trevor's casual interest in the journal underwent a subtle change, replaced by a growing curiosity over this unusual turn of events. He also began to experience a feeling of empathy with the journal's keeper, and sensed the change in his manner to a darker, more sombre mood.

5th. September

The nights are drawing in and the scratching is more persistent than ever. Mama still cannot hear the noise, and it unsettles me greatly. I mentioned it to the gentleman next door and asked him if he had problems with rats in his house. He told me that he had not (he seemed quite put out by my question), and invited me to inspect his cellar to prove the point. I then made a startling discovery which puzzles me greatly. His cellar comprised two rooms whereas our cellar only has one.

I have measured the cellar and have come to the conclusion that there is another room there — but it has been sealed up. I assumed that the door of this sealed room would be in the same position as the one in the cellar next door, and began a preliminary inspection, chipping away a small portion of the plaster. I was correct in my assumption, and came upon wooden boards beneath the plaster surface. It was the door. And then I heard the scratching again. It came from the other side of this sealed door.

Trevor pondered over this discovery with rising excitement. 'Why was the room sealed? Who or what lay beyond the door?'

It was the stuff of criminal detection stories, of innocent victims murdered and hidden away, and, thanks to this latest development, all thoughts of his College project were immediately suspended. He read on.

7th. September.
The plaster was cleared away at last and the door uncovered. I discover that it is locked and I now have to find a key or break it down.

12th. September.
Mama found a rusty key hidden away behind a cupboard whilst cleaning the pantry, and by a fortunate coincidence it fits the mysterious door (although I wonder why the key was hidden away in the first place). I am relieved to find that the unearthly scratching has stopped for the time being.

I opened the door without any difficulty and entered the room with much trepidation. The air was stale and musty and a deep carpet of dust covered the floor. To my surprise I found no fixtures or material fittings of any kind, or for that matter any sign of rats. I thought I glimpsed movement in the candlelight, a white shape in the farthest darkened corner, and momentarily drew back in alarm. But it was a figment of my imagination, and on closer inspection I found the room to be empty. Then my search revealed a most disturbing feature.

On the reverse side of the door I saw marks on the panels, deep incisions which scored and disfigured the wooden surface. I was somewhat troubled by this grim discovery, and could not help but wonder if this strange phenomenon was related to the constant scratching. I bent down to examine them more closely and at that moment (as if some door had just been opened) a sharp draught of foul air swept into the room, raising a cloud of dust and swirling around me. The candle flickered wildly and was suddenly extinguished, leaving me in the dark. Recalling the white shape I fled the room in panic. As I scrambled up the cellar steps I had the distinct sensation that something was close on my heels. I reached the parlour, slammed the door shut, and pressed my weight against it for some moments, whilst slowly recovering my composure. The recovery was short-lived when I realized that I had committed a fatal error. I had forgotten to close and lock the inner door of the cellar.

This revelation had a similar effect on Trevor. His imagination began to play tricks on him and he began to feel uneasy, glancing at the door. He found himself listening intently, straining to hear the faintest sound in the house beyond. All was quiet.

'At least we haven't got a cellar,' he thought, heartened by this fact. He turned to the next page of the journal.

13th. September.

Today I plucked up courage and went back down to the cellar. The door was still open and with the benefit of extra lighting from oil lamps I was able to see more of the secret room. The extra lighting also revealed another disturbing feature, one which I had not noticed on my first inspection. The layer of dust on the floor had been disturbed, and an irregular furrow-like impression led away to the far right hand corner of the cellar (where I thought I had seen the white shape). I followed this trail and discovered another unsettling thing — a rusty iron ring. It was attached to a trap door. Although the hinges were rusted and wooden barrier well and truly set in the stone floor, I concluded from the absence of dust around its edges that it had recently been opened. At that moment Mama called me and I decided to leave further exploration for the time being.

14th. September.

Last night was dreadful. I awoke from a terrifying night-mare and I have not slept since. I feel decidedly unwell. In my dream I saw the white shape in the shadows at the bottom of the stairs. It began to crawl painfully up towards the landing, a daunting spectacle in the flickering candlelight. As it neared the top of the stairs I finally realized what that the white shape was — a grotesque figure wrapped in a shroud, arms outstretched and talon-like fingers gripping the stair carpet, drawing itself forward towards me. I raced back to my bedroom and barricaded the door. I heard its approach along the passage, and then I at last found out what the nerve-wrecking scratching was. This sound came from the other side of the door, as the creature's finger nails slowly scraped along the wooden surface — that irritating and disagreeable scratching so familiar to my ears.

How long I suffered this awful assault in my dream I cannot say, but I awoke with a start and lay trembling in my bed until sun-up and the blessed relief that daybreak brought. Unfortunately this feeling was quickly reversed when I saw the deep score marks on the other side of my bedroom door.
Something has to be done.

17th. September.

The cellar continued to intrigue me and I returned to solve the mystery of the trap door. When I at last levered it open a blast of fetid air belched out, striking me in the face and I reeled back from the overwhelming foul stench, choking and gasping for breath. After the air partially cleared I returned and held the oil lamp over the opening. Its light fell upon a narrow shaft leading down into the bowels of the earth. Iron rungs, pitted with rust, were set into the side of the shaft at regular intervals and disappeared from view into the dark pit.

This development greatly excited Trevor. This was the first hint of the sort of thing he was searching for, and ideal for the College project.

'This could be worthwhile, after all,' he thought.

He read on.

Then I heard a sound, faint and distant, a sound so familiar to my ears. The scratching came from the depths below, and grew louder as I peered into the black hole. Was the 'thing' down there? I broke into a cold sweat at the thought — and then reeled back in shock. I was sure I saw a movement way down in the shaft, and my nightmare became reality when a vague white shape began hauling itself up the rungs — up towards me. My resolve failed. I slammed the trap door shut and ran from the secret room, this time making sure to close and lock the door on my way out. I have not told Mama of these haunting events for fear of upsetting her. She in turn seems quite happy in our new home.

I am not!

21st. September.

Some days have passed since the discovery of the trap door and events in the cellar, and my nervous system has been partially restored by the passing of time. Once again the secret room exerts its powerful influence and I am firmly resolved to investigate further, intending to enter the shaft at the earliest opportunity. Preparations have been made — oil lamp, spare candles, crow bar and a length of stout rope have been collected. What lies below remains to be seen.

The following extract banished all doubts in Trevor's mind as to the suitability of this unusual house for inclusion in the College list of projects. What he read definitely fulfilled the "unearthing urban myths" concept.

24th. September.

I chose a time to explore the shaft in the cellar when the house was empty, on Mama's night out at the Institute. I raised the trap door and lowered the oil lamp on a length of rope, listening intently for any sound of movement below. All seemed well, and I carefully descended the narrow shaft, checking each iron rung with my weight before proceeding. To my surprise I found that the shaft was not as deep as I had first thought and I soon reached the bottom — and dropped into a small square chamber. I was astonished to see that this eerie chamber was lined in brick, measured approximately eight feet by eight feet, and had ornate brick-patterned arches on two opposing sides from which narrow tunnels led away into the depths of the earth. A coating of thick mildew covered most of the chamber's surface, vying with flaking brickwork and loose mortar which covered the floor. It was quite obvious that this mysterious chamber and tunnels had not been used for many, many years. The stench was quite nauseous and I stood there for some while, pressing a handkerchief to my nose and mouth, adjusting to this strange and frightening environment.

Why was it there? Who had built it? Why did a shaft in the cellar of Number 38 lead down to it?

These questions flooded my mind and there was no apparent answer.

Which way to go? Which tunnel to take — left or right?

It was a difficult decision to make. The tunnels led away in each direction, into the overpowering blackness way out of reach of the puny yellow rays of my oil lamp. Then I felt a strange sensation, as if a hidden presence in the depths of the tunnels were urging me on — to take the left way. This persuasive feeling drew me forward and I moved off through the decorated arch and away from the shaft, my crunching footsteps echoing in the confined passage. Moments later I was confronted by another problem when I reached a bend in the tunnel. At this point the tunnel split into two, branching right and left, and I paused momentarily. Again I felt drawn to the left branch and continued down that path. As I progressed I was conscious of a growing feeling of unease — as if I were close to some unknown danger.

And then the pale light from my lamp fell upon a brick lying in the dirt ahead of me and, mindful of safety and possible roof collapse, I cautiously approached this section of the tunnel. I examined the wall and saw a small breach, about five feet up from the floor, where this brick had been displaced. I raised my lamp to examine this area of wall expecting to find solid bedrock behind the brick lining — but to my astonishment I found a small vaulted room beyond. This vault had been bricked up — and I saw the reason why. It was lined with an assortment of coffins piled one upon the other, dust-covered and streaked with the ravages of mould and decay.

The riveting account so far had exceeded all Trevor's expectations and he could not but tremble with excitement at this latest development.

'Jack must have stumbled on a secret burial vault beneath a church,' reasoned Trevor. "Now that certainly would be an unusual urban slant on the tunnel project.' He turned the page and found that it was not as simple as that.

This particular urban slant took a more sinister turn.

And then I saw something else through the breach in the

tunnel wall. In the far recess of this burial vault there crouched the apparition of a man in a long cloak, his back towards me — and he was engrossed in a most peculiar and gruesome activity. His ear was pressed firmly against the lid of a coffin — as if he were listening intently to some noise within. I stifled a gasp of horror at this weird scene — and he straightened up and turned to face me. His eyes, glinting in the lamp light, met mine and I detected undisguised rage in his piercing glare. This malevolent spectre started towards me, no doubt bent on supplying another body for that deathly chamber, and I reacted accordingly. I fled back down the tunnel in a bid to escape this vindictive creature, and as I raced away I could hear him coming after me, the sound of his footfalls echoing and merging with my own in the confined space. Further along the tunnel this mad chase soon developed into something even more hair-raising when I realized that I had lost my bearings and taken the wrong branch — and I was now totally lost in this terrifying labyrinth.

When I suddenly stopped — my assailant stopped, and the tunnel fell silent.

And when I moved forward quietly — he did the same, yet slowly gaining on me. It became a monstrous game of cat and mouse, and he knew these tunnels better than I. Exhaustion and fatigue now began to take their toll and, to top it all, the oil in my lamp dwindled and the flame gradually dimmed and spluttered — and then gave out. I was left in a state of panic and despair, staring into the blackness as 'he' edged closer and closer.

All seem lost.

I reached out with my hands in the pitch-blackness, vainly searching for the wall — and touched something cold and leathery.

It was another hand.

Long, bony fingers grasped mine and began to drag me on, leading me down the passage — away from 'him'. I followed in a frenzied shuffle, blindly stumbling and lurching along, unable to see my silent, mysterious saviour, or anything else for that matter. All the while 'his' footsteps dogged us, closing the gap. Suddenly my hand was released and I lurched to a halt. At this moment of release something brushed past me, and I briefly touched the waving folds of a finely textured, sheet-like garment.

Again I was alone.

And then I perceived a soft glow in the distance and stumbled towards it. As I neared this beacon of light my spirits rose — for I saw it was coming from the shaft — the light streaming down from the cellar of Number Thirty Eight. I raced into the chamber, leaped onto the iron rungs and pulled myself clear of the tunnel. 'He' was close behind, but not close enough. I clambered up and reached the safety of the cellar, slamming the trap door down just in time. Trembling with fear and exhaustion I literally dragged myself out of that secret room and locked the door. I realized there and then why the previous owner had sealed it — and why the house had remained untenanted for all those years.

Yet I know not who had guided me through the darkness and saved me? Whoever it was still remains down there in the tunnel with 'him', and I have no desire to return to that place.

I must find some way to persuade Mama to seek fresh accommodation. She often tells me that the furnished rooms suit her admirably — unfortunately I have to say the burial vault beneath our house has the totally opposite effect on me.

<u>26th. September.</u>
Last night my already nervous constitution received

another shock and my tenuous grip on the situation took a turn for the worse. I have nailed down the trap door and re-sealed the cellar room. The door has been re-plastered and concealed as a barrier against unwanted visitors, either 'into' or 'out from' the secret room. In the early hours I returned home from an evening spent with friends at the theatre. My mother had retired to bed and I immediately went up to my room. There I received an additional blow to my already troubled mind.

My precautions have failed.

I found someone in my room — in my bed!

I could see the shape beneath the bedclothes — and this shape slowly rose to greet me. The bed sheet fell away, and I was confronted by the most horrific sight. A haggard spectral creature in a tattered mouldy shroud, arms outstretched, leathery hands torn and blood-stained swayed painfully across the room and reached out to embrace me.

Could this ungodly creature be my saviour from the tunnel?

I decided to reject this show of tender affection out of hand — and fled from the room.

The final extract in the journal had a similar effect on Trevor. It was quite short and ended abruptly — in mid sentence. There was no indication to show whether Jack had gone on to write a sixth journal, and whether he had finally persuaded his mother to leave the haunted house for another property in a different part of the city.

27th. September.

I find it difficult to express my feelings at this moment. My bedroom 'visitor' has been joined by 'another'. 'He' knows that I have witnessed his actions and his intentions towards me are perfectly clear. In fact I swear I hear 'his' footsteps coming up the stairs to my door and . . . .

The rest of the pages were blank.

* * *

Trevor Foster arrived with the journal.

"Well — what did you think of it?" I asked him.

"Really weird — unbelievable, in fact," he answered gravely. "Were there any more journals in that bundle of old music?"

"No — just the one."

"What a shame," he replied in a disappointed voice. "We don't even know the name of the street — only the number of the house — or what eventually happened to Jack and his mother."

"That's right," I nodded, "although you must bear in mind that the house might be long gone by now — especially after the wartime bombing. A lot of property was destroyed, you know."

"Property yes — but not the tunnel. In fact, when I mentioned it to the lecturer, she immediately thought of the Williams tunnels. In fact she had already organized a College trip to see them." He handed me a College bulletin. "Do you think she could be right?"

History Department
(Planned Visits - Term 2)
(3) Archeological Site — Williams Tunnel Complex
(Proposed Date and Time to be announced)
Details of a Tunnels Visitor Centre has recently been unveiled to the general public, the latest stage in the promotion of what is seen as a unique and ambitious tourist attraction. Thanks to the vision and tireless efforts of the Joseph Williams Society, a dedicated group of enthusiasts who banded together to secure European funding for extensive renovation work, a valuable piece of the City's historic and architectural heritage had been saved for future generations.

These tunnels, 'lost' for many years, are unique, there being
no others like them in the country, and an unusual 'double'
tunnel is the only one of its kind in existence. On completion
of this exciting project visitors will be able to walk deep into
the heart of these dark passages and see how they were carved
from the solid rock. Special arrangements for architectural
students and other like-minded groups to view the progress
of the work so far have been agreed with the contractors.
Please fill in the attached booking slip.

"I'd say it was very likely," I nodded after reading the details.
"Yes, very likely indeed. There seems to be many tunnels, and it
looks as if Jack found an entrance to one of them in his cellar."

"But do you believe what he saw down there?" Trevor asked me.
"It could have been a Victorian hoax. The contractors haven't found
anything out of the ordinary so far."

"Well, I don't think Jack made it up," I declared, recalling the
description of his chase and escape. "The end of the journal was a
bit mind-boggling. If we could lay our hands on the other journals,
and journal six in particular, it might shed some light on it all. At
least it would be an interesting addition to your college project. Let
me know how you get on with the visit."

Trevor promised to do just that.

I, in return, promised to contact the Joseph Williams Society for
more information on the originator of these strange tunnels.

The Society, by return, sent me the following extract.

Thank you for you inquiry.

If you want to know more or become involved in the work
we do, you can look for "Friends of the Williams Tunnels"
on the internet.

<u>THE MOLE OF BORDER HILL</u>
Joseph Williams (born 1769 — died 1840 supposedly of

*'water on the chest') was born in Warringforth and came to
Liverhead in 1780 to work in the Tait tobacco factory. He
married Elizabeth, the daughter of the owner, and his eccentric
ways began to manifest themselves even at his wedding. He
attended the ceremony in hunting pink, and then galloped off
to the Liverhead Hunt. He was also obsessed with arches
and tunnels (he wore moleskin clothes), spending vast sums
of money on his 'hobby' when he retired from the company
in 1818. He began from his own cellar, with a small shaft,
and excavated a labyrinth of tunnels and vast underground
halls, vaults, pits and chasms with the help of a great number
of unemployed men (demobilized soldiers returning from the
Napoleonic Wars). In "giving charity to the poor by giving
work to the unemployed" he became a unique public
benefactor of his time.*

*These underground passages stretched for several miles,
with additional blank-walled or circular passages which
returned to a starting point: there was no apparent reason or
plan for their tortuous routes (like the tunnels of a mole). The
locations of these tunnels were forgotten or 'lost' over the
years, until rediscovered in the early 20th. Century by building
workers. Joseph Williams was laid to rest in the Tait family
tomb in the yard of St. Michael's Church (demolished in
1905), and his portrait can be seen in the local library.*

I enclose a membership form and subscription details.

This "Mole of Border Hill" was eccentric in the extreme, judging
by his description, and so were his tunnels.

I decided to contact Trevor, and it was at this point, on reading
an article in the local paper, that I became aware of his unfortunate
dilemma.

* * *

It was on the third page of the Southbeach Visiter. It was short and of general interest to its readers. However, to readers of Journal Number 5, written in 1908, the contents were, to put it mildly, quite astounding.

STUDENT'S STRANGE DISCOVERY

A student from Southbeach College stumbled on a gruesome relic of the past at the weekend. He was one of a group from the Collage visiting the Williams Tunnels, the latest tourist attraction in the area. He wandered away from the main party and came upon an unknown section of the tunnel not yet discovered by the contractors in charge of renovating this unique architectural site. There he found a vault and uncovered a mystery. The vault had been stacked with coffins and then sealed up.

However, it turns out that this type of burial was not uncommon before 1834. When the small city graveyards were full (caused by the rapid growth in city populations and high mortality rates) the church authorities resorted to placing the bodies of the deceased in other locations (cremation was unknown at that time) and they found this part of the Williams catacomb-like tunnels eminently suitable for this purpose. The 'burial' problem was overcome when an Act of Parliament allowed private cemetery companies to operate, followed in later years by cremation.

The article had not mentioned Trevor by name but I was convinced that it was him. A visit from "the student" in question proved the case when Trevor, pale and shaken, arrived at my door within the hour.

"Was it you, then?" I asked, waving the newspaper.

"It was," Trevor replied with a despondent air. "But it didn't tell you everything."

"Everything — you mean there's more?"

71

"Yes, I'm afraid there is," he replied dejectedly, and then went on to describe the events leading up to his discovery.

The party of students from the College arrived at the proposed site of the Visitor Centre. They were greeted at the tunnel entrance by the consultant in charge of the development and given a general description of the history and layout of the tunnel system, followed by a brief appraisal of the work to date and safety requirements, "Do not stray from the group" being the primary instruction. The party then entered the as yet unfathomed labyrinth, making their way along brick-lined passages and through high-vaulted chambers into the depths of the earth. They came to the end of the lighted section of the tunnel system where the remedial work had so far progressed, and carried on into a part of the system using the lamps on their safety helmets to light the way.

It was at this point, near a fork in the tunnel that Trevor became detached from the main party when he stopped to adjust his lamp, which had developed an intermittent fault. Unfortunately he chose the wrong branch and eventually arrived at a section of the tunnel blocked by a roof fall. He heard a noise on the other side of this barrier, and thinking the College party were on the other side, scrambled through a small gap at the top of the pile of rubble. He dropped down on the other side and found to his astonishment that he was in a small chamber.

It was all too familiar to him.

The decorated arches, the shaft with iron rungs, the mildewed bricks, the bend and left-hand branch were the tunnel split in two were just as Jack described them, all those years ago. And further on he too came upon a small cavity in the wall, the sealed vault in the fifth journal. He peered into the gap in the brickwork, the light from his lamp falling upon dust-laden coffins ranged round the walls, one piled upon another, and he half expected to see the strange apparition crouched in the corner, ear pressed against the lid of a coffin.

However, what happened next wasn't described in the journal. *He found himself face to face with something so horrible that he froze on the spot, unable to move.*

A woman's face, ravaged with decay and covered in strands of long white hair, rose up from the behind the wall. A hideous expression of torment and rage, eyes glowing with pain and anguish greeted the terrified student. Their eyes met and her tormented expression instantly softened to one of gladness and relief, as if at long last someone had found her. Then a leathery hand emerged from the black hole, a hand withered and emaciated, its fingers torn and nails broken. It gently reached out to touch him, and Trevor jerked back, his safety helmet flying from his head to hit the ground with a resounding clatter. The light was immediately extinguished and Trevor found himself in the darkness.

He staggered away, groping the sides of the tunnel, remembering Jack's predicament all those years ago. At this very moment Trevor was sure he heard footsteps in the darkness behind him. However this time it wasn't the guiding hand or the light from a cellar shaft which aided him, but the distant lamp light from a search party coming to look for him.

"That's an experience you'll not forget in a hurry," I observed grimly, "You won't have any doubts about the journal now!"

"If I had — then they were swept away last night," Trevor replied. "I woke up around one o'clock and thought I heard a scraping noise outside my bedroom. When I opened the door this morning I found several deep scores in the wood — possibly scratches."

* * *

Trevor is faced with a growing dilemma.

A second article has appeared in the local newspaper, and reveals the unnatural and monstrous circumstances within the sealed vault.

GRUESOME DISCLOSURE

Following on from a previous article ("Student's Strange Discovery"), the Joseph Williams Society has informed us that there has been a further development in the case. It seems that when the secret burial vault was fully opened a skeleton wrapped in the remains of a shroud was found lying on the floor behind the sealed wall. A coffin with a displaced lid was also found nearby. It was empty. At this stage another gruesome discovery came to light when it was found that the underside of the coffin lid bore deeps scratch marks, indicating that the incumbent was actually alive when interred in the coffin and had tried to break out. Medical opinion suggests that it was one of those rare cases of mistaken symptoms of death due to that rare medical condition, catalepsy (a state of deep insensibility linked to bodily rigidity).

The identity of this unfortunate person was found on a brass name-plate. It is one Alice Sherbourne, and records indicate that she was the wife of a Doctor Sherbourne, a medical practitioner and surgeon in the city, and that she died suddenly in 1863. An inventory of the other coffins reveal that they were all placed there before 1832, and so it remains a mystery as to why that particular coffin came to be placed in the sealed vault over thirty years later.

I have also examined the City Archive records for that particular period with a certain medical practitioner in mind. From various entries and letters I have gleaned some interesting pieces of information on which I now base my theory concerning the strange happenings in Number Thirty Eight. It seems that Doctor Sherbourne, an aspiring surgeon of the time, sought rapid advancement in the stuffy world of medicine, but he lacked the necessary influence, and such high ambitions were well above his means — until he married a young woman with a very large fortune.

Unfortunately he hit a snag.

Her fortune was held under strict trust laws, and he was unable to benefit from it — until he discovered his wife's unfortunate condition — catalepsy.

Unlike today, the laws of the period gave the husband full rights over his wife's property and fortune on her death, and when Alice 'died' suddenly in 1832 Doctor Sherbourne inherited this considerable fortune. It would seem, bearing in mind the recent gruesome discovery, that Alice was not dead but in a deep trance, and that the villainous doctor had taken advantage of this, issuing a death certificate and consigning her to a burial plot in the local church yard (the church and grave yard have long since vanished, displaced by modern development). However, it did lead to some speculation and mounting suspicion about the circumstances of her death at the time.

As to the conundrum of her final resting place in the tunnel vault, I can only surmise that Doctor Sherbourne found the shaft in the cellar of his house, and when he discovered the burial vault, long disused, in the tunnel he saw an ideal opportunity to cover up his villainy by secretly moving the body of his departed wife from her grave in the church yard to this underground tomb.

How did he manage this damnable transfer?

A possible explanation lies in a particularly odious medical practice of the time. During the early Victorian Period many advances in surgical skills came from a new understanding of the anatomy of the human body. This in part was brought about by the dissection of corpses, often stolen from church yards by grave robbers or 'body snatchers' (as they were termed in the press). They supplied surgeons with fresh corpses, usually exhumed within hours of internment, and it was a very lucrative trade. It is most likely that Doctor Sherbourne (considering his ambitious nature) was one such surgeon who used their services, and no doubt, did so on this occasion. And, if Jack's account in his journal is anything to go by, Doctor Sherbourne, the crouching apparition in the vault, listened to his wife's frenzied scratching and muffled screams of terror as she desperately tried to escape the confines of her coffin before he bricked up the vault.

When she did eventually mange to break out of this horrendous wooden confinement she found herself walled-up in a dank, mildewed *prison* built by an eccentric and charitable old gentleman some thirty years previously.

Madness swiftly overtook the unfortunate woman, followed by a lingering death.

As to the *good* doctor, it seemed his rise in the medical profession was curtailed. He indeed did become extremely wealthy, but at the same time withdrew from the world of medicine and became a recluse (there was an obscure medical reference to paranoia, severe melancholia and disordered mental state due to hallucinations about nocturnal visits from of his departed wife), never leaving the house — almost as if he were guarding the premises. The sealed room in the cellar would suggest drastic preventative measures against some incursion from below rather than above.

The reclusive doctor lived at Number Thirty Eight into the next century, a lonely guardian, until his death some forty years later, and the house remained empty until Jack and his mother came to live there several years later.

And now to Trevor's present dilemma.

If the current pattern of events conform to those which took place in 1910 (so vividly described in the fifth journal), then the deep scoring on Trevor's bedroom door could be an ominous forewarning of an amorous visitation from one so callously misused centuries earlier — to be followed by an angry visitation from another well versed in the dissection of the human body.

As for myself — I am waiting patiently for Trevor Foster to call.

SCARISBRICK

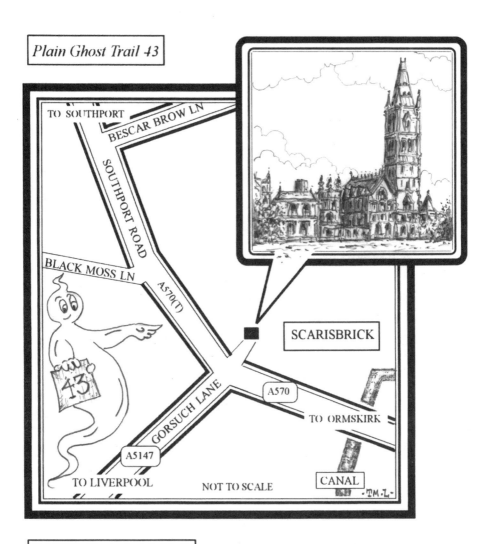

Plain Ghost Trail 43

TO SOUTHPORT

BESCAR BROW LN

SOUTHPORT ROAD

BLACK MOSS LN

A570(T)

43

SCARISBRICK

GORSUCH LANE

A570

TO ORMSKIRK

A5147

TO LIVERPOOL

NOT TO SCALE

CANAL

INSET *Scarisbrick Hall*

THE SACRED CROWN

"What is it?"

"Hmm — a sort of tin can, I think."

"Where did you find it?"

"In the college woods — near the canal."

The pair, sitting in a secluded corner of the Bridge Inn lounge bar, examined the unusual object: it was battered and severely dented.

"It has been knocked about a bit," observed the younger of the two.

The older man nodded. "A couple of blasted kids — they were belting hell out of it with a large stone. I had just settled down to an afternoon's peaceful fishing when they turned up and started to make a right old din. So I got up to give them a piece of my mind."

"Were they from the college?"

"Yes — scarpered sharpish when one of the masters suddenly came out of the trees . . . ." The older man paused for a moment. "At least I think it was one of the staff. It was a bit misty at the time so I couldn't be sure. But I'm certain he was wearing one of those old-fashioned gowns, like the sort those public school teachers wear — and he looked in a right bad mood."

"So they took off before he could get his hands on them?"

"Took off — I'll say they did — shot right past me absolutely terrified," the older man replied with a grin. "I didn't think teachers could put the fear of God into kids these days — but he certainly did!"

"I had a teacher just like that — related to 'Old Nick" himself,

79

so we thought at the time," the younger man chuckled. "What did the teacher say?"

"That's the odd thing about it all," the older man replied. "Nothing — he just disappeared into thin air. One minute he was there, next minute he was gone — vanished into the mist."

"Probably doubled back to catch them at the Hall gates."

"He would have to be quick about it — those kids were certainly moving fast," he answered with a chuckle. "Anyway, I went into the wood to investigate what all the fuss was about and found this old can next to the stone in the long grass."

They contemplated the battered metal canister.

"I wonder where those kids found it?"

"Maybe it came from the college," the older man surmised. "The County Council is doing some preservation work at the Hall at the moment, and perhaps those young blighters found it — must have thought there was something valuable inside."

"So what are you going to do with it, Stan?"

"Good question, Bill," Stanley Talbot, the older man, replied. "I think I'll take it home for the time being," he decided, placing the canister in his fishing bag, "— and hold on to it until I see those two college kids again — find out where they got it."

"Do you think it could be worth a bit?" asked Bill Watson.

"Don't know," Stanley sniffed, as the pair left the pub and set off home. "I'll take it round to that dealer in Southbeach. He might know something about it."

Meanwhile the two very frightened kids in question, junior pupils of Scarstone Hall Independent College, crouched in the long grass behind the imposing wrought iron gates next to the gatehouse at the Hall entrance. They peered anxiously down the misty tree-lined drive, searching for any sign of their pursuer, at the same time seriously debating whether it was wise to return to the old Hall.

Their recent escapade with the mysterious canister in the Hall grounds had seemed so exciting at the time, and the possibility of valuable treasure within their grasp had built up such a fever of anticipation, that is, until the sudden appearance of a terrifying gowned figure bearing down on them out of the mist. This ghastly figure had immediately put an end to all that childish speculation — and given them an extremely unpleasant shock into the bargain.

This silent apparition was, to put it mildly, both malevolent and hostile, and in the opinion of the two unhappy pupils — *long dead*!

* * *

The renovation of the ancient building had begun some weeks previously, and a considerable sum had been allocated for this purpose by the County Council, or, as the local newspaper put it, "*the money is entirely for the protection and preservation of those works of art contained in the Hall which are currently owned by the Council*". It also stated that "*part of the cost of restoration of the Hall itself is being met by the new owners, Mercian Independent Education PLC, and undertaken in full consultation with County Heritage*".

On the advice of the representative of County Heritage it was decided to remove certain artifacts and paintings for safe keeping while the work was in progress, and it was during this initial stage of restoration in the Great Hall that the two young students, Alistair and William, stumbled on the root cause of their current predicament.

This part of the building was out of bounds to the all college students, but the inquisitive pair, while on an errand for the college bursar, could not resist the temptation to see what was going on in this interesting room. They made a detour and crept into the south porch and hid behind the medieval screens just in time to see three workman removing a substantial wood carving from the west wall of the Great Hall. The work was so complicated and demanding, considering the weight and valuable nature of this medieval carving, that their attention was entirely taken up with the removal procedure.

Because of this the workmen initially failed to see a small cavity in the wall behind the carving — but the sharp-eyed boys didn't.

"Look, there's a hole in the wall," whispered William excitedly. His companion nodded.

"I think there's something in it," he replied. "I'm going to see what it is."

"Be careful," advised William, glancing round to see if the coast was clear. "We've had it if some one finds us in here."

By the time he turned back Alistair was already half way across the room, and seconds later arrived at the cavity. He swiftly reached in and withdrew a grimy cobwebbed object.

William gasped in a mixture of excitement and tension, for the workmen, up to now completely oblivious to what was in progress, were about to return. Alistair made it back to the screens just in time, and the pair beat a rapid retreat from the ancient hall, Alistair clasping the mysterious *find* tightly beneath his blazer. Breathless and relieved at their narrow escape, they reached their dormitory in the junior wing and immediately wrapped the object in Alistair's football shirt, stashing the bundle in his bedside locker before hurrying back to their classroom.

Meanwhile an argument had broken out in the Great Hall.

"There was definitely some one here, I tell," one of them declared.

"Well, I didn't see anyone, mate," the second replied.

"But there was — I'm sure of it!"

"What did the bloke look like?" asked the third.

"It's hard to say," the first replied. "I only caught a glimpse of him — really ancient and wearing a dusty old gown — didn't like the look of him at all. I'm sure he wasn't one of them masters."

"Blimey, mate," the second declared, "I bet you've just seen a ghost."

"Get out of it!"

"It bet it was. Everyone knows all these old Halls are haunted. I

82

blame it on that old religious carving. It gives me the creeps, just touching it. In my opinion we should have left it where it was."

"Never mind all that baloney, you two," the third interrupted irritably. "Let's have a look at that hole."

What they found was unusual, to say the least. The cavity contained three plates, tarnished and covered in grime, and a rotting leather pouch which crumbled in the sunlight. Several misshapen coins spilled out, bouncing and rolling across the floor in a mad whirling clatter.

The workmen quickly recovered the hoard and placed the coins on one of the plates.

"What a turn up," the first gasped in astonishment. "What should we do with it all?"

"Got to hand it in," replied the third.

"Perhaps there'll be some sort of reward for finding the stuff?" reasoned the second.

"Doubt it — it all belongs to the Hall," replied the third.

"Mind you, on second thoughts I don't want anything to do with it," remarked the first, contemplating the strange dirt-encrusted collection on the table.

"Why's that, mate?"

"Well — it might belong to that weird bloke I saw. Ghost or no ghost, I certainly don't want anything to do with him, I can tell you."

Alistair and William, sitting together in a classroom in the distant junior block, had yet to reach that very same conclusion — but they eventually would.

*　*　*

"What do you think it is?" wondered Alistair, unwrapping their *find*.

The boys stood contemplating the grimy canister-like object on the bed.

"Search me. It's definitely a container of some sort," replied William, picking it up and giving it a shake,"— and I think there's something inside it."

"It could be some sort of treasure — jewels and stuff, like the one in that book you got from the library."

"You mean "The Canterville Ghost" and the family treasure?"

"That's the one," replied Alistair. "This could be the same sort of thing, couldn't it? This old tin could have been hidden behind that weird carving for years."

"Right — so it looks as if we've found the Scarstone family treasure,' declared William gleefully. He wiped the container with the cloth and examined the top. "It's dead old and it has been sealed up. How can we open it?"

The pair pondered the problem, and came to the conclusion that it would need a certain amount of brute force, possibly in the form of a hammer and chisel, to overcome the problem.

"Try bashing the edge on the end of the locker," Alistair suggested. "That might do the trick."

"Good idea," William replied. "Just check the stairs and see if the coast is clear. The others will be coming out of the dining room any time now." The pair had purposely missed their lunch to come up to the dorm to examine their *find*, and there wasn't much time to spare.

Alistair went out and looked over banisters at the stairs below — and gave a start. The "coast" was not clear, and the treasure hunters were in imminent danger of discovery.

He was astonished to see a strange figure ascending the stairs from below, and there was something very disturbing, not to say downright menacing, about this eerie person. Because Alistair looked down upon him from above, the boy's view was partly obscured by the double flight of stairs. But it was the way in which the figure moved, silently and purposefully, pale bony fingers sliding up the banister rail at each step, that cast Alistair into a state of sheer panic, further exacerbated by the sight of straggling wisps of bleached hair falling upon a dusty and cobweb covered gown.

The eerie figure would soon reach the landing and then all would be lost.

"Quick — or we've had it!" cried Alistair, racing back into the dorm. "Let's get out of here. Some one is coming up the stairs!"

A startled William considered for a moment. The way out down the stairs was blocked.

"The fire escape — we'll have to use the fire escape," he decided, grabbing the container and making off down the corridor, closely followed by his shaken and pale-faced companion. In a flash they shot down the fire escape stairs and across the lawn, into the shelter of the surrounding woodland. A light mist was rising and swirling through the trees and once they were well away from the Hall the pair halted and drew breath.

"Phew, that was a narrow escape," William panted. "Was it one of the teachers?"

"Definitely not," returned a shaken Alistair. "I've never seen a teacher like him in school."

"Well, no one will see us here," said William, spotting a large piece of sandstone lying in the long grass. He picked it up and, laying the canister on tree stump, turned to a very nervous Alistair. "Let's see if this will work. Hold the tin steady while I hit the edge."

William began to bash it with the stone, badly denting the sides but having no immediate effect on the sealed lid. Unfortunately the noise was quite considerable, the clash of stone against hollow metal echoing through the leaf-less trees and December gloom, and it made Alistair even more nervous. He became anxious and fidgety, constantly looking over his shoulder and peering apprehensively into the mist.

"I — I don't think this is a very good idea, William," he stammered. "I'm — I'm sure some one will hear all this noise. I think we ought to . . . ." His voice trailed away and he turned white as a sheet.

85

"Oh no!" he cried. "I think we ought to get the hell out of here."

Flinging the canister into the long grass he took off into the trees. William, astounded by this sudden strange behaviour, turned round to see what the fuss was about — and gasped in horror at the sight of an unearthly creature, covered in dust and cobwebs and plainly furious, emerging silently from the mist and bearing down on him.

"Wait for me!" William yelled, and sprinted after his friend.

In the meantime Stanley Talbot, peacefully fishing in the nearby canal, had been disturbed by the awful din.

He got up to investigate, moving into the misty wood just in time to see one of the boys drop the canister as one of the college masters came up on them. The boys raced blindly past the astonished fisherman in a state of terror and panic, and he watched them disappear into the mist before turning to meet their teacher.

To his surprise the master had also vanished into the mist.

* * *

"Do you know what it is?"

"Well — I've got a good idea." The elderly owner of the "Everything Bought And Sold" corner shop nodded as he cleaned his spectacles and examined the tin canister. "Where did you say you found it?"

"In the woods near Scarstone College," replied Stanley. "You know — that private school on the way to Ormsley."

The dealer looked up and regarded him somewhat curiously.

"The woods, you say — not in the Hall?"

'That's right — in the estate woods by the canal."

"Hmm — unusual — very unusual." The dealer turned back to the canister and continued to turn it round and round. "I must say you were a bit heavy-handed when you tried to open it."

"It wasn't me," retorted Stanley. "It was like that when I found it."

86

"Well — if you say so. It has been knocked about a bit, I'm afraid?"

"Yes, I know that," replied Stanley in an exasperated tone of voice. It had to be said that his patience was wearing a bit thin by this time. "But what is it?"

"At first glance I would have said that it was an small urn — or a funeral urn to be exact," the dealer replied, "but . . . ."

"But what?"

"Now I'm pretty certain it isn't — a funeral urn, I mean." The dealer looked very puzzled. "I have some tomb and altar accessories over here in the corner, so you can see for yourself."

He pointed to a corner of the jumbled room where various dusty objects balanced precariously on some rather unstable shelving. Large and small urns and goblets, caskets and candlesticks vied for living space with porcelain flower bowls, chalices and several grimy wine vessels. It was immediately apparent to Stanley that his "urn" was somewhat on the smaller side when compared to the urns on the shelf.

"For a start," the elderly dealer went on, "most of these accessories are made out of brass, copper or pewter for general use, but expensive ones can often be made out of silver and even gold. Yours is a bit of a mixture which is very unusual." The dealer reached up and took down one of the urns. "And another thing — it is much smaller that this one, which is the usual standard size. So I don't think it is a funeral urn."

"There definitely is something inside it. Could it be cremation urn — for someone's ashes?"

"No, I don't think so," replied the elderly dealer with a chuckle. "Cremation only became possible in the Victorian Period, some hundred and fifty years ago, and I'm pretty certain this container is a lot older than that."

He noticed Stanley's disappointment. "Sorry I can't be of more help," he continued sympathetically.

At that moment his attention was taken up by someone arriving at the door, an indistinct shape outlined in the begrimed glass pane. The figure didn't enter, but seemed to hover, undecided, possibly wishing to consult the dealer privately. Business had been slack and he didn't want to lose valuable custom. He abruptly brought his conversation with Stanley to a close.

"What you really need," he advised quickly, "is an opinion from some one more familiar with earlier religious accessories. Mr. Jones, the owner of Ormsley Antiques, might be able to help you. I have heard that he is well up on this sort of thing."

Stanley thanked him and left the shop — and to the dealer's disgust the hesitant figure went after him.

"He looked a bit of a weirdo anyway," he sniffed, somewhat annoyed at a loss of revenue. "Probably not even interested in buying anything."

The dealer was right on that score.

Some half an hour or so later Stanley arrived in Ormsley and immediately set off in search of the antiques shop. He arrived at the premises just as Mr. Jones, the proprietor, was locking up.

"I'm sorry sir," the proprietor said, shaking his head, "but I'm closing for the rest of the day."

"Oh dear," replied Stanley rather dejectedly. "I came for an opinion on this." He pulled the canister out of his carrier bag, and held it out. Mr. Jones took one look at it and immediately changed his mind.

"Ah yes — I see. Do come in," he smiled, inviting Stanley in and placing the "closed" sign in the window. "Now let's see what you've got there."

The preliminary conversation covered the same ground as that with the elderly dealer. However, on this occasion Mr. Jones was definitely better informed. He pored over the metal object, closely examining it with a magnifying glass, turning it this way and that, his face gleaming with undisguised pleasure.

"My word, you really have got something here," he chortled, rubbing his hands together. "Do you mind if I do a test on it."

"No — be my guest," Stanley replied, "— as long as you can tell me what it is."

"Oh I think I'll be able to satisfy you on that score," the antique dealer beamed.

He produced a tin of cleaning fluid and began to polish a small portion of the surface. It had an extraordinary effect on the metal. Gleaming streaks appeared on the dull surface, and Mr. Jones drew his breath.

"Just as I thought," he murmured. "Different metals."

"Different metals?"

"Yes. The basic container is made of ordinary pewter — but silver has been added to it, hence the gleaming streaks." He turned to Stanley. "I have to tell you," he observed in a serious tone, "I haven't seen anything like this before. It really is a very unusual, not to say exciting, piece."

"So is it a funeral urn?"

"Oh no, old chap," he replied in a hushed voice. "This is something much more interesting than that. I'm sure this is a reliquary."

"A reliquary — what the Dickens is that?"

"A container for relics."

"You've got me there, I'm afraid," replied a puzzled Stanley.

"Relics are belongings or parts of the body of a saint which are usually kept in a church or monastery as objects of reverence after the saint's death ," Mr. Jones told him seriously.

"So there are bits of some old saint in this old tin?"

"Perhaps — but this container, or urn as you call it, is very singular. Some of these reliquaries are normally very ornate, highly decorated with delicate filigree of vines and holy figures, and often made out of gold or silver, while others are of an elegant and simple design. However, in this case we have a very basic, almost crude design, and the pewter metal has been infused with silver — so in religious terms what do you think that means?"

"Absolutely no idea," returned Stanley. "I'm not into all this religious stuff."

"Well, if you think back to your bible stories, one of the most famous references to silver is that of Judas and the coins he received for betraying Jesus to the authorities — the notorious thirty pieces of silver."

"Ah, yes — I remember that — after they had their supper."

"Not quite — but near enough," chuckled the antique dealer, swiftly realizing that biblical history was not one of his customer's strong points.

"In my opinion this simple reliquary is made out of a mixture of pewter and thirty pieces of silver . . . ." He paused for a moment, savouring the conclusion. "Which means that the remains inside this reliquary might not be those of an ordinary saint — but of Jesus himself."

"Blimey!" Even Stanley, with his basic understanding of religion, could see the magnitude of this disclosure.

"Unfortunately there is a slight drawback," Mr. Jones went on in a more sober fashion. "During the early Christian era there were lots of fake relics. Many dubious reliquaries were sold for large sums of money by travelling tinkers and bogus monks, especially after the Crusades in the Holy Land, and I'm bound to say that this could be one such fake."

He picked up the cloth and vigorously cleaned the base of the holy object.

"Ah — I think we have something here — some incised letters, I think." He took his magnifying glass and spelled them out. "L-a-c-o-u-r-o-n-n-e-s-a-c-r-é-e. Now what does that mean?"

The pair pondered over the words.

"It's double-dutch to me," Stanley reflected. "I've no idea."

"Well I think I do," answered the antique dealer. "It's French and I'm sure it says "la courone sacrée". That means "the crown sacred" or "the sacred crown".

However, he seemed disappointed at this development. "That's a pity," he sniffed.

"Why's that. At least it tells you something more about it."

"Unfortunately it's the language. To be authentic and from those early Christian times the words ought to be in Hebrew, or possibly Greek or Latin." He pondered for a while. "Although it is still possible that these words were added some centuries later, only extensive testing will prove that, I'm afraid. Perhaps you could leave it with me and I'll . . . ." Mr. Jones paused, open mouthed.

Looking over Stanley's shoulder he suddenly became aware of a customer standing outside by the window, his face pressed against the glass pane. This grimacing face was indeed awesome, with skeletal cheek bones, cavernous mouth, and wisps of white hair which straggled over gaunt cheeks and down to hunched shoulders covered with a dusty old gown.

The malevolent creature fixed the antique dealer with a piercing glare.

"Did you bring some one with you," gasped Mr. Jones, paling visibly.

"Bring someone with me . . . .?" repeated Stanley, perplexed by this sudden change of tone and conversation. "No — not as far as I know."

"You're absolutely sure," cried the anxious man, and Stanley began to feel uneasy.

'What's the fellow on about? Is he mad?'

At that moment a skeletal hand emerged from the folds of the cobwebbed gown, pointed at the reliquary, and then slowly reached for the shop door handle.

"I think you ought to leave — right now — this minute — go!" The frightened antique dealer's voice rose to high pitch.

"What's the matter," demanded Stanley. "Is there someone outside?" He turned to face the door.

There was no one there.

The customer had vanished.

Mr. Jones stood behind the counter quivering with emotion. He began to regain his composure and confronted Stanley.

"Well — if you didn't bring him along," he declared hoarsely, shoving the reliquary back towards Stanley, "— then that thing did!"

He pulled himself together and pointed to the door. "I'm sorry, but I can no longer help you. Please make your own way out."

"But — but what do you think I should do with this reliquary?"

"Do with it — do with it!" retorted the pale man, the vision of the daunting spectre at the door burned into his memory. "Put the damned thing back where you found it — and if I were you I'd be quick about it."

At the time Stanley didn't think much of this advice, coming as it did from an hysterical antique dealer with most peculiar mood swings — but some days later he had occasion to remember it.

By then it was a different story.

* * *

The Scarstone estate was centuries old, originally given to Giles de Scarstone by his brother Stephen de Grebheart in 1238. Giles chose to build the first hall in an unfortunate position, for it lay too close to Martyn Mere, a large inland lake with its mists and damp, unhealthy atmosphere. However, in 1595 Edmund de Scarstone built a new house on higher ground and the present Hall now stood on these same foundations. The building was altered in 1813 by Tobias Scarstone and 1833 remodeled in the Gothic style by his son Charles, who inherited the estate on the death of his father. The new owner began his purchases of land and other estates, becoming, it was widely thought at the time, the richest landowner in the county. He also improved the estate farm, building several cottages for his workers and extending the stables.

The Hall remained in the family until 1946, when it was sold for use as a training college. In 1963 it was sold again and became a private school. It had recently been acquired by Mercian Independent Education PLC for use as a private college, incorporating both boarding students and day pupils. However, the estate lands and farm had been sold separately in 1946 and became known as Home Farm. Stanley Talbot recently moved into one of the farm cottages as a tenant, and now worked for that concern.

It was on one of his customary patrols around the estate, checking the fencing and old stone perimeter walls that he once again spotted the two boys in the woods near the canal. They were so busy occupied with their endeavours that they failed to see him approach.

"Hey, you two!" he shouted. "What are you doing!?"

The boys hesitated, deciding whether to make a run for it, and then, for reasons of their own, decided to stay put.

"Well — what are you boys up to?"

"We've lost something," one of them answered, "— and we've come back to look for it. Perhaps you've found it?"

'So that's why the blighters didn't take off,' thought Stanley.

The boys looked at him rather nervously, and one of them became very fidgety, continually glancing back into the woods towards the Hall.

"Now then — let me see, replied Stanley in a solemn voice. "Was this "something" small, round and made of metal?"

"That's it!" cried the other boy. "So you have found it!?"

"I have, young feller — and it's in safe-keeping"

"Can we please have it back?" the nervous boy begged. "We've got to put it back."

"Put it back? No, not until you tell me everything — where you got it from and why you scarpered the other day," declared Stanley with authority. "Come on now — let's hear all about it."

William and Alistair looked at each and nodded.

"All right then," William declared, "but you must promise not to tell anyone else, or we're in big trouble with the headmaster and our parents."

"And *him* too," added his companion. "Don't forget *him. He's* worse that the others."

"I'll think about it," replied Stanley in his most serious manner. "Well — let's hear it."

The boys revealed everything, the events in the Great Hall, the eerie figure on the stairs, their attempts at opening the sealed container in the woods and a graphic description of the master who discovered them.

"We just don't know what to do," Alistair moaned. "He definitely isn't one of our masters, that's for sure — because he's dead. We've seen him again, and we're going to run away from the college."

"Now don't be too hasty, lads," Stanley reassured them. "I'm sure it's just your imagination playing up. I'll keep hold of the reliquary for the time being before I decide about our next move."

"Reliquary — what's that?"

"Oh, didn't I tell you?" replied Stanley. "You hit the jackpot with that little container. I've been told it could be an extremely rare and valuable bit of religious gear."

"Gosh!" exclaimed William. "As important as that."

"I don't care how valuable it is," muttered Alistair. "All I want to do is put it back where we found it."

"And I'd like to know why someone hid it away in the first place," declared Stanley.

"So would we," answered the boys, and they parted company, Stanley promising to get back to them as soon as he had any further information about the ancient religious artifact.

"Don't forget — sit tight, lads," he called back as he left the wood for the towpath. "I'm on the case now."

Future developments would reveal that it was indeed quite a case — possibly one which Stanley might not be able to handle.

Later that night, just after midnight, Mr. Jones, the owner of Ormsley Antiques, was disturbed by a commotion in the shop below. He had not been sleeping well and his nerves were still in a very bad way after that harrowing experience a couple of days earlier, so much so that he had temporarily closed the shop until his state of health improved.

The trembling man tiptoed quietly down stairs to investigate the noise, reaching the heavy chintz curtain which separated the main shop from the back room. His condition worsened dramatically when he peered through the curtain and was confronted with a most bizarre sight.

Illuminated in the orange glow from a street light which shone into the room he beheld an astounding figure, one which he immediately recognized from his study of historical collections and old antiquities. This figure was bearded and brutal in appearance and beneath a cloth surcoat, a type of military tunic from the Middle Ages, he wore a coat of chain mail. In his hand he held a short bladed sword, which the antique dealer immediately recognized as a falchion, a type of weapon which he had seen belted to suits of armour in many historic collections. Mr. Jones instinctively sensed a connection between this intruder and Stanley Talbot's gowned companion.

'*Were they searching for the same thing?*'

The military man seemed to be probing for something amongst the objects in the shop. With the tip of his sword he picked up the cleaning cloth which Mr. Jones had used to polish the reliquary and examined it. He gave a nod and satisfied leer, flicking the cloth onto the floor and Mr. Jones inwardly cursed himself for not getting rid of the link with the reliquary sooner. The intruder in chain-mail armour began to rummage through the items on top of the counter, but seemingly couldn't find what he was searching for. He gradually became more furious and started to lash out in a fierce temper. The way this medieval fighting man slashed and swung his sword, smashing and destroying Mr. Jones's valuable collection of antiques, caused the horrified dealer to be prudent rather than brave — his head could easily go the same way.

This villainous figure was, on no account, to be confronted or disturbed, and Mr. Jones wisely decided to withdraw by way of the back door, and the safety of a friend's house.

The badly shaken man's opinion on the beneficial influence of reliquaries upon the human spirit had undergone a complete change, and his passionate interest in antiquarian pursuits had also taken a severe knock — one from which he would never fully recover.

* * *

Stanley Talbot was surprised at the size of the cavity in the west wall of the Great Hall; the boys' description of events had left him with an impression of a much larger opening. There were also signs of recent repair work around the edge of the cavity where the plaster surface had been renewed and was now in the process of drying out. He bent forward to examine the interior.

"Excuse me — what are you doing here?"

The voice spoke in a refined accent and with some authority, the words echoing around the Great Hall.

Stanley turned to see a middle-aged officious-looking lady standing by the wooden screens at the far end of the hall .

"What are you doing here?" she repeated, hurrying across the floor to confront Stanley. "Don't you know this part of the building is out of bounds to the public?"

Stanley, somewhat taken aback by her imperious manner, hesitated for a moment before answering. He noticed the identification tag clipped to the lapel of her tweed jacket and the heavy framed spectacles hanging on a gold chain around her neck. The tag declared her name in red print and status in black; *Mary Winstanley - County Heritage*.

She glared at him "Well . . . .?"

"I'm here to help out," answered Stanley, trying to think of an excuse for his unauthorized presence in this part of the building, "— with the renovations. I live in a cottage on the drive at the back of the Hall." Mary Winstanley's aggressive stance began to relax. "And I'm a member of the estate management team."

This latter piece of information had the desired effect.

The officious custodian's haughty expression began to soften, and she actually broke into a semblance of a smile. It worked. Stanley was only a labourer on the estate farm but the title "estate management team" suggested a position of some importance, one which her type of officialdom could relate to. In her eyes he now became eligible for the outward sign of his new-found status — the ubiquitous name tag.

"We all have to wear one of these tags, you know," she said importantly. "I'll see that you get one. Now what did you say you were doing here?"

Stanley had to think fast.

He was sure he couldn't fool this sharp-eyed harridan with any old tale. He glanced nervously at the cavity, desperately trying to think.

"Oh, I — I was — I was just checking — checking on the state of this plaster-work."

It was an inspired reply.

"Oh, so was I," the County Heritage official declared. "I think it is coming on nicely. Do you think it will be ready for the ceremony tomorrow?"

"The ceremony . . . .?" Stanley had no idea what she was talking about. "Ah, the ceremony tomorrow. Hmm — well er . . . ." He bent forward and lightly touched the plaster surface.

"Yes, I think it might."

"It's such a novel idea, don't you think?"

Stanley still didn't know what on earth she was talking about.

"Er — yes — yes it is."

"We discussed it with the Council Conservation Department, you know," she went on, luckily for the bemused man, "and we decided, considering the negligible worth of the plates and coins, that we would return them to their resting place behind the wood carving. We thought it would add some mystery to the ambience of the Hall."

"Right — I see," nodded Stanley, beginning to see the light at last. So it would seem that the medieval plate and coins were destined to be replaced in their original position. "A jolly good idea on your part."

The lady warmed to the compliment. "And then there's the novel talking point for the visitors."

"The — the talking point?"

"Yes — the origin of the hoard. We think we've discovered where the artifacts came from," Mary Winstanley enthused. "I must say these last few days have been so interesting, especially the research into the personal documents of Charles Scarstone."

She went on to tell Stanley all about it, while he thought it prudent to keep quiet about his own recent *interesting* research.

It was a wise decision.

However, her account did interest Stanley, and added a further dimension to the unusual reliquary.

She told him that when Tobias Scarstone died in 1833, his son Charles, a History undergraduate at Oxford University, inherited the estate. Charles also continued to acquire more land, coal mines and developed the local resort of Southbeach. His annual income was such that he was said to be the "richest commoner" in the counties, and with this vast increase in his income he began to collect antique objects and works of art. Soon the Hall was filled with paintings (at least seven hundred and fifty of them were later put up for auction), carvings, furniture, prints and drawings, armour and weapons, ceramics and glassware, and piles of antiquarian books.

Although his religious beliefs often caused much speculation his taste was firmly rooted in the fashionable Gothic Revival Movement of the Victorian Period, a movement embracing the romantic principles of the Middle Ages. He went so far as to engage a famous "Gothic" architect of the time to re-design and refurnish the Hall in that style when he returned from Oxford.

Then, for some inexplicable reason, he began to change, exhibiting certain eccentric habits and becoming reclusive, so that he eventually lived in the Hall alone, avoiding contact with others, even to the point where he would not meet his own estate steward. Mary Winstanley discovered that the beginnings of this disturbing personality change coincided with a strange hoard unearthed on part of his land reclaimed from the sea near a coastal village some ten miles distant. A local ferry man uncovered the secret cache whilst digging his garden. He found plate, coins and an unusual sepulchral urn which Charles Scarstone, with his passion for antiquities, claimed and had them removed to the Hall. The Master of Scarstone Hall judged them to be pre-Reformation in origin, possibly thirteen century altar plate and currency, except the mysterious urn, and could not explain how they came to be buried near the sea shore.

So, from this time on it would seem that Charles Scarstone became a changed man.

"I combed through the inventory of his possessions after his death," Mary Winstanley ended, 'but there was no mention of this particular collection to be found anywhere in it. Now I know where part of it went — he hid it behind the religious carving on the west wall. It also answers another peculiar entry in his last will which puzzled everyone at the time."

"Oh, really — something to do with the altar plate?"

"Yes, I believe so. He specified that on no account should the wooden altar carving ever be moved or sold, and now you can see why."

She paused to contemplate the cavity. "I've taken photographs of them, you know — to be displayed on the wall next to the carving. What a pity about the unusual urn, though. Unfortunately I can't find any reference to it — or if it still exists."

'Believe me, it certainly does,' thought Stanley to himself, '— and it isn't any old common or garden sepulchral urn either. If only she knew what it really was she would burst her corsets.' He gave an inward chuckle at the hilarious sight of name tag, spectacles and tweed jacket flying in all directions.

"Will you be coming to the ceremony tomorrow?"

"Oh, yes — most definitely," Stanley Talbot replied with a wry smile. "I wouldn't miss it for the world."

Later that evening, as he turned in for the night, Stanley Talbot happened to glance out of his sitting room window which over-looked the tree-lined rear driveway to the Hall. It was a chilly mid-December night with a full moon, light mist and ground covering of hoar frost.

He was surprised at what he saw. A hazy figure appeared at the distant bend in the drive and approached in a measured pace through the light mist towards the cottage.

'That's strange,' mused Stanley thoughtfully.

The figure grew closer, the moonlight casting its silvery light upon his frost-covered form. "It's a bit odd for a master from the college to be wandering about at this hour."

Then he uttered an astonished cry.

"My God — it isn't frost — it's cobwebs and dust!"

This solitary figure had already been described to him in stunning detail by two very frightened pupils. Stanley instantly recalled Alistair's words *"he definitely isn't one of our masters, that's for sure — because he he's dead"*, and drew back from the window in alarm and dismay. The *dead* master of Scarstone Hall glided by the window and moments later a sharp rap on the front door announced his arrival. The hollow sound resounded through the cottage, shaking the very foundations of the house, and throwing Stanley into an advanced state of panic. The frightened man was trapped.

What should he do?

Then something else caught his eye which made an immediate decision imperative: drastic measures were required.

Another figure suddenly appeared on the edge of the driveway, one who used the trees which bordered the drive as cover. In this case the alarming figure crept forward, tree by tree, glinting in the moonlight — and this glinting light wasn't caused by the frost.

Stanley realized why.

This menacing stranger was enclosed in chain mail armour which reflected the moon beams as it moved. He was bearded, brutal in appearance and wore a surcoat belted at the waist — and he grasped a short sword in his fist. It was obvious from his demeanour and stealthy movements as he crept along the edge of the drive that his visit was not going to amicable — but very painful indeed.

Stanley reacted in the same way as the frightened boys and the terrified owner of Ormsley Antiques. He took off by the back entrance and headed for his friend's house in the village.

Bill Watson opened his own front door to find his friend crouching on the steps, trembling in a state of panic.

"I'm sorry to disturb you, Bill," the pale and breathless man gasped. "Could you put me up on your sofa for the night. I've had a spot of bother at the cottage — with a couple of blokes. I think they want to get their hands on that tin can I showed you last week."

"Going by the state of you, mate," his friend declared solemnly, "it looks as if they want to get their hands on you as well."

It was a simple observation, and probably right. It gave Stanley pause for thought and cause for anxiety.

All the indications would suggest, judging by the evening's intimidating experience, that he wouldn't have long to wait before they did.

* * *

The assembled guests gathered at the west wall of the Great Hall. Here lay the reason for the gathering. Medieval coins in a red leather pouch, polished church plate and a parchment scroll in a small glass case were neatly arranged on a small table awaiting official internment. Above the table a metal rail supported a small yellow curtain with a corded draw string, hiding the cavity from view and giving the occasion that extra aura of importance. Unfortunately the ceremonial opening had to be delayed due to the absence of the Chairman of the Council. It was lucky break for Stanley, who had also been late in arriving for the ceremony. He had only partially recovered from the previous night's hair-raising encounter, having returned from Bill's house to the cottage some twenty minutes earlier to change for the ceremony.

In the meantime the assembled company had been handed a sheet of paper setting out the agenda and describing the main participants in the ceremony and an updated visitor guide book. Stanley took this opportunity to browse through this newly printed booklet. On page twenty four he came across a black and white illustration of a religious wood carving, with a caption and description underneath.

A group of words immediately caught his eye. They were in French and all too familiar: *"La Courone Sacrée"*.

CROWNING WITH THORNS
(La Courone Sacrée des Épines)

This massive 17th century composite wood carving hangs on the west wall of the Great Hall. It is the largest remaining item from the collection of Charles Scarstone (who stipulated that it should never be moved or sold) and is reputed to come from Antwerp Cathedral, Belgium. It is an altar piece depicting Christ crowned with thorns. In accordance with religious tradition, a sacred relic (in this case thorns from the original sacred crown) would sometimes be placed behind this type of altar for public reverence.

Such holy relics, placed in receptacles called reliquaries (often said to contain body parts of saints, splinters of wood from the holy cross, and even the blood of Jesus) were of inestimable value to the church authorities (the Middle Ages equivalent of modern 'pulling power') although it has to be said many such items were in actual fact completely bogus.

This unforeseen link with the altar piece and the reliquary made a startling impression on Stanley, and he recalled the weird behaviour of the Master of Scarstone Hall.

It all began to make sense.

Perhaps Charles too, on claiming that hoard for himself, had been faced with the same disturbing visit from an enraged armoured knight, no doubt a possible cause of his increasingly eccentric behaviour. The wealthy gentleman had resolved his dilemma by secretly placing the reliquary behind the 'Crown of thorns' altar piece, stipulating that the Flemish carving should never be moved or sold.

And then a century and a half later came the renovation in the Hall and the curiosity of two school boys.

The boys had been right about one thing.

The reliquary had to be put back in its original secret resting place, or as the proprietor of Ormsley Antiques had so vehemently declared — *"Put the damned thing back where you found it — and if I were you I'd be quick about it."*

But how could Stanley achieve this end before the large carving was remounted on the wall, thereby sealing the cavity for years to come.

At that moment the Chairman of the Council arrived and the ceremony commenced. It was quite short, with speeches from various dignitaries and the ritual of internment photographed by a representative from the Ormsley Gazette. Fortunately for Stanley, the first part of his dilemma was partly solved, thanks to the tardiness of the Council Chairman. Because of his delayed arrival the ceremony had fallen behind schedule and time was now running out for the remounting of the heavy carving on the wall. This task was postponed until the following morning.

The curtain was closed, the cavity remained unsealed and the guests began to leave the Great Hall. By chance Stanley glimpsed Miss. Winstanley, the County Heritage representative, talking to the newspaper photographer. She in turn saw Stanley and pushed through the crowd to speak to him.

"I'm glad you could make it to ceremony," she said. "What did you think of it?"

"Splendid," answered Stanley. "Exactly the right thing to do." The lady beamed. "And I think the new guide book is excellent as well."

"Oh, do you really. I'm so glad you like it. I helped with it, you know," Miss. Winstanley enthused. "In fact I was just talking to the Gazette reporter about it. I had another small item for the guide but unfortunately I missed the printer's deadline."

She opened her folder and produced a sheet of paper. "Tell me what you think?"

A striking piece of evidence, found in one of Charles Scarstone's personal papers, has come to light which might have some bearing on the secret collection found in the west wall of the Great Hall. The document states that in the year 1333 a certain John de Grebheart, squire of Grebheart Manor (destroyed by fire in 1816), with blood ties to the Scarstone family line, was charged with "robbery on the King's highway" and the murder "by blows from his short sword upon the person of Adam de Cockerham, a Canon of Laythom Priory", and "this foul act witnessed by Thomas

Brookacre, called Bayman". The Canon was travelling to Penworthley Abbey by way of a coastal track in existence at that time (this track, shown on an early map of the period, disappeared due to the inundation of the sea and changes in the coastline in the fourteenth century).

It was thought that the cleric chose this lonely and isolated route because of the secret nature of his mission: to deliver something of great religious value to the Abbey. However, somewhere along this ancient track the pious cleric was waylaid by the squire and robbed of his sacred burden. John de Grebheart hid the treasure and managed to escape the clutches of the High Sheriff, although he was later pardoned for the offence, such was his influence in the county.

The sacred treasure was never recovered.

Charles Scarstone came to the conclusion that the hoard found on his reclaimed land on the coast actually belonged to the unfortunate Canon, brutally murdered in 1333 by his distant relative, and Charles concealed it in the Great Hall. It is plain that he was wrong in his assumption that this was the Canon's treasure, because the church plate and coins recently discovered in the west wall were of insignificant money or religious value, and not the sacred burden.

Stanley was absolutely gob-smacked.

Could this villainous John de Grebheart be the armoured apparition of the previous night?

The menacing night visitor certainly looked the part, and it would seem his gowned companion was in fact the ghostly Master of Scarstone Hall himself.

However, the document was totally wrong in one respect.

What Charles had hidden in the west wall with the plate and coins was of great, perhaps inestimable, value. The snag was that it had been removed by two schoolboys and presently resided in a battered cardboard box in a small cottage on the estate.

"What do you think?" Miss. Winstanley repeated.

"I — I — I don't know what to say," stammered Stanley, still trying to come to terms with this compelling supposition. "It is absolutely fantastic. I have to admire your dedication, Miss. Winstanley. Your investigation must have taken hours of painstaking work."

"It did — and I haven't finished yet," she replied. "Charles Scarstone left a massive number of private papers and family documents, some of which have remain unread since his death. There is, of course, one aspect of the Scarstone story which I would like to clear up."

"What's that?"

"The unusual sepulchral urn," she replied. "I would dearly like to know what became of it."

"Ah — that is a mystery," Stanley Talbot spoke carefully, trying to remain calm. 'And you never will,' he muttered under his breath, '— not if I have anything to do with it.'

Miss. Winstanley was called away, and Stanley left the Great Hall with a seemingly insuperable problem. He had to find a way back into the Great Hall that very night to replace the sacred relic, but this could prove difficult, especially where a modern burglar alarm system was concerned.

Time was running out, the morning deadline inexorably approaching.

The two boys, waiting for him by the rear driveway, solved the problem.

"It is going to be a difficult job, lads," the dejected man told them. "It's the burglar alarm in the Great Hall — activated by movement."

"Don't worry about that," William smiled. "It has been switched off because of the renovations."

"That's a real bonus," declared Stanley, his spirits rising. "So I just have to think of a way to get in."

"That's no problem either," returned Alistair with a grin. "We'll open a window for you. You can climb in through that window in the lower school corridor, the one with the dodgy catch."

"And then we'll show you the way to the Great Hall," added William.

The boys drew a rough plan of the part of the building where he would enter, and the time and place were discussed and final arrangements completed.

"All we need is a bit of luck, lads," ended Stanley, before setting off down the driveway towards his cottage. "And don't forget — we now have the living as well as the dead to contend with — so keep your fingers tightly crossed."

That was one thing the two pupils did for the rest of the day.

* * *

Once again the night proved clear and frosty, with a light mist covering the silent estate under the gentle rays of a full moon. This mantle of light enabled Stanley to use the edge of the woods as cover, thus avoiding detection, and he was able to approach the school block by way of the trees line. The boys were waiting by the window as planned and moments later, after muffled scramblings and scrapings, Stanley slid down onto the corridor floor and the trio set off through the silent school, the reliquary in a holdall, the boys in pyjamas and slippers and Stanley in his stocking feet. They were aided in their unusual journey by the rays of the full moon which shone through windows, casting a soft rainbow of colours on walls and floors.

They reached the Great Hall without any problem and the boys stood guard while Stanley went over to the ceremonial curtain and pulled the chord. The curtain slid open and Stanley reached into the cavity and removed the pouch, church plate and scroll, carefully laying the items on the table. He took the reliquary from the holdall and prepared to place it where it belonged.

The next instant he heard a stifled gasp, and Alistair raced across the hall to join him, totally unnerved.

"Quick — he — he's coming," he stuttered. "That scary master — he's coming down the corridor." William joined the pair.

"Alistair is right," he hissed. "He's coming right enough."

They stared in terror at the screens at the far end of the Great Hall — waiting. The Master of Scarstone Hall glided into view, and in the moonlight the terrifying apparition looked even more frightening than on those previous occasions.

The grisly apparition began to advance across the room, and the boys clutched Stanley's arms in sheer panic and terror.

"We've had it!" cried Alistair in despair. "There's no way past him."

The Master came on, slowly and intently, his purpose all too clear. He raised his arm and clenched his bony hand in a gesture of anger, shaking it and releasing clouds of dust from his mildewed gown.

It was now or never.

Stanley turned and swiftly cast the reliquary into the bottom of the cavity. This 'spur of the moment' action had an immediate effect on the alarming situation.

The spectre halted and slowly unclenched his fist, his arm falling to his side.

"Quick — get the other stuff," cried Stanley, taking advantage of this favourable development, and the boys grabbed the other items which he quickly placed on top of the reliquary.

This action also had its effect on the ghostly apparition, for the ghost seemed to briefly waver, shimmering in the moonlight, and then, to their utter astonishment and relief, it slowly began to fade away, leaving a haze of dust particles swirling and eddying over the spot where it once stood.

A mournful sigh filled the air, rising in volume and lingering in the moonlit hall for some moments before dying away.

The trio were left standing in the silent empty room, each one feeling a huge sense of relief and gladness, as if some great burden had been lifted from their shoulders.

"Phew, I think we've done it, boys," Stanley murmured at last, still coming to terms with the outcome of the ghostly confrontation. "Yes — I do think we've pulled it off."

He grasped both their hands in admiration at their fortitude under such trying conditions. "Well done, you two — well done."

Stanley closed the ceremonial curtain and they made their way back through the school.

"I bet you're both glad that's all over," he whispered as he stood on the frosty lawn below the corridor window. "We got away with it this time — but for heaven's sake don't try another stunt like that again."

They both nodded.

"No fear of that," Alistair replied grimly. "Once is enough."

Stanley left them by the open window and looked back when he reached the edge of the trees. The window was now closed, and the boys back in their dorm.

If he thought he had finished with ghostly activity for the night he was sorely mistaken, for on the way back along the border of the wood he saw a most peculiar sight.

On the north side of the Great Hall a window opened and four figures dropped out onto the lawn. They were followed by a long wooden box, which they carefully lowered to the ground.

Stanley was astounded at the sight.

He couldn't believe his eyes.

The men, roughly dressed and bareheaded, picked up the box, one at each corner and bore it away across the lawn, through a hedge and across the adjoining field, their course following a direct line towards the distant village. It was an eerie sight in the moonlight, and to Stanley in some way it had all the appearance of a funeral. He stood there shivering with cold and pondering over this strange activity, watching it until it eventually disappeared into the mist.

By then Stanley Talbot had seen enough of ghostly appearances and disappearances to last him a lifetime and he set off home, weary and cold, tumbling into bed fully clothed and immediately dropping off into a deep slumber.

* * *

The college had closed for the Christmas recess and the old Hall lay silent and empty, as if in suspended animation, patiently awaiting the Spring term and the return of clattering footfalls in the corridors, lesson bells and youthful voices in the classrooms.

Stanley Talbot took this opportunity while the building lay dormant to return to the Great Hall, to view the completed renovation, and more especially to see the altar carving on the west wall.

The Great Hall did indeed look quite splendid, antique paintings cleaned, oak panelling and minstrel screen polished and mosaic tiled floor gleaming under a coating of wax. However, the altar carving held pride of place, and its principle feature, the crowning of thorns attended by carvings of Mary Magdalene and St. John the Evangelist at the base, glowed with a religious intensity. Stanley could not help but feel deeply moved by the scene.

The reliquary was indeed in its rightful place — and the *Gothic* Master of Scarstone Hall was thankfully in his.

But as Stanley stood pensively in the silent hall nagging doubts began to assail him, doubts that *another* was not in *his* rightful place.

In the meantime two letters were forwarded to Mr. Royston-Snell, the Principal of the Mercian Independent College at his London address.

The first letter caused a certain amount of concern.

Dear Mr. Royston-Snell,

I am sorry to inform you that our son William will not be returning to Scarstone College after the Christmas break. Due to circumstances beyond our control, and in no small measure due to our son's reluctance to leave our home overnight, we have decided to enroll him at a local comprehensive day school. I am sure we can come to some suitable arrangement with regard to the balance of our son's outstanding college fees.

I would like to end by thanking you for your kindness and support while our son was in your care.

Yours faithfully,

J. Smallwood.

The second letter made matters worse, especially the obscure reference to the college.

The contents followed almost word for word that of the previous letter, except for the offending paragraph on the second page.

Such is the state of Alistair's nerves of late that we have been compelled to seek medical help. The poor boy seems to have a fixation about masters in school gowns and funeral urns hidden behind walls. We put it all down to bad dreams and vivid nightmares, possibly caused by something or someone at the college, but he still persists in believing that these figments of his imagination are real. We have been advised that it could be some time before Alistair is well enough to continue with his studies.

At about the same time Miss. Winstanley, the County Heritage representative and avid investigator of ancient family affairs, discovered a curious item in a leather-bound family bible. It was a note concerning an ancient and superstitious belief in the power of relics and was penned by the wealthy landowner and reclusive *Gothic* Master of Scarstone Hall himself.

> *In the course of conversation with several of my tenants I have discovered that it is a widely held belief in some parts of my estates that certain holy relics have a hidden force, in as much as these sacred objects have the power to heal the sick in mind and body. It is highly inadvisable, so I am told, to tamper with these religious artifacts in any way. In committing such a sacrilegious act one risks a living state of purgatory and in some extreme cases the resurrection and vengeance of the dead. Recent personal confrontations of a most terrifying nature lead me to such a conclusion myself, and I have undertaken certain precautionary measures to resolve my unfortunate dilemma, including certain specified conditions and deportment for my own funeral.*
>
> *No traditional shroud but instead my University College cap and gown. No undertaker to be employed, no invitations to relatives or mourners to attend, no hearse or bell, choir or hymns, and a plain home-made wooden box will suffice for a coffin, to be carried by four of my trusted keepers. It will be carried at break of day in a direct line from the Great Hall to the south west angle of the graveyard wall, openings to be made for my passage to my own eternal place of rest and a simple mass will be said at the graveside, to be followed by a swift internment.*

On the fly sheet of this old bible Mary Winstanley found a scribbled entry in pencil in a rough hand, presumably written shortly after the funeral by one of the participants.

> *The Master's wishes were carried out to the letter. The*

planned route of the coffin from the oak table in the Great Hall passed through the north window, across the main lawn, through a gap cut for this purpose in the boundary hedge, through the wheatfield and the low pasture, and across the far potato field, through the back garden of Mother Jackson by way of the brick wall, again partly demolished along with a part of the church wall for direct passage, and thence straight to the graveside.

Finally there was the question of Stanley Talbot's ruined Christmas celebrations, thanks to the sharp-eyed vigilance of his close friend, Bill Watson.

On Christmas Eve he had called in on Stanley with a small present.

"You really shouldn't have, mate," Stanley told him disapprovingly. "You know you can't afford it — what with the car repairs and that new carpet in your front room."

"Get away with you, Stan," Bill answered, brushing the snow from his overcoat. "It's something I thought could be very useful after what happened the other week."

Stanley removed the Christmas wrapping and found a box: the contents were described as "Home Security Light complete with diagram and fittings".

"And I'm sure you're going to need it," Bill continued. "I noticed a weird bloke hanging about in the drive. I think he might be watching the place."

"Weird bloke?" gasped Stanley. "What did he look like?"

"Hard to say — he was hiding behind a tree," Bill Watson mused. "I think he had a beard and he was wearing a fancy dress costume — a funny sort of cloth coat."

Stanley's nagging doubts returned.

"Fancy dress . . . .? Was . . . . was he carrying anything?"

Bill thought for a moment.

"I don't think so, although I could be mistaken. At first I thought it looked like a sword — but people don't go around carrying that sort of thing in this day and age, do they? "

Stanley didn't answer, but went straight to the window in the front room. He drew the curtain to one side and peered down the snow-covered drive towards the Hall.

His previous nagging doubts were immediately put to rest.

The crouching surcoated armoured figure in the trees was, of course, very familiar and partly expected. It was also clear that he was definitely not in his *rightful place*.

It would seem that the sacred power of the holy relic, hidden for centuries behind a religious carving in Scarstone Great Hall, had worked its spell in 'spades' and resurrected the vengeful dead.

And so it would appear that the spirit of an enraged knight was out and about, looking for a suitable candidate to vent his anger.

The Master of Scarstone Hall was again at rest in a graveyard some miles from the Hall, and two mischievous pupils had now left the College, never to return — so that left poor old Stanley Talbot to "carry the can".

However, unlike Stanley's generous friend, this menacing visitor carried no wrapped Christmas gift.

On the contrary, the medieval squire expected one instead.

This expected gift, which presently lay behind a medieval altar carving in the nearby Hall, had a direct link with the Christmas Birth.

As far as that venerable ancient reliquary, the Sacred Crown, was concerned John de Grebheart was out of luck — and so, it seemed, was Stanley.

ORMSKIRK

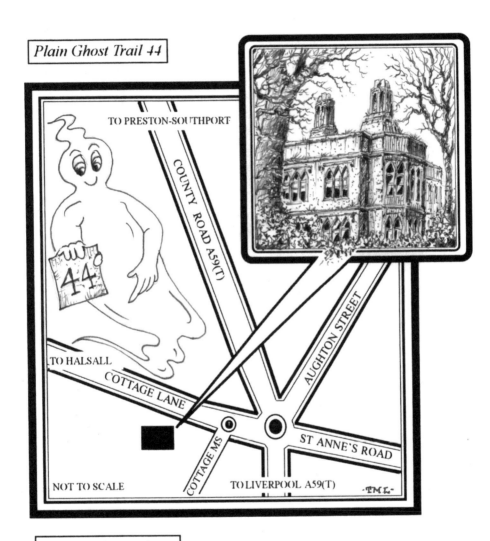

TO PRESTON-SOUTHPORT

COUNTY ROAD A59(T)

AUGHTON STREET

TO HALSALL

COTTAGE LANE

COTTAGE MS.

ST ANNE'S ROAD

NOT TO SCALE

TO LIVERPOOL A59(T)

INSET *The Rookery*

115

AN INHERITED PECULIARITY

So it was true.

"MYSTERY MRS. MOP SWEEPS UP A JACKPOT"

This unusual caption finally banished all rumour and speculation concerning the fate of the old house. The newspaper headline was accompanied by a brief article which supplanted rampant gossip with plain fact and finally confirmed a widely held opinion in the neighbourhood that the old property had a new owner at last.

"The story of a cleaning lady who inherited a fortune from an elderly customer hit the headlines this week. Speaking to our reporter exclusively the lady in question asked not to be identified, and we are happy to oblige. However, we can reveal that this local 'char lady' is the sole heir in the will of a wealthy antique dealer who left her the Grange, a Grade 11 listed mansion, along with valuable antiques and cash worth half a million pounds."

Janet Ellis, the "char lady in question", was just as gob-smacked at the enormous bequest as the rest of them. This startling development, it seemed, came right out of the blue and was totally unexpected. Considering her mundane life-style and hand-to-mouth existence Janet Ellis could hardly believe her good fortune, and found great difficulty in accepting the fact that not only was she now a person

117

of substantial means, but also one of high standing in local society.

Some days later, when she arrived for an appointment at the offices of Rankin, Jessel and Large, the firm of solicitors handling the legal affairs of the late owner, the shy and somewhat nervous lady expressed her reservations about this strange inheritance to Mr. Large, a senior partner in the practice .

"Why me?"

"Hmmm — an interesting question indeed, Mrs. Ellis."

"I wasn't related to him, you know — or any other member of the family for that matter," the incredulous cleaner explained to the pensive executor of Arthur Binsley's estate.

"Yes — I am aware of that, Mrs. Ellis," Mr. Large replied.

"So — why me?"

"I honestly don't know," the old gentleman answered with a shake of his head. "I can find no explanation in the will, or in any of Mr. Binsley's correspondence with us relating to the property. His relatives are all stunned and angered by the whole business and have threatened to contest the will."

"Oh, dear," Janet replied timidly, "— so I won't get anything after all?"

The old solicitor smiled, and raised his hand.

"Come now, Mrs. Ellis — that is not the case. Arthur Binsley's will is perfectly legal and above board, I can assure you," he told her. "No — it all belongs to you, and the family have no legal right to any part of it."

Mr. Large paused. "It's just that . . . ."

Janet Ellis waited for it. 'Here comes the catch,' she thought to herself. 'It has all been too good to be true.'

"It's just that . . . ." He hesitated, trying to find the appropriate words. "It's just that all this unusual business has happened before with that particular property."

"Happened before . . . .?"

"Yes," he replied with a puzzled frown, "— on three separate

118

occasions, in fact." He held up a bundle of papers bound in a red ribbon. "I came across this peculiarity in the deeds. At various times in its history and for some unspecified reason the Grange has been passed on to people totally unrelated to the family."

"You mean — passed on to people like me?"

"Yes, it would seem so — but I can't find any explanation for it in any of the documents. However, there is one unusual clause attached to these peculiar bequests," the solicitor added. "In order to fulfill the conditions of the inheritance you are required to take up permanent residence in the property for the period of one year."

"You mean I can't sell it — or let it out to someone else?"

"No, I'm afraid not," answered the solicitor, shaking his head. "It states categorically that in order to qualify for the inheritance you must live in the house for one calendar year."

"Was that the case with those previous owners?"

"Yes — it would seem so," Mr. Large replied.

"It does seem very odd."

"I suppose it does," he continued, "if you also consider the fact that each beneficiary who fulfilled the one year residency clause then went on to live in the house for the rest of their lives. In my experience I have never come across this peculiarity before."

Janet Ellis, the reserved and wealthy "Mrs. Mop", was now set to continue this "peculiar" tradition.

She had just inherited a desirable Grade 11 listed building and a small fortune, but to her eventual consternation she would find that this unexpected inheritance also included a "peculiarity" not found in the deeds of the old mansion — or, for that matter, of this world.

* * *

Over the following days Janet Ellis had time to reflect on her dramatic change of circumstances. As an elderly person of very limited means, living in a small maisonette on a run-down council estate she found great difficulty in coming to terms with this sudden upheaval in her life. Her first thoughts on learning of her good fortune were that it had to be some terrible mistake and that she was bound to lose her job and a valuable source of much-needed income. But, in the event, it was indeed true, and the shy and retiring 'Mrs. Mop' began to accept the fact that this new found wealth would change her life.

One thing was certain. Janet would no longer need to continue her menial career as a domestic. In fact she was now in a position to employ one herself, and, since she had to move from her modest maisonette into a grand mansion to fulfil the terms of the bequest, she quickly realized that she would need assistance in running the place. She made plans accordingly and advertised for domestic help.

However, unbeknown to the shy owner of the Grange, others were also making plans, devious plans intended to scupper the unusual terms of the bequest. The aggrieved relatives of the late Arthur Binsley had no intention of losing their inheritance to an old 'char lady' and concluded that the new owner had to be persuaded to leave the Grange before the year was up. They plotted to overthrow this menial usurper from within.

Arthur Binsley's niece Henrietta Worthington and her husband Byron applied for the position of resident servants and arrived at the Grange dressed accordingly for such work. Janet took them into the spacious drawing room for an informal interview. She began hesitantly, somewhat nervous of the sombrely dressed couple sitting opposite her.

"Have — have you done anything like this before?"

"Oh yes, Mrs. Ellis," Henrietta declared, handing Janet a set of false credentials. "As you can see from these references we have had considerable experience of domestic service." Although the forged credentials were glowing and impressive they certainly didn't reflect the fact that Henrietta and Byron Worthington were used to giving orders to domestic servants rather than taking them. Nevertheless the couple were very plausible indeed and completely deceived the gullible and unsuspecting owner of the Grange. They were accepted and moved into a room at the top of the house the very next day.

They immediately prepared to put their devious scheme into practice.

"We'll have to be careful, Byron. We don't want to alarm the silly old girl," Henrietta advised her husband. "I don't know how she managed to inherit the Grange. She's such a mediocre common person, without any character or style, and certainly not up to the social position this place deserves."

"I'll second that my dear. We'll settle in and watch her," replied Byron. "Try to find her weaknesses — what makes her nervous — that sort of thing."

During the course of the following weeks the pair of tricksters patiently watched and waited, and soon came to the conclusion that it would be all too easy. They discovered that their employer was the most shy and timid of people, easily swayed and influenced by others. She was also extremely nervous into the bargain, which suited their scheme admirably. In this respect the Worthingtons couldn't understand why such a nervous person would want to live in a large house, with its many gloomy rooms and dark passages.

"You'd think she would be frightened of living here all alone," commented Byron. The strange house had already begun to exert its influence on the avaricious man. "I noticed it as soon as we moved in. There's definitely something odd about the place — something not quite right. It gives me the creeps, especially at night."

"Don't be a silly ass, Byron," Henrietta rebuked him. She obviously wasn't on the same wavelength as her husband, and was unaffected by the gloomy atmosphere. "It's only an old house, after all."

"But you must admit I do have a point. Perhaps we could try something on those lines."

"Like what?"

"Think up something to scare the old lady," Byron mused. "She's such a nervous creature so it wouldn't take much to frighten her."

"Well, I think you might be wasting your time," his wife said. "She doesn't seem in any way nervous about the Grange — only us."

Byron replied. "I wonder why?"

He had a point.

From the very first moment Janet had entered the Grange all those years ago she had felt at home, so much so that she was often reluctant to leave at the end of the day. There was something about the atmosphere in the house, as if a kindly presence inhabited the rooms and passages, creating a feeling of well-being and peace. Flowers and plants seemed to do extraordinarily well, the scented aromas from their blossom wafting through the rooms and their colourful blooms lasting for longer than usual. There were even occasions when Janet swore she heard faint sounds of music drifting through the house, especially after Arthur Binsley's wife passed away.

As his health declined the wealthy old man now began to depend more on Janet, and she in turn was only too pleased to take on the extra responsibility for the invalid as well as her domestic duties. On the other hand Arthur Binsley's relations never came to see him and to all intents and purposes he was now all alone in the world. Janet was his life-line and link with the outside world, and the atmosphere in the house seemed to reflect her devotion and care.

And so Henrietta's assessment of her mistress was spot on. Janet was extremely happy and at ease in this gloomy old house, and the Worthingtons couldn't understand why.

Unfortunately the heartless couple were also completely insensitive to the ambience of the house itself and failed to realize that their callous plans to unsettle the mind of their kindly employer could upset the harmony and balance of the Grange. It didn't occur to them that a house which seemed to react to kindness with warmth and affection could also react to evil intent in equally proportionate measures.

In other words the scheming couple completely failed to understand the nature of the inherited peculiarity of this unusual property — and so their unseemly plans were destined to backfire in no uncertain terms.

* * *

"Well, Henrietta — where should we start?"

The Worthingtons sat at the kitchen table debating their next move. How to get Janet out of the house before the year was out.

"Have you noticed the old dear is very set in her ways," Henrietta mused, "and likes everything in its rightful place."

"Yes, I have," Byron sniffed. "It's a bit of an obsession with her, isn't it? She's very fussy — doesn't like anything to be moved — as if its some sort of house rule. It's quite obvious nothing has been changed for donkeys years."

"Hmmm — that's given me an idea," his wife replied. "If we move one or two things around tonight after she's gone to bed, she'll come down tomorrow and wonder what's happened."

"That's a great idea," Byron nodded. "How about the table and chairs in the dinning room. You can bet she would spot any change in the furniture straight away."

"And we wouldn't know anything about it, would we?" smirked Henrietta. "Now I'm sure that would really unsettle her."

The plan was put into operation that very night. The table and chairs were quietly moved to the far end of the dinning room, and Byron's previous observation was confirmed by the state of the carpet. Judging by the marks and large faded sections it was glaringly obvious that the old furniture had not been moved for donkey's years. It would also be glaringly obvious to Janet, when she came down to breakfast the next morning, that her precious furniture was not in its usual place.

Early next morning the mischievous couple heard Janet leave her bedroom and make her way downstairs for breakfast. The pair waited in the kitchen with growing anticipation for the shrill sound of her startled voice.

It didn't come.

Instead they heard the strident buzz from the room indicator board on the kitchen wall. Janet was ringing from the dining room.

"That's odd," commented Byron, mystified by it all. "She seems to be taking things calmly enough."

The Worthingtons hurried from the kitchen and found Janet sitting in the dining room as usual waiting for her breakfast.

"A boiled egg today, I think," Janet smiled, "and perhaps two rounds of toast with . . . ." She paused, taken aback by the expressions on the Worthington's faces. "Is — is something the matter?"

The Worthingtons didn't reply, but stared at the table and chairs in disbelief.

The dining room furniture was back in its usual place and looked as if it hadn't been moved in years.

"The — the table and chairs," Henrietta spluttered.

"Yes, what about them?"

"You haven't moved them, have you?"

"Moved them," answered a bemused Janet. "Certainly not. You know my thoughts on that subject, my dear. I like everything in its proper place, as you well know."

"But surely . . . ." Henrietta halted, totally perplexed by the situation. She came to an obvious conclusion. Someone else had returned the furniture to its original position in the night.

But who?

Later that evening Henrietta had her first sense of this "someone else" in the house — a fourth person. The Worthington's room lay at the top of the house, reached by a narrow flight of stairs. It led to a small landing outside their bedroom door and then continued up to the attic. As she climbed these stairs she caught a fleeting glimpse of a vague shape, its outline irregular and its movements erratic, slipping into the bedroom.

"Byron," she called out apprehensively. "Byron — is that you?"

There was no reply, and then she remembered her husband was outside in the garden.

So who was the intruder in her room?

"Who's there . . . . ?"

She quietly climbed the stairs to the landing and cautiously entered the bedroom.

It was empty — *but someone had recently been there.*

The bedroom furniture had been totally rearranged. Furthermore the bedclothes were in complete disarray and the contents of the drawers scattered on the floor. Henrietta Worthington surveyed the jumbled scene with growing alarm. It was covered in a mantle of dust, which struck her as very peculiar since she had only cleaned the room the previous day. However, in her present shocked condition she failed to notice several larger flake-like particles in the dust.

These yellowed flakes left a trail which led out of the bedroom and up the narrow stairs to the attic.

Within minutes these small particles had turned to a fine powder, soon to be dispersed by a sudden draught which swept down the narrow stairs from top of the house.

* * *

"I don't like it, Byron," Henrietta declared nervously. "If you didn't do it, then someone else has been up here and moved the furniture."

"Do you think it could have been Mrs. Ellis?"

"Janet —moving heavy furniture at her age," his wife retorted impatiently. "No, definitely not. With her obsession "everything in

125

its right place" that's the last thing she would get up to."

"But you did think you saw someone at the top of the stairs — near our bedroom."

"I was so sure at the time, but perhaps it was a trick of the light, or possibly my own shadow," Henrietta shuddered. "But it gave me quite a turn, all the same."

"I can believe it," agreed Byron, shaking his head. "I didn't realize how gloomy this old pile was, with its narrow corridors and dark corners, until I came to live here. And now it's beginning to give me the creeps, I can tell you. I can't understand why the old girl wants to live in a place like this."

"Neither can I," declared his wife. "But she seems perfectly content. In fact you never see her in a bad mood or unhappy about anything, do you?"

"That's right, now you come to mention it," Byron nodded slowly.

It was true.

The old lady was perfectly content, and it would be difficult to shift her. "Anyway," he continued grimly. "You can be sure that once we've got her out the Grange this place and everything in it will be sold by the end of the year — and we'll have all that lovely money to spend."

"So where do we go from here?"

"Well there's just got to be a way to unsettle her."

"We'll wait for a few days and then try something else," said Henrietta.

"What about hiding some of her favourite ornaments," Byron suggested. "That usually upsets people — losing personal things. She seems especially fond of those figurines in the drawing room."

"Ah, yes — the ones she dusts herself," nodded Henrietta. "She says Aunt Jessica gave them to her, but as far as I'm concerned she's making it all that up. Those figures are much too expensive to give away to a cleaning lady."

126

"Yes, it does sound a bit odd to me," Byron said thoughtfully. "Anyway, she's bound to notice if they go missing. We'll hide a couple of them, and see what happens."

And so the following week Byron Worthington crept nervously down stairs in the middle of the night, pausing every now and then to listen intently. All was quiet and peaceful. He entered the darkened drawing room and crossed to the large glass cabinet which displayed Janet's treasured figurines. As he opened the cabinet to select the figures he saw the reflection of the drawing room in the glass pane — and a dark irregular shape framed in the doorway. Then he saw the door slowly swing back and close with a soft thud. The startled man spun round, peering into the darkness.

Had someone just entered the room — or left it?

"Is that you, Henrietta?"

The reply which reached his staining ears was not from his wife. Instead he heard a most unusual sound — a sound not unlike the harsh grating of old dry wooden joints moving after many years of inactivity. This strange sound was accompanied by a rustling noise, of softer material.

The unseen intruder was on the move.

Byron heard a sharp intake of breath — and a low snuffling, not unlike that of a dog casting around for the scent of a cat.

Whatever it was had picked up Byron's scent — and the tempo of the grating, rustling and snuffling increased.

It was closing on him.

He reacted swiftly, snatching two figurines from the glass cabinet, and dashed for the door.

He was just in time, for as he crossed the drawing room he brushed against something — and was enveloped in a soft and downy embrace — almost feather-like to the touch. He burst from the grasp of intruder and fled from the room, down the dark corridor and up the stairs, all the while conscious of the other presence close behind him, dogging his footsteps.

At last Byron reached the sanctuary of his bedroom, slamming the door shut and gasping for breath. His wife, on the other hand, slumbered peacefully through all this commotion, unlike her shaken husband who spent the remainder of the night in a restless state of mind and body. The precious figurines were hidden away at the back of a chest of drawers and Byron Worthington was satisfied that no one would find them in a hurry — or so he thought.

Unfortunately the next day disclosed alarming developments which further fuelled Byron's growing phobia about the Grange and was yet another blow to his mental state.

The couple were confronted by the sight of a smiling Janet Ellis opening the door of the glass cabinet in the drawing room.

Instead of a cry of disbelief at the loss of two valuable treasured figurines the Worthingtons were greeted by "I think I'll run a cloth over my babies after breakfast, Henrietta. It's a while since I dusted them."

In the cabinet Byron Worthington contemplated a full set of figurines.

None were missing.

However, later that day the already troubled couple were exasperated by a similar situation. Byron couldn't find his expensive wrist watch anywhere, and Henrietta searched high and low for her favourite valuable necklace to no avail. These personal items were missing.

"I tell you," a shaken Byron put it to his wife, "there's something very peculiar about this damned house. The sooner we get the job done — then the sooner we're out of here."

In Byron Worthington's case it would be sooner than he thought.

* * *

Byron's appearance had begun to change quite noticeably, and he became more morose and embittered as the each day passed by, unlike his wife who seemed to mellow under the benign influence of Janet and the old house. He couldn't wait to get his hands on the old lady's fortune, and the expensive and valuable antiques which cluttered the Grange were a constant reminder of such wealth just waiting to be realized.

He now decided that more drastic measures were required, unlike his wife whose disposition, in contrast to that of her husband, became increasingly gentle and content as time went by. And, to the annoyance of her husband, Henrietta was becoming more and more disenchanted with the whole idea.

"I think we are being too hasty, Byron," she told him. "Janet doesn't deserve all this trouble. I think we should forget the whole idea."

But Byron was not to be swayed by his wife's gradual change of heart. His mind was made up, and he couldn't be reasoned with. Something had to be done, something which would look like a common place household accident — and Byron had the answer.

"That's it — the stair carpet."

"The stair carpet?" his wife returned, looking somewhat puzzled.

"Yes, the stair carpet," Byron replied, and went on to reveal his plan to his wife. "Loose stair carpets are a common cause of accidents in the home, especially when it comes to older people."

Henrietta immediately saw what he was getting at. "You don't mean you would go to those lengths!" she cried. "That really is too drastic!"

"I can't see any other way out," her husband retorted. "I know you haven't felt the hostile atmosphere in the Grange in the same way that I have, but there's something very disturbing about this place — something or someone here in the house that keeps on thwarting us. We've had no success so far."

"But to think of causing such an accident," Henrietta replied, obviously shocked at this latest cruel scheme. "Poor Janet could be badly injured — even die. No — oh no, I don't like that idea at all!"

"No, not badly injured if I loosen the stair rods part way down the staircase," Byron explained reassuringly. "When she slips she won't have as far to fall, and her injuries will be slight, hopefully enough to need the services of a nursing home — which means she'll have to leave the Grange."

"Oh, no Byron," his wife replied. "I've become rather fond of Janet. You'll have to stop all this nonsense now."

But Byron's mind was made up. The old lady had to go.

Later that evening his malignant plan was put into practice. The appropriate stair rods were removed, a copious amount of floor polish inserted under the carpet and the rods loosely replaced. Byron tested the carpet with his foot, and nearly went sprawling himself as the carpet shot from under his foot. He managed to grab the stair rail in time to save himself from the nasty fall.

"Well, if that doesn't do the job," he gasped, "I don't know what will." As he made his way quietly back to the bedroom at the top of the house, tiptoeing carefully up the flight of stairs, a faint rustling and grating sound reached his ears.

Recalling his previous late night experience in the drawing room he threw caution to the wind and hastily completed the remaining stairs in leaps and bounds.

The strange sound grew louder.

What was it?

It seemed to come from the top of the old house.

Something was stirring — and then he had a rather nasty shock.

As Byron grasped the handle of the bedroom door a sudden flurry of air accompanied by a violent swishing sound wafted down from the stairs above and before he could turn round to confront this frightening disturbance someone or something grabbed him by the neck.

He felt the painful burning sensation of claw-like fingers digging into his skin and heard a low guttural snarl close to his ear.

He automatically reacted by turning the door handle. The door flew open and he fell into the bedroom with a startled cry of terror. His wife sat up in bed and responded in a similar fashion.

"What on earth is the matter!" Henrietta yelled. "You almost scared me to death!"

Her husband didn't answer.

Instead he scrambled to his feet and slammed the door shut, leaning back against it, arms spread out.

"What's the matter with you, Byron?!"

"Something is out there," the terrified man choked. "Something awful is in the house — and it's outside the door."

"Calm down, for goodness sake," his wife responded in a shrill voice. "I can't hear anything." She listened intently. "Are you sure?"

"There's something out there, I tell you — and it just grabbed me."

Henrietta climbed out of bed and pulled him away from the door.

"Nonsense — we'll soon see about that."

"Don't open it," Byron begged her. "Don't open it — don't let it in!"

She grabbed the handle and yanked the door open, the light from the room piercing the darkened space beyond. The landing and stairs were empty.

All was silent. There was no one there.

She turned and after some well-chosen words of reassurance she at last managed to calm her shaking husband. He eventually regained his composure and climbed into bed. However, he neglected to tell his wife about the loosened stair rods and carpet. Everything was now in place, ready for the following day and had she known about the dangerous situation Henrietta would have put a stop to it, he was sure. So it was best that she didn't know.

The next morning he awoke early and lay there listening for Janet to rise. He heard her bedroom door open followed by her footsteps as she made her way to the head of the staircase.

She began to descend — and Byron lay there in anticipation and dread. He grasped the coverlet of the bed, drawing it up to his chin as he waited for the terrified scream and rumble of a body rolling and tumbling head over heels down the stairs.

It didn't happen.

There was no scream — no crash of a falling body. Nothing.

He arose and hurriedly dressed, and, on making his way to the top of the stairs, saw Janet come out of the drawing room unscathed.

How could it be?

He soon found out, for when he ventured carefully down the stairs to the place where he had loosened the rods he saw that they were untouched — soundly fixed and totally safe.

Once again something in the house had thwarted his designs. The embittered man was still no nearer to getting his hands on the family fortune — but that state of affairs was soon to change.

* * *

Byron slowly turned the handle and quietly opened the door to Janet's bedroom. He paused on the threshold for a moment before entering, peering into the darkness, listening to the gentle breathing of the occupant within, sound asleep in her bed. As if on cue a shaft of moonlight, suddenly released from its mantle of cloud, pierced the darkness, entering through a gap in the curtains to fall upon an unusual four-poster bed, an antique piece of Victoriana of neo-gothic design collected by the original owner of the Grange.

To the modern eye this unique four-poster was no longer fashionable, but to Janet it was cosy and warm, especially on a freezing winter's night when westerly storms whistled round the chimney stacks, or bitter north winds blanketed the old house in a mantle of deep snow. And so with heavy velvet curtains drawn tightly together to counter those winter draughts, and a large hot water bottle to warm her feet Janet found these unusual sleeping quarters very cosy indeed. She slumbered peacefully on, unaware of the approaching danger.

The moonlight also highlighted something else, sparkling on the bedside table.

It was an empty glass.

This glass had contained Janet's customary hot chocolate drink, of which she was so fond at bedtime. However, on this occasion the chocolate concoction had been laced with a strong sedative, one which Byron's wife had been prescribed for "nerves", a condition which had developed when she began working in the old Grange.

That was before her change of heart and mind.

Now his wife slept like a top, and had no need of sleeping draughts. However, this medicine was ideal for Byron's devilish purpose, and he had administered a strong dose to the unsuspecting owner of the Grange at bedtime. It had the desired effect and Byron, now satisfied that all was clear, edged into the room and tiptoed towards the four-poster — to perform the most drastic action of all.

The peculiar events of the previous months, the strange forbidding atmosphere and deep hostility which pervaded the house had taken its toll on Byron's constitution. His overwhelming obsession to get Janet out forced him to consider more desperate measures. In short, as each of his carefully-made plans were thwarted by that unknown presence in the Grange, and the family fortune still remained in Janet's hands, the unfortunate man began to lose his grip on reality — and became completely unhinged.

But now all that was going to change.

Nothing would stop him now.

He approached the bed, gently drawing the heavy curtains apart to contemplate the sleeping innocent for a moment. He leaned over, and the moonlight also highlighted something in his hands.

This object was rather bulky and floppy. It was also soft and downy.

133

It was in fact a large pillow, and it was destined to be used for a diabolical purpose — Byron Worthington's final solution to his problems — suffocation.

As he raised the pillow over Janet's face Byron's lips parted in crooked smile, unmoved by her soft expression of contentment and peace. 'There's no one here to help you now, madam,' he thought to himself.

This was it.

He began to lower the soft fabric down onto the face of that defenceless creature — and suddenly halted in utter astonishment.

Something small and white fluttered down from above, wafting from side to side like a snowflake to come to rest on the forehead of the sleeper. This "snowflake" was soon followed by another, and this time the puzzled assailant managed to grasp it. He examined it in the moonlight — and found that it crumbled into a powder at his touch.

What in Heaven's name was it?

Where on earth had it come from?

Byron Worthington looked up into the dark confines of the drapes, tracing the path of these white flakes — and uttered a strangled gasp of dismay. In the semi-darkness his eyes gradually encountered something which broke his already strained constitution.

A pair of gleaming blood-red eyes met his.

They belonged to a gruesome creature nestling in the folds of velvet at the top of the antique four-poster — and this creature was now on the move. And as it began to descend its sharp talons gouged the bed posts and small white flakes detached themselves from its leathery form.

Byron came face to face with an alternative final solution.

The horrified man flung the pillow at this vision of retribution, and fled from the room, heading for the stairs and escape by means of the front door. He reached that part of the staircase where he had set that ingenious trap for Janet the previous night. But now someone else had interfered with it, for the rods gave way, the carpet slipped forward, and Byron gave an almighty yell, falling headfirst, tumbling head over heels to the bottom of the stairs. He was badly shaken but unharmed — until he saw the small white flake flutter past his head to come to rest on the carpet beside his nose.

He rolled over to scramble to his feet — but it was too late.

In the meantime Byron's wild cry and resulting loud tumble had resounded through the house and awakened his wife. She immediately rushed from her room onto the landing. What she saw at the bottom of the stairs caused her to faint on the spot.

In the dim light she saw a shape, part human, part something else (or as she put it later "I think it had wings") lying at the base of the staircase, face down.

It gripped and grappled with something beneath it.

And then she saw a pair of feet sticking out, kicking wildly about. One foot had lost its shoe and she recognized the patterned sock.

It belonged to her husband.

And then there was the awful choking sound, the gasping for air and the muffled screams — and then the feet at last became still. At that moment the light from Janet's bedroom flooded the hallway and she looked out of her door, yawning and rubbing her eyes.

"Is that you, Henrietta?" Janet yawned, her voice echoing in the hall. "What was that noise? What's the matter?"

The bright light and her voice had a desired effect — and the spell was broken. And as Henrietta Worthington's head began to swim she saw the fearsome creature slide quietly away out of the light and into the darkness, leaving the body of Byron, her husband, his bulging lifeless eyes staring up at her, crumpled and twisted on the stairs.

Byron Worthington had his final solution — and left his wife a complete nervous wreck.

She fled the house that very day, and, much to the surprise and bewilderment of her gentle employer, refused to take any of her belongings with her, and that included the balance of her wages. Her parting remark puzzled Janet.

"No, I couldn't take anything with me," Henrietta Worthington declared with a shudder, recalling the awful appearance of her late husband. "I can't take the risk of *it* — *it* finding me as well."

* * *

"Good morning Mrs. Ellis," Mr. Large greeted her warmly. "I'm glad to see that you are keeping well, considering that recent unfortunate business at the Grange."

"Yes, it was very upsetting, Mr. Large," Janet Ellis replied. "A tragic accident, so the coroner eventually concluded after studying all the evidence — although there was one thing that puzzled the police, and me, for that matter."

"Oh, so the verdict wasn't as straightforward as it sounds?"

"No, I'm afraid not," Janet confided in a hushed voice, and went on to recount the ghastly events.

When Henrietta fainted on the landing at the top of the stairs, Janet was the first to reach the poor man. His face was bloated and swollen, as if he had choked to death, and there were small white particles, not unlike flakes of white paint, round his lips and mouth. Janet later heard that the police doctor found particles of rotten wood lodged in his throat, but decided that a severe heart attack was the probable the cause of death.

"Really — that is very odd."

"That's what I thought," Janet nodded slowly, "— but by the look of him and his bulging eyes I'd say he died of fright."

"That must have upset his poor wife. I have to say that it was very generous of you to provide for her after her nervous break-down, Mrs. Ellis," the solicitor replied, quickly changing the rather gruesome subject, "considering she is unrelated to you."

"Well, I can assure you that Mrs. Worthington has the best care and attention — it seems the right and proper thing to do."

"Well, there's no doubt you can afford it, now that you have completed the terms and conditions of the will," Mr. Large smiled, handing her a substantial brown envelope. "Here are the final contracts, signed and sealed, and I am pleased to say that the Grange now officially belongs to you." Janet thanked him, taking the envelope.

"What do I do with them?" she asked nervously.

"Such important documents should be kept in a secure place, your bank perhaps — or you could leave the deeds with us for safe keeping."

"Oh, that would suit me, Mr. Large," Janet replied very relieved.

"In that case I'll take them back and place them in our vault," he said. "However, there are one or two interesting items which I thought might interest you."

He withdrew a small folder from the envelope and passed it across the desk.

"You can take it with you, if you like," he continued, "and return it at a later date. The folder belonged to my father — part of a bundle of old newsletters and magazines which were discovered in the attic of the old rectory of St. Michael's Church when it was demolished in 1970. Our firm handled the contracts, you know, and the bundle was handed to my father who took a keen interest in these sort of antiquarian matters. He was particularly interested in a series of articles, aptly titled *"Where are they now"*, written by Mr. Harold Aitkin, an antiquary and founder member of the Ormsley Historical Society. The articles appeared in the society newsletter, and dwelt on the whereabouts or demise of unusual antiquarian features in the district."

Later that evening Janet Ellis opened the folder and read the contents. Since she wasn't really interested in historical or antiquarian matters Janet initially found them rather boring.

The first item, from an architectural magazine, told of a Mr.

Osbourne and the Grange, a new property in Cottage Lane.

ARCHITECTURE REVIEW 1868
DOMESTIC TUDOR GOTHIC — LANCASHIRE COUNTY

A recent addition to this popular style can be found in the small quaint market town of Ormsley. This secluded property, aptly named the Grange, is situated in Cottage Lane, a quiet back road on the outskirts of the old town. The house is constructed of pebble-dash render on brick, with cement dressings and hipped roof with two chimney stacks incorporating tall clustered octagonal chimneys. The building comprises two storeys and with plinth, rusticated quoins, first floor sillband, string courses and parapet. Three windows are set in casements with arched lights, quoined surrounds and hoodmoulds while the doorway has fluted pilasters, frieze and a door with two arched glazed panels. The owner, Charles Osbourne esquire, makes no secret of his passion for all thing Gothic and is in the process of collecting appropriate furnishings and fittings for the interior in keeping with the mock Tudor design of the Grange. It will indeed be most interesting to view the property on completion of his endeavours.

The second article dealt with a local church.

HAUGHTON OLD CHURCH (CIRCA 12th CENTURY)
(Dedicated to St. Michael)

The ancient church stands on the site of an earlier Saxon place of worship. Rubble found under the south west part of the church indicates a building constructed of mud, reeds and wood circa 840 AD. Over the centuries much rebuilding and remodelling has taken place. The tower was constructed in the 14th century, the chancel rebuilt in the 15th century and the Rector's vestry added in the 17th century along with 3 cottages and a school in the churchyard. In the 18th century a choir gallery was placed at the west end of the nave and 4 bells installed in the belfry, while in the 19th century the graveyard was twice extended (the cottages and charnel house demolished for extra space) and the interior of the church remodelled. The old wooden angels (circa 14th century) in the chancel were replaced by stone carvings, high box pews replaced the old benches and the stone-work was covered with thick white plaster. This covering was later stripped away in the early 20th century when the church was renovated and a Lady Chapel installed.

The third item was devoted to a description of ancient wooden angels.

ST. MICHAEL'S ANGELS

The rebuilding of the chancel of Haughton Parish Church was completed in the latter part of the 14th. Century and part of the refurbishment included the erection of 12 wooden angels in the nave roof. These unique carvings (presented to the church by certain members of the congregation known locally as custodians) were set on the beam ends, probably as a measure to ward off evil influences, calamities such as the Black Death and attacks from bands of marauding soldiers who ravaged England during the Wars of the Roses. Others thought it was a reference to the 12 apostles and the Last Supper. However, contrary to religious practice, each wooden angel bore a strange heraldic emblem, both obscure in design and meaning, which none could decipher and thought to be pagan in origin, possibly from the early Saxon period.

Over the intervening centuries these unusual guardians of the ancient church gazed down upon the congregation, and eventually became known as the "old ladies" of Haughton. Unfortunately their saintly and sacred position could not protect them from the ravages of time, and over the years wood rot and the beetle took their toll. Many "ladies" lost noses, eyes and part of their wings. They became so unsightly, frightening the younger members of the congregation, that they were eventually coated in a thick layer of whitewash. In 1886 the chancel was once again remodelled, and the angels were removed and replaced by stone carvings which now support the principals in the roof. In 1893 several of these angels were still in existence, for an article in the Parish Magazine mentioned the purchase of one of them by Mr. Osbourne of the Grange, Cottage Lane as an addition to his already large collection of Gothic antiquities. Since that time the whereabouts of the other "old ladies" remain a mystery.

Then she read the final item which differed from its companions in that it was handwritten in manuscript form on yellowed parchment, the hand writing rather meandering and crude in style.

'When the winter wind howls round the thatched eaves and thick walls of the poorest cottage and whistles down the crooked chimney, scattering sparks and smoke from the fire, those humble folk gathered around the hearth on those stormy nights oft tell of the Old Ladies of Haughton. 'Tis said that in bygone times, when the country was in such turmoil and chaos, the Black Death reached this part of the county. As the awful pestilence gradually drew near, decimating the surrounding countryside, the Parson realized the peril of the situation, and overcoming the reservations of his flock, turned to a wise old man in the parish for help, a certain

Apothecary, a doctor who, it was rumoured, was well versed
in the Black Arts and held in awe by all.'

The parchment went on to disclose that the Apothecary accepted
the invitation and came to survey the village from the top of the
church tower. The wise doctor concluded that the Black Death
could only be held in check by *"guardians"* set around the village
as a barrier against this evil monstrosity. He instructed that twelve
angels be carved as quickly as possible from the sanctified wooden
beams in the church roof above the altar. He also instructed that
each angels should have an emblem with a pagan sign carved upon
it as an extra precaution, and on completion of this formidable task
the unusual guardians were blessed by the Parson and set in place
around the village. It seemed that the apothecary's plan worked, for
the Black Death failed to appear and the village was saved.

For a while the Old Ladies were placed in the custody of certain
ancient families, just in case the pestilence should return to strike
again, but the doctor advised that the angels should be returned to
the nave of the church when times where more settled and peaceful.
The narrative ended with a disturbing warning.

''Tis said that these very angels have the power to protect
the innocent and good, who are rewarded accordingly for
their kind deeds, but woe betide persons of evil nature or
intent who would try to harm in any way those souls under
the protection and watchful eye of these ancient guardians.
Their just reward leads to the tomb and everlasting sleep.'

* * *

Later that year Janet Ellis, mindful of the previous exceptionally
cold and miserable winter, decided to install central heating in the
Grange. Money wasn't the problem now that she had fulfilled the

legal requirements of the inheritance. She could certainly afford it, but it was the prospect of all that disruption and mess that put her off. Nevertheless Janet went ahead with the decision, and invited a local plumbing and central heating firm to stop by and give her an estimate for the work.

The firm's representative, in the shape of a middle-aged plumber in blue overalls, duly arrived and proceeded to measure rooms, corridors and stairs with great efficiency. He then asked to see the attic at the top of the old house to check the area where the water tank for the heating system would be situated.

At this point the plumber noticed a small trap door in the ceiling near to the chimney breast.

"Do you know what's up there?" he asked Janet.

"I haven't the faintest idea," she replied.

The plumber decided to check it out — and hit a most unusual snag.

He found that this small trap door into the loft had been well and truly sealed with wax, as if to prevent any access to this isolated part of the old house. The perplexed and rather disgruntled man could find no apparent reason for this rather sinister development. Eventually, after much mumbling, spluttering and grumbling, he managed to free the door and disappeared into the dark confines above. Janet listened apprehensively to the muffled shuffling and tapping, peering up at the cavity in the ceiling.

After a while the plumber reappeared, his overalls covered in cobwebs and grime, and slowly climbed down ladder.

"My word, it's a real mucky hole up there — never been disturbed for years, by the look of it. The supply tank will have to go up there," he explained to Janet Ellis. "That's the best place for it."

"Will it be a difficult job?"

"Not really," the plumber replied. "Just a bit more expensive — the extra time it will take soon adds up, you know."

"Oh, don't worry about the expense," Janet declared, "— just make sure you do a good job."

"We always do a good job, madam," he returned, rather miffed at the implication. "We use top quality materials and don't cut corners."

"I'm glad to hear it," she said, "and I would be grateful if you don't make too much mess — or disturb anything while you are working."

This remark caused the plumber to glance back up to the trap door.

"Hmmm . . . ." The plumber paused and scratched the back of his head. "Well, I'm afraid there could be a bit of a problem in that department . . . ."

"Oh, really," Janet replied nervously, her obsession about "*every thing in its rightful place*" gathering momentum. "What sort of problem?"

The plumber paused for a moment, pondering this development. "There's not much space for the water tank up there," he explained. "I might have to move that funny old carving out of the way first."

"Funny old carving?"

"Yes. At least I think its a carving — fixed onto the roofing timbers," he answered. "There are bits broken off it — and under the dust and muck it looks as if it has been covered in whitewash."

"Does it look like an angel?" gasped Janet.

"I suppose it might," the plumber replied, "but it's much too ugly for an angel — almost creepy, in fact. It gave me quite turn when I came face to face with it." He shuddered. "And there's another thing that's most peculiar," he continued. "I'd say someone went to a lot of trouble to hide it away in that recess behind the chimney breast. You wouldn't know that old carving was there unless you went searching for it."

"I suppose I have always known — I mean I've always felt there was something special about the house," murmured Janet and lapsed into silence.

So this was Charles Osbourne's angel, purchased all those years ago when the building of the Grange was completed.

She recalled the words in the manuscript ' *'Tis said that these very angels have the power to protect the innocent and good, who are rewarded accordingly for their kind deeds*'.

'Could this be an explanation for my recent good fortune,' she wondered, possibly her reward for the affection and unstinting care and happiness she gave to a lonely old man and his wife in the latter part of their lives.

'But what about that warning at the very end of the manuscript' she pondered. '*But woe betide persons of evil nature or intent who would try to harm in any way those souls under the protection and watchful eyes of these ancient guardians. Their just reward leads to the tomb and everlasting sleep.*'

Janet remembered Byron Worthington's crumpled body lying at the bottom of the stairs in a state of everlasting sleep and she shuddered at the awful question "Was this his reward — and for what?"

"On second thoughts," she addressed the plumber after a moment, her obsession taking control. "I think I'll leave things as they are for the time being."

"Are you sure?" the man replied in a disappointed tone. A lost sale wouldn't go down well back at the office. "I could re-site the tank somewhere else, I suppose."

"No — I've made up my mind," she replied with a hint of a smile.

She realized that she had found something much more beneficial than central heating — something which must never be disturbed.

The plumber looked slightly bemused by her sudden change of mind. As he left the house he turned and spoke.

"What do you think that weird old carving is?"

"What is it?" Janet smiled, partly to herself. "I suppose you could say it's — it's an inherited peculiarity."

"Never heard of one of those before," he sniffed.

Janet closed the door and sighed.

She was no longer alone in the house — and there was another "*old lady*" from a bygone age up in the loft to prove it.

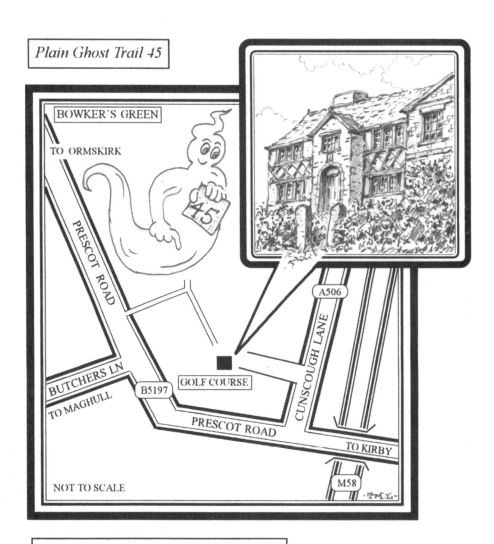

Plain Ghost Trail 45

BOWKER'S GREEN

TO ORMSKIRK

PRESCOT ROAD

BUTCHERS LN

TO MAGHULL

B5197

GOLF COURSE

A506

CUNSCOUGH LANE

PRESCOT ROAD

TO KIRBY

M58

NOT TO SCALE

INSET *Mossock Hall (now demolished)*

DUST

Love of money is the root of all evil.

It is universally accepted that this oft-quoted adage alludes to the desire for money and the evil consequences which can arise when it becomes a total obsession. The lives of those innocents who are ensnared in these 'roots' can be blighted and, in extreme cases, destroyed. The roots can be buried away for centuries, their malign influence lying dormant as time passes them by, until one day a set of unusual circumstances occur. Perhaps trivial and ordinary, or momentous and earth-shattering, these circumstances collide — and awaken this malevolent desire. Thereafter the evil scourge is released to wreak havoc upon an unsuspecting victim.

The circumstances in this particular *collision* encompassed a special engagement gift together with the discovery of a long lost hoard. The gift in question was given by a bride-to-be to her intended as an expression of devotion, just as the elusive Charlamont Hoard, missing and sought after for centuries, was finally uncovered.

Then the nightmare began.

* * *

As night drew near and the setting sun gradually dipped below the distant horizon the dwindling rays of parting day fell upon a young woman, immobile and deep in thought, sitting on a weather-worn seat in a secluded part of the old garden. Rosemary Morton, the pensive woman in question, was in a troubled state of mind, as she tried to recall the exact moment when things had started to change — or,

147

more to the point, when *he* had begun to change.

Simon Courtly, the 'he' in question, was her intended, the love of her life and hopefully her future companion for years to come. He had proposed some months ago, had been accepted, and had sealed the bargain with a beautiful diamond engagement ring much admired by Rosemary's close circle of friends. In everyone's opinion, including critical in-laws and aged aunts, the couple were ideally suited and could look forward to great happiness and a contented, blissful married life.

Then shortly after the engagement party things began to change, subtle changes at first hard to define but now, some months later, hard to ignore.

Simon Courtly, it seemed was a changed man.

Subsequent events had taken their toll on the model relationship, and the young woman sitting pensively on the weather-worn seat had, at last, been forced to accept the previously 'unthinkable'.

The expensive wedding, in its final stages of planning and preparation, was off.

She held a small engraved black box in her hand. The box contained the expensive engagement ring, recently admired by one and all — now to be returned.

But what had caused this drastic state of affairs — *and why*?

Rosemary Morton opened the box and contemplated the ring, the expensive gem stones sparkling in the last rays of the setting sun. And what an occasion it had been, a perfect engagement party to savour in later years. Then she recalled her own engagement gift to Simon, her fiancé. His taste in jewellery was almost non-existent, and eternity rings and the like were definitely not his style. And so, after much deliberation over the sort of present he might like, she set off in search of the ideal gift, scouring numerous shops and department stores in the process.

Rosemary eventually found it — but unfortunately the unsuspecting love-struck girl didn't realize at the time that this 'ideal' gift would eventually turn out to be the root cause of her present alarming dilemma.

* * *

"What is it exactly . . . .?"

Rosemary pointed to an item partly hidden beneath an untidy assortment of rather cheap and vulgar jewellery piled on the tray

"Well it is hard to say," the lady in charge of the bric-à-brac stall replied with a shake of her head. "I suppose you could say it is two pieces joined together — a silver chain and a rather unusual cuff link." She handed it to Rosemary, who examined the customized piece of jewellery in the light.

It was indeed an unusual piece.

She perused a silver chain fitted with ornamental clasps at each end and a curious cuff link which had been set into its centre. The link was larger than its modern counter-part, thus belying its age, and took the form of an heraldic shield and cuff supporting clip in the design of a sword and crown.

"Yes, I must say it is an odd piece of jewellery," Rosemary replied, "and I wonder why the cuff link has been fixed to the chain?"

"The most likely explanation is that the other link had been lost and the owner made this one into a waistcoat chain," the lady guessed. "Probably there was some romantic involvement — may be a token of love." Rosemary smiled to herself. That was just the sort of thing she was looking for. The stall keeper's next observation settled the matter.

"You can see the shield has a sort of monogram engraved on it."

"Yes — 'SC'," Rosemary breathed in delight. "Would you believe it? They are my fiancé's initials — Simon Courtly."

"Same initials — that is a coincidence, I must say," smiled the stall keeper. "Then I suppose it would make a very suitable present

— not too fussy, if you know what I mean."

Rosemary certainly did, recalling her boyfriend's comments about jewellery and effeminate men. But this gift would be 'just up his street', with its macho connotations of shield, sword and crown.

To Rosemary's delight Simon Courtly was absolutely bowled over by his engagement present, and immediately went out to buy a suitable waistcoat to see how the old silver link would look. It was now the turn of Simon's friends and acquaintances to admire his engagement gift, and it received the same accolades as Rosemary's diamond engagement ring, much to his surprise and undisguised pleasure.

"It goes well with that waistcoat, old chap," one of his mates remarked on seeing the silver link chain for the first time. "Don't you think he looks a changed man, Rosemary?"

Rosemary put her arm round her fiancé, and gave him a squeeze. "A changed man — I hope not!" she declared. "He suits me just the way he is."

Unfortunately she didn't realize at the time that this flippant remark "changed man" would soon come back to haunt her.

Rosemary noticed this subtle "change" about a week or so later.

"Have you been dying your hair, darling?"

"Dying my hair!" he snorted. "Certainly not! What gives you that idea?"

"Well it looks different in this light," Rosemary answered with a puzzled frown. "Not your usual shade — sort of darker really."

"Well I haven't," he spluttered indignantly. "Dying my hair indeed. Surely you don't think I'm going grey already. We haven't been married yet."

Rosemary laughed, but all the same there was something different about his hair. Taking into account a woman's perspective on matters concerning hair tints and colouring, she was adamant, as the week progressed, that the shade of his hair had darkened, and had begun to thicken with a hint of waves. And it had to be said that up to now

Simon's hair had always been sleek and flat. But there it was — the first sign of a curl.

And then there was this new habit that Simon had developed over the following weeks. Rosemary could not help but notice that he began to fondle the old link in moments of absent-mindedness, running the silver chain through his fingers like a string of rosary beads, a persistent trait which he seemed to be unaware off.

Unfortunately these character changes were also accompanied by a more worrying, not to say disturbing, pattern of behaviour.

It took the form of a growing addiction to gambling and ever increasing bouts of heavy drinking, something which greatly surprised her, considering his strong dislike of excessive alcohol. It caused much concern, leading, as it did, to an aggression and rage which often bordered on the 'physical' and ultimately began to frighten Rosemary. It was all so totally out of keeping with her fiancé's calm and pleasant nature and refined social manners.

What was happening to him — and why?

Then it all began to dawn on her — but it didn't make any sense. She began to notice that for some reason Simon's mood swings and change of personality only took place when he wore his treasured silver link.

Perhaps the answer lay there?

Rosemary began her strange quest by revisiting the antique stall.

"Do you remember me?" she asked the lady. "I bought a small piece of jewellery for my fiancé some weeks ago — a silver chain and cuff link."

"Ah, yes," the stall keeper replied. "An engagement present, if I'm not mistaken. I do hope he liked it."

"Yes, he does," Rosemary nodded. "He has become very fond of it in fact, and I would like to try and find out more about it. Do you know where the silver link came from?"

"Oh, now that is a difficult one, my dear," the lady replied, shaking her head. "— very difficult indeed. You see a lot of this bric-à-brac and jewellery comes from all sorts of unusual places, but house clearances in the main."

She reflected for a moment.

"Ah, now I remember," she continued. "I'm almost certain some of the pieces on that tray came from a farm cottage near Ormsley."

"Near Ormsley — do you know where?"

"No, I can't say I do," came the disappointing reply. "However, I do recall that it was from an attic clearance. All sorts of junk dumped in the top of the house, I gather — going back a long time, so they say."

"Nothing else?"

"Well, I'm fairly sure the old chap who died had connections with an old Hall." She paused again for a moment. "I was told he found the silver link in the roots of a thorn tree."

"Can you remember the name of the Hall?"

"Oh, now let me see," the lady pondered. "It could be Mossley Park or Hall. I think I read that it had been sold to be turned into a leisure complex — a sort of Country Club."

"In the newspaper?"

"That's right," the lady nodded. "The local newspaper — and you might be in luck, if you wait a moment." She turned away and reached under the table, thumbing through a pile of old papers. "Yes, here it is," she muttered. "It is a bit tatty, I'm afraid, but you'll be able to read all about the place on the centre page." Rosemary thanked her for her help and went on her way.

Luckily the article was quite intact, and the stall keeper's earlier recollection concerning the future of the old Hall proved correct.

Under a banner headline the colourful advertisement described the various attractions on offer at the new Country Club, as well as membership fees and introductory inducements. It then went on to describe the Hall, including a summary of its chequered history.

Rosemary read *"The Mossley Story — Part One"* with growing interest. Usually she found such articles rather boring, but in this

152

case she had a distinct feeling that she was on to something — and perhaps Mossley Hall held the key to her dilemma.

The Hall lies some distance from the old high road, just within the boundary of Bickersley (mentioned in the Doomsday book) and the wealthy Stanlon estates. Surrounded by varied timber and straggling hedgerows this ancient building stands on a small rise of land in what can be described as a remote and lonely situation, a place to be avoided on a dark and stormy night. This rather foreboding structure is built partly of brick and timber (in a style so common place in the county at the time) and has a noticeable feature in the form of a very large chimney which takes up a considerable space in the house. Primitive construction in the form of clay floors and wattle and daub walls were also a feature of the interior of the Hall in earlier times.

By the end of the 17th Century it had acquired such a sinister reputation for ghostly sightings that it became known locally as 'Boggart Hall', a dismal place haunted by those restless spirits from beyond the grave. The ghost of a distressed lady dressed in a white gown wailed and moaned around the entrance to Hall, slamming the door behind late night visitors, and this supernatural event was often followed by the sound of rattling chains and shuffling footsteps which approached the Hall from the old barn.

It is also said that Mossley Hall has not abandoned these 'other' unseen tenants from bygone times. 'They' still reside within its walls and remain free to roam this lonely and deserted rise of land.

On the eventual demise of the Charlamont family (a branch of the noble Mossley line whose lineage could also be traced back to the Doomsday Book) the building had many tenants and recently fell into disrepair, being sorely neglected and

*eventually abandoned to its last tenant, a reclusive farm
labourer. It is now in the hands of a building consortium,
who are in the process of turning the estate into a golf course
and the Hall into a Country Club with full facilities.*

Unfortunately the article finished at this point, but the editor
went on to mention that a further article on the Hall would appear
in the next edition.

So there it was, plain to see. A lurid piece of local folklore and
an enthusiastic promoter who would have her believe that 'Boggart'
Hall was a most singular place, with hauntings, boggarts and
colourful past.

'I suppose it is another way to drum up membership,' she
thought cynically. 'Teeing off at midnight with some headless ghost
as your caddie would cause quite a stir in golfing circles, I suppose.'

Rosemary was equally sceptical about the pleasures of golf and
'unearthly' matters, finding it difficult to accept that the supernatural
could exist — until her own hair-raising experience later that
evening.

After such a busy day the exhausted girl decided to put her feet
up and spend the evening by herself, curled up in a comfortable
armchair with the latest edition of 'Modern Brides'. It was one of
her favourite magazines, a glossy expensive publication mainly
devoted to Grand Society occasions, wedding dresses and ornamental
three-tier cakes. A cup of tea was in order and Rosemary went into
the kitchen with this in mind, leaving 'Modern Brides' on a handsome coffee table, a premature wedding present from colleagues at
the office. She returned with the simmering tea and settled down in
her chair, reaching out for the magazine to continue her reading —
and from that moment her sceptical opinion on the supernatural
underwent a change.

The coffee table was empty — *and the magazine gone!*

Rosemary looked for it on the floor, under the table and down the back of the armchair.

No luck.

She then went back to check the kitchen. Again there was no sign of the publication.

'Modern Brides' had completely vanished into thin air.

Rosemary sat down and frowned, deeply puzzled by this mysterious turn of events.

'I know I put it down here,' she told herself reassuringly. 'I can see the outline of it in the dust.'

Dust?

That was odd. There shouldn't be any dust. The room had been thoroughly dusted and cleaned that very morning.

But there it was, plain to see, on the table top — a fine coating of a dry, powdery substance — *dust*!

Unfortunately this domestic mystery didn't end here. To her astonishment the apprehensive girl found other powdery traces of that 'housewife's nightmare' — and tangible evidence of an intruder.

A faint line of hand prints were plainly visible on the dusty stair rail, their irregular outline pointing to a culprit with an emaciated hand and long crooked fingers.

As Rosemary started up the stairs, following this disturbing trail, a disgusting smell swept down from above. The nauseous odour filled the air, an overpowering stench of decay which caused Rosemary to draw breath and splutter, choking uncontrollably in the rancid atmosphere.

Rosemary covered her nose and mouth with her handkerchief and carried on, following this eerie trail up to the landing — and stumbled over something on the floor. The 'lost' magazine, 'Modern Brides', lay on the carpet at her feet.

But how did it get there — *and who had taken it*?

Suddenly alarmed at the prospect of some odorous lunatic with a penchant for nuptial 'gear' roaming around her flat Rosemary halted on the landing, debating whether to go on.

She stood and listened for some moments, straining to pick up any sounds of disruption or commotion in the flat.

Her ears met with a wall of silence.

A light scattering of dust lay on the landing carpet, and the trail led to the door of the small box room at the far end of the passage.

This door now stood slightly ajar — but Rosemary was quite certain she had securely locked it earlier that day.

She stored her wedding dress with other sundry wedding items and gifts in this room, well away from prying eyes, and it was strictly out of bounds to all but the selected few. And now she saw the door standing well and truly open — open to unenlightened prying eyes. And judging from the alarming sounds which now reached her ears whoever was in the box room was up to no good. Rosemary listened with grave misgivings to mournful groans and sighs rising and falling in volume, dying away to whispers.

" My wedding dress . . . .!"

Rosemary, alarmed at the prospect of someone interfering with her expensive dress and disrupting the preparations and plans for the 'best day of her life', threw caution to the winds and burst into the box room to confront her uninvited guest — and became a firm believer in the after-life on the spot.

The room looked as if it had been hit by a tornado and a nauseous, overpowering smell accompanied a haze of dust which swirled round and round, coating every thing in white particles. Bridesmaids dresses lay scattered all over the floor, along with the cute little page boy outfit.

And there the middle of the room, stroking Rosemary's finely-made wedding dress with long taloned fingers, hovered the intruder responsible for this unholy mess.

And what's more, the contrast between the beautiful dress and the intruder's appearance was quite startling. It was painfully obvious to Rosemary that this creature, partially covered in tattered mouldy rags in their final stages of disintegration, was *no more*.

Yellowed skin and bone of a severely withered frame poked through jagged rents in the material of a once highly ornate garment which, to Rosemary's growing horror and consternation, had all the hallmarks of a marriage gown — that the apparition was clothed in the remnants of her own wedding dress.

The unearthly 'being' regarded Rosemary with hollow, mournful eyes and reached out to touch the terrified girl with long, emaciated fingers.

Rosemary recoiled in horror, her back against the door.

The ghostly bride's pallid face and deathlike features were partially concealed beneath long strands of matted white hair, wrapped at intervals in once-fine ribbon — and with each movement the creature displaced particles of fine dust and mould which swirled around her withered shape.

The spectral 'bride' hovered before Rosemary, a pitiable and sorrowful sight, and the frightened girl, to her relief, began to sense that this ghostly 'bride' meant her no harm.

The gruesome spectre's mouth slowly opened and she drew breath with a great deal of pain. Harsh rasping sounds arose from the hollow depths of her being, and at first Rosemary had difficulty in understanding the words.

Then she understood why, shuddering at the grim reason for this unfortunate condition.

Ugly crimson marks were plainly visible on the bride's neck, marks which encircled her wrinkled throat and were, no doubt, the primary cause of her afflicted speech and present condition.

It was obvious that the ghostly creature in the tattered wedding dress had, at some time in her past, been strangled.

She had not spoken in centuries, but she made another painful attempt to do so, drawing breath and scattering dust in the process.

'What is she trying to tell me?' the astounded and fearful girl cried inwardly.

The words gradually became more comprehensible.

"Fly away — away from him and his accursed line. Fly before it is too late," the trembling creature rasped in a mournful tone. "Fly away, my dear, I beg ye — now while ye still have the power to do so . . . ."

And with that sombre warning the spectral bride began to glide forward, and, before Rosemary could dodge aside to avoid her, the unearthly visitor glided through her like an icy draught of air, out of the room and on to the landing, leaving a cloud of dry dust and mouldy particles swirling in her wake.

Down the stairs and out of the flat into the night air swept the bride, leaving Rosemary spluttering and gasping from mouthfuls of dry, choking dust.

She stood there, shivering with shock and numb with cold, nervously contemplating the chaos on the dusty, box room floor.

And all the while Rosemary was vaguely conscious of the spirit's hollow voice fading into the distance, her haunting warning lingering on in the empty flat.

"Fly away — fly away, I beg ye — fly away . . . ."

* * *

From then on Rosemary refused point blank to stay in the flat.

She withheld the reason from Simon and went to stay with her parents for several weeks, citing gastritis rather than nervous depression as the cause of her illness. A warning from a ghostly bride to cancel the wedding was not something she wished to discuss at that particular moment in time. Feeling safe at home in the company of her parents helped to soothe her nerves and restore her confidence, and slowly she began to recover from the shock of the ghostly confrontation.

One afternoon Rosemary made her way into Ormsley and, remembering the article on Mossley Hall, called in at the newsagents and bought the latest edition of the local newspaper.

She thumbed through the pages, searching for the relevant article, and eventually found it under the caption *"The Charlamonts of Mossley Hall"*.

This second article dwelt on a particular dark and disturbing period of its history.

Not only did Mossley Hall acquire an unsavoury reputation during the latter part of the 17th Century, but it also marked a gradual decline in the Charlamont family's fortune and influence. The reason for this perilous state of affairs was plain to see and could be laid firmly at the door of the young Lord of the Manor, Simon Charlamont. The only son of William Charlamont, who had inherited the Mossley estate through marriage, the new owner of Mossley Hall was tall and handsome, with thick luxurious curls of bronze-coloured hair which fell to his shoulders and was the envy of many a young buck in his London club. He was also a thoroughly dissolute and avaricious character, the proverbial 'black sheep' of the family, causing his family much distress on account of his gambling and spendthrift ways.

Simon Charlamont inherited the estate on the death of his father and immediately set about reducing the family fortune to the point of bankruptcy. Within two years of inheriting the title this 'noble' Lord had reduced the family fortune to a level unheard of at the time. The coffers were soon emptied to pay off the gambling debts, crackpot wagers and, disturbing as it seemed at the time, to silence growing rumours of irresponsible behaviour, which some said bordered on insanity, even sorcery. Matters came to head with angry creditors clamouring at the Hall door, and on the advice of the family lawyer and in order to rectify this disastrous situation the scheming Lord undertook an expedient so favoured by the penniless upper classes — that of taking a rich wife with a substantial dowry to clear his debts and fund his dissolute ways. He began to look for a rich heiress of substantial means — and the obvious solution to his financial problems. He was in luck.

Gossip and title-tattle in his London club brought Eleanor Haysmith, the only child of a wealthy London merchant, to Simon Charlamont's notice. It seemed her doting father, Jasper Haysmith, had aristocratic pretensions and sought to marry his daughter off to a suitable candidate with an upper class pedigree as a first step towards a peerage. By deceit, lies and blatant trickery Simon Charlamont played on the vanity and snobbish pretensions of the merchant and the outcome was the marriage of the daughter to the Lord of Mossley Hall, sealed with a handsome dowry.

Unfortunately the second part of his initiative, the acquisition of this suitably large dowry, faltered. The "handsome" dowry of gold, silver and jewellery, it seemed, completely vanished, as did Eleanor, his bride, some months later. It was all very suspicious and caused much speculation at the time, ending any chance of his rehabilitation. Lord Charlamont was arrested for the murder of his wife, and taken to Lancaster Castle in chains. However, the penniless aristocrat still had one or two favours to 'call in', and he turned to influential acquaintances for support — and, in the absence of a body, not surprisingly he got off.

The dowry, or Charlamont Hoard as the broadsheets later described it, was never found. The Lord of Mossley Hall, unable or unwilling to leave the family seat, became a recluse for the remainder of his days, and it was said that his vengeful ghost roams 'Boggart' Hall in chains, searching for the lost hoard of gold.

This illuminating article on the history of 'Boggart' Hall ended on a supernatural note, the editor promising to return to the story the following week.

* * *

Some weeks later Rosemary had recovered sufficiently from her ghostly encounter to realize it was time to pick up the pieces and return to her flat. It was strange at first, as she relived that horrendous night, but once she had overcome her initial nervousness she set about cleaning the flat, tidying the box room, vacuuming the dust and polishing the furniture. Her mind was awash with thoughts, ideas and unanswered questions about the supernatural.

In Rosemary's mind the connection between Simon Courtly and the 'noble' Lord was obvious. Their initials 'SC' were both the same, and, in her opinion, the silver sleeve link currently adorning her fiancé's flashy waistcoat and the one found centuries earlier by a workman in the roots of a tree near the hall were one and the same.

'I'm certain the silver link belonged to that notorious toff,' she mused, '— but, more to the point, how did he come to lose it under a tree in the first place?'

After a relaxing hot bath she settled down in her armchair with a cup of tea and a biscuit. She phoned her fiancé and found that he had made other plans for the night, no doubt involving excessive drinking and riotous behaviour totally in keeping with his recent 'change', and so a meeting was arranged for the following day.

Imagine her surprise when, later that night, she heard someone approach the front door of her flat, followed by her caller trying without much success to insert his key in the lock.

'Oh no — he told me he would be busy tonight," she muttered rather irritably, recalling her conversation with Simon. "And now he has turned up well and truly sloshed. There goes my peace and quiet for the night.'

Reluctantly the disappointed girl rose from her comfortable

chair. The last thing she wanted was a violent confrontation with Simon, and she began to have second thoughts about letting her fiancé into the flat, knowing all too well the aggressive streak in his newly established volatile nature.

Unfortunately she couldn't hide. He knew she was there, and she had no alternative but to let him in.

Rosemary made her way down the hallway towards the door. She could see his figure swaying unsteadily backwards and forwards on the other side of the glass, a dark shape framed in the frosted panel.

He tried the key again — without any luck.

'He is in a worse state than I first thought,' Rosemary groaned inwardly, for the inebriated fiancé was still having trouble with the lock — as well as keeping his temper under control.

It was to no avail.

He began to bang loudly on the door with his fist, making such a racket that Rosemary, terrified of what the neighbours would think and complaints of domestic violence to the police, panicked and quickly opened the door.

At that very moment her healthy scepticism in "unearthly matters" took another fatal blow, as a malodorous stench swept in from the darkened hallway and she came face to face with the noisy caller.

It wasn't Simon!

Sure enough the tall gaunt figure exhibited some of Simon's changed characteristics — *or was it the other way round*?

Although the style of his clothes was noticeably different there was no doubt about the similarity between those luxuriant curls and Simon's recent change of hairstyle.

And then she was alarmed to see another similarity, in this case not with Simon, but with the spectral 'bride'. A fine coating of dust, mildew and cobwebs covered his clothes.

The intimidating stranger swayed from side to side, breathing heavily and much the worse for wear, the key in his left hand.

And it was no wonder he had trouble with the lock.

This rusty key was most unsuitable, and would never, in a month of Sundays, open her Yale lock. In fact its old-fashioned design made it more fitting for the spring lock on a huge, heavy door in a church crypt.

And then there was the cuff link.

This was large, made out of silver, and held flounces of linen in place — and the heraldic shield was an exact copy of Simon's link.

It had the same monogram engraved on its surface — 'SC'.

The visitor lurched forward, reaching out with his other free hand, intent on entering — and Rosemary reacted swiftly, slamming the door and trapping his arm. She gasped with terror when she saw the linen folds of his fine shirt hanging loose and slightly torn. The silver link for this sleeve was missing — ripped out.

"Go away — go away!" screamed Rosemary, thrusting all her weight behind the door.

The violent intruder snarled with anger and withdrew his arm in a flurry of dust. Rosemary secured the door and retreated to the living room, shaking with fright and shock.

Her respite was not to last long, for the sound of a key in the lock of the hall door announced the return of her visitor.

This time he had managed to open the door.

His footsteps came down the hall, and Rosemary crouched in her chair, her wide eyes glued to the living room door.

It slowly opened — and Rosemary sprang to her feet in panic.

"What are you up to, darling?" enquired a tipsy Simon, entering the room, a puzzled frown on his face. He contemplated the terrified girl. "And where did that pile of dust by the front door come from?"

Now, as far as Rosemary was concerned, that was a question with no credible answer — not for the moment, anyway.

* * *

"Have you decided where you would like the reception,

Rosemary?" her mother asked.

"No, I haven't decided yet," Rosemary replied, now back at home with her parents. "I've had such a lot on my mind recently." That was an understatement, to say the least.

"Well, you'll have to make up your mind soon, dear," her mother advised. "These places are usually booked up well in advance."

"What about this venue," remarked Simon, holding out a colourful brochure to his future mother-in-law.

"The Mossley Country Club?"

"Yes, a new development near Ormsley," Simon replied. "It has just opened, so we might be lucky with an early booking."

Rosemary's mother read the brochure which listed the various activities on offer, describing the facilities in the leisure complex and stressing the refined quality of style and decoration associated with such a high class venue suitable for all occasions.

"Yes, it does look promising."

"We could visit the restaurant and check out the catering," Simon suggested. "It says they do a Sunday special."

The arrangement was confirmed with a phone call and a reservation made for the following Sunday.

In the event Rosemary was glad she went, especially when she saw a small exhibition of photographs and drawings in the foyer of the restaurant. The display was arranged on the walls and consisted of interesting features associated with the renovation of the Hall. There were several views, before and after renovation, and some were of the interior of the building.

THE GREAT SCREEN

This elaborate Medieval screen was designed to partition the Great Hall for religious and secular purposes. The Mass was held in secret during the years of religious turmoil and persecution.

THE GRAND STAIRCASE

The grand oak staircase is one of several unusual features to be found in the Hall. It is not so much admired for the quality and breadth of its Medieval carving, but more on account of its size. It is rather large and somewhat incongruous when compared to other furniture in the great hall, and this architectural inconsistency is further highlighted by the supporting balustrades. They are indeed substantial.

Then another illustration on the opposite wall by the door caught her attention. It was a small ink drawing of a gentleman's cuff link, and it bore the initials 'SC'. She read the accompanying description beneath this drawing with mounting excitement.

THE SILVER LINK

This sleeve link was found embedded in the roots of a thorn tree near the entrance to Mossley Hall. It was probably lost by someone planting the tree, ripped off when he caught his sleeve on the thorns. A gentleman's cuff link of 17th Century origin, it was larger and heavier than its modern counterpart. The main plate was in the form of a shield embossed with intertwined letters 'S' and 'C' and decorative vines, and was attached by means of a finely moulded silver link to a cross piece incorporating a dagger and crown. It was one of a pair, obviously made for a singular person of wealth and influence (possibly a Charlamont, a 17th century owner of Mossley Hall), whose initials were 'S C'.
This unusual link seems to have had supernatural associations. The workman who found it kept the silver link for only a short time. He made it into a waistcoat chain and then, in apparent haste, sold it. However, since there was no sign of its companion, the value of the silver link was more than halved, but he did not haggle about the price, and seemed

glad to be rid of it. He said he was plagued with 'visitations', and refused to go near the Hall or speak of it again. Unfortunately the whereabouts of the silver link are presently unknown.

"Well — that's wrong for a start," Rosemary muttered under her breath.

On the other hand the reference to *visitations* was right on the mark, and she gave an involuntary shudder as she watched her fiancé absent-mindedly fondle the silver link on his waistcoat.

What was to be done?

* * *

Rosemary decided that she could no longer live in the "plagued' flat.

However, she knew she would have to return at some point in the future to retrieve her wedding dress and other items needed for the ceremony. She did not dare to go alone and arranged to meet Simon to help with the task. While he found a parking space further along the street she made her way to the flat to wait for him.

She found that someone had already called to see her.

The visitor had left a 'calling card' by the door.

Rosemary gazed in dread at the sprinkling of white dust on the door mat, and debated what to do.

Perhaps 'he' were still inside — *waiting*.

As she hesitated, peering through the frosted glass door panel, her suspicions were confirmed.

A dark shape emerged from the shadows, emaciated hands pressed against the glass to be followed by a pale skeletal face, partially covered by strands of dank hair and contorted with fear. A second, taller shape, then appeared from the darkness and strong hands grasped the terrified creature by the neck, fingers tightening round her throat. To her dismay Rosemary watched the creature's pale lips part in shrieks of agony and terror as she struggled violently to escape, but her attacker was too strong for her. In an instant the tall figure wrenched her from the door and retreated into the darkness, dragging his senseless victim behind him.

This awful scene settled the debate and Rosemary turned and ran from the flat, straight into the arms of her alarmed fiancé. Leaving her in the car to recover, Simon returned to the flat — but found no-one there. Moments later he appeared with the wedding dress and other items.

"Did . . . . did you see them?"

"No, love," he declared. "The flat was empty — no sign of any-one." He paused. "I must say the place is in a right old mess — covered in dust."

Later that evening, safe and sound in her parents' house, Rosemary contemplated her lamentable predicament. She could not help but wonder if these same *visitations* had also plagued the unknown workman who had originally found the silver sleeve link.

The workman had rid himself of it without delay.

Perhaps it was time for she to do the same — if she could persuade Simon to part with his favourite piece of jewellery.

* * *

The newspaper dropped through the letter box onto the hall carpet with a soft thud and Rosemary went to pick it up. The headline immediately caught her eye, and she in turn caught her breath.

A LOCAL HALL GIVES UP ITS SECRETS

On Tuesday morning workmen discovered the remains of a body on the old Mossley estate. The workmen were engaged in draining a section of land as part of a scheme to widen the Hall drive for the new Country Club. While clearing the ground prior to levelling they uncovered the remains under the roots of an old thorn tree. We have been informed that they are those of a woman and a preliminary examination indicated that she was relatively young when she died. The body was in a poor state of preservation, partly because of the nature of the marshy ground and partly due to the fact that it had been interred without the protection of a coffin. There was no clue as to her identity or the cause of death, but it can assumed from the position of the body that the woman died in suspicious circumstances. The fine quality of the remnants of clothing would suggest a person of some wealth and status while the age of the ancient thorn tree, which stood near the entrance to the Hall, would indicate that the body was extremely old.

However, there is a strong possibility that it could be that of Lady Eleanor Charlamont, who mysteriously vanished without trace in the early 18th Century. DNA testing and forensic investigations continue for the moment, but the lack of any substantial evidence and length of internment do not offer much hope for a positive identification of the mystery woman or an early solution to this unusual crime. In the meantime the body has been re-interred in the Charlamont family tomb, and the baffling case put on file for the time being.

Rosemary considered the facts of this "baffling" case and her own horrifying encounters.

'As far as I'm concerned there's no doubt about it. Lady Eleanor was strangled by her husband and buried under the tree,' she mused, remembering the dark shapes behind her front door. 'It has puzzled everyone for years, but they didn't have the benefit of a supernatural enactment of the crime.'

In the next edition of the paper the following week she came across a letter to the editor.

It was written by a Mr. Arthur Wingate, a local historian and antiquary. His researches into the family letters, journals and private papers of the Charlamonts had uncovered certain family secrets.

Under the title "*A proverbial wolf in sheep's clothing*" this letter dwelt on Simon Charlamont and his part in the affair.

Dear Sir,

In my opinion the remains found in the grounds of Mossley Hall are definitely those of Eleanor Haysmith. Her union with the Charlamonts was an unmitigated disaster. It was abundantly clear from the total change of her husband's behaviour and his callous treatment of her early on in the marriage that Lord Simon had only married her for the large dowry to settle his vast debts and continue with his dissolute ways. Too late the poor girl realized her mistake and so she sought to deprive her villainous husband of her large fortune, hiding the dowry in some secret place.

It can be assumed that the enraged Lord, suspecting his wife had a hand in the affair, relentlessly persecuted her both mentally and physically. Her mysterious disappearance some time later and his subsequent arrest and trial for her murder caused a public scandal and brought the name of Charlamont into disrepute.

The facts of the trial are common knowledge, and the missing fortune, which became known as the Charlamont hoard, has never been found.

Rosemary sat in deep contemplation. In her mind there was no doubt as to the identity of the ghastly and forlorn spectre in the box room — and the reason for Lady Elenor's visit now became clear.

It would also seem that the silver cuff link was a portal to the past and the villainous Lord, and its unearthly influence on Simon Courtly was all too apparent.

Simon's character had changed dramatically since Rosemary gave him the engagement gift, and from that moment on he started to exhibit all those disagreeable traits and pernicious behaviour of the black sheep of Mossley Hall — to the point where his physical appearance also began to resemble that of the noble Lord himself.

In Rosemary's eyes Simon was slowly turning into another 'Lord Charlamont' — and the 'dusty bride' from 'Boggart' Hall had returned with a warning, a stark warning not to be ignored. Rosemary recalled those haunting words with a shudder.

"Fly away — fly away, I beg ye — fly away . . . ."

There was no doubt about it.

It was clear to Rosemary that she had to break off the engagement and cancel the wedding without delay.

However, there still remained the other reason for her present *nightmare* — Lady Elenor's fortune, the Charlamont hoard.

Another interested party, one from an aristocratic family with a total obsession for money and devilish ideas on how to spend it, had tracked down a new 'bride-to-be' and was now intent on claiming what he regarded as rightfully his.

And he had already paid one call with this in mind.

* * *

And so as night drew near and the setting sun gradually dipped away below the distant horizon the dwindling rays of parting day fell upon Rosemary Morton, immobile and deep in thought, sitting on a weather-worn seat in a secluded part of the old garden.

She held a small engraved black box in her hand. The box contained an expensive engagement ring, recently admired by one and all — now to be returned.

'How would Simon react to the decision to cancel the wedding and the return of his ring?' she wondered. 'He has changed out of all recognition — and his weird and aggressive behaviour really frightens me.'

She opened the black box and contemplated the ring, glittering in the last rays of the setting sun. The grating sound of the garden gate announced the arrival of her intended, and she look across the lawn to the line of trees.

The tall figure of her fiancé appeared in the distance, a dark silhouette against the setting sun, casting a long crooked shadow on the dew-soaked grass.

Rosemary rose to her feet, suddenly feeling apprehensive — ill at ease.

'What was it about him?'

There was something out of place.

The figure seemed taller, and then there was his hair. In the half-light it seemed luxuriant and curly — and it fell to his shoulders.

The figure drew near.

On the right hand sleeve of his long coat she saw a silver link glinting in the sunset.

It bore the initials 'S C' — and she realized her mistake.

It certainly didn't belong to her Simon Courtly.

Instead it was the other 'S C', the vengeful owner of this silver sleeve link, who purposely crossed the lawn. Having long departed this world and now aroused from his eternal slumber beyond the weather-beaten door of the Charlamont tomb, the 'dusty' spectre was now on the loose, bent on finding his hoard.

Another thing disturbed Rosemary greatly.

It was the rusty spade which the figure then withdrew from the folds of his long coat. The cuff of his left hand sleeve was loose and open, the frills of his silk shirt stained with soil and hanging untidily astray.

He had recently lost the other cuff link.

It was now perfectly clear to Rosemary how the body of Lady Charlamont, without the protection of a coffin, came to be at eternal rest under a straggling thorn tree.

However, before Rosemary could open her mouth to utter a cry of alarm or turn to escape, the tall apparition spoke in a hoarse cavernous voice, malignant and threatening.

"The dowry, my Lady, if you please . . . ."

* * *

"Have you heard the latest . . . .?"

"Heard — what?"

"It's all on again."

"Ah . . . . You mean Rosemary? That is surprising."

"Yes, I thought so when I first heard the news," replied a young secretary, rising from her desk. "— especially after her recent nervous breakdown."

"Poor Rosemary," her companion nodded. "It was a really odd business, wasn't it — made her very ill, so I've been told."

"It did indeed," the first girl agreed, "— but then she made a remarkable recovery and got back with Simon again."

"So the wedding is back on?"

"Yes, I'm glad to say."

It certainly was a "funny business".

On the evening of those traumatic events Simon was late for his appointment with Rosemary, and as he entered the garden through the rusty iron gate he glimpsed a figure in the distance which he, at first, thought was Rosemary. However, he soon realized that it was not his fiancée, for this figure was dressed in the tattered remnants of a long gown — covered in a fine coating of white dust.

The figure stood for a moment, sadly contemplating a dark shape on the grass, before turning to glide away across the garden into the trees, disappearing from his sight.

Simon, somewhat unnerved by this ghostly interlude, cautiously advanced towards the ominous dark shape by the weather-worn seat — and, to his astonishment, discovered his fiancée lying there in a

172

crumpled heap on the grass. Rosemary was in a semi-conscious condition, babbling incoherently and trembling with fear.

Her dreadful confrontation with that malignant supernatural force had left her in a state of nervous collapse, and the poor girl was confined to bed for several weeks.

However, one profound thought seemed to dominate her recovery. Something had to be done about the cause of all her problems.

The silver link had to go.

And so her remarkable recovery was, in no small way, aided by a peculiar task undertaken by Simon, her reinstated fiancé. He was totally puzzled by her strange request, but followed her instructions all the same.

These instructions were brief and quite specific.

The 'ceremony' took place in the parish graveyard, at the entrance to the Charlamont family vault. Simon knelt on the bottom step and cleared the accumulation of moss, ivy and dead leaves from the base of the weathered door. After careful scrutiny he found a small gap in the corner where the sandstone had corroded, leaving sufficient space to slide the silver link into the vault. He inserted the silver link into the gap and was about to give it a poke with his finger when something quite extraordinary happened.

"I couldn't believe it," he told the anxious patient. "I was just about to push it through the gap into the vault when I heard a sort of shuffling noise on the other side of the door. It was really scary, I can tell you."

By this stage of the narrative the patient had turned quite pale. "And would you believe it," Simon went on, to the patient's growing concern. "The next instant the silver link disappeared, pulled into the vault — and a puff of dust shot out from the hole."

From then on Rosemary made a remarkable recovery, except for her singular aversion, bordering on revulsion, to dust.

As to the wedding itself she refused to wear the lovely white wedding dress, preferring instead a dark informal frock, much to the bewilderment of her parents and friends; and when it came to the bridegroom's attire she made Simon undertake a solemn pledge.

He would never ever, under any circumstances, wear cuff links again.

* * *

Love of money is the root of all evil — and in the case of the Charlamont hoard this particular root was eventually uncovered.

Once again the headline in the local press announced the astonishing fact to the public with the headline "*At last the secret is out of the bag*".

The Managing Director of the Mossley Country Club has informed us of the outcome of a well-kept secret.

The decision to incorporate fittings and fixtures from the old Hall into the interior designs of the new building uncovered a secret which ended centuries of speculation. Last year, during remedial work on the medieval staircase, a craftsman, experienced in the art of wood carving, was hired for this delicate undertaking, and it was during the dismantling stage of the work that he discovered something quite unusual, long concealed in the old staircase.

One of the balustrades was hollow — and it contained a most remarkable find.

Gold and silver, jewels and small ornaments, wrapped in velvet or enclosed in leather pouches, were discovered in the cavity and carefully withdrawn. The items, patiently unwrapped and placed on the great hall table, glittered and sparkled in the light of day, rescued from their long period of confinement.

The Charlamont Hoard, missing and sought after for centuries, it seemed had at last been found.

174

The hoard was removed to a safe and secure place, and, because of the laws relating to treasure trove, rights of ownership and the danger of vandals breaking into the property, everyone involved in the discovery was sworn to secrecy. In the meantime work continued on the new Country Club as normal.

However, investigations into ownership and a valuation of the treasure have at last been completed, and, since there are no living descendants of the Mossley or Charlamont Families to challenge the right to the treasure, the Court has ruled in favour of the new owners.

The Charlamont hoard officially belongs to the Consortium. It is worth a substantial sum, and it has been decided to keep a selection of the finer pieces of jewellery for display and auction the rest of the hoard, the proceeds to be used to raise the old Hall to its former glory.

However, there is one descendant of the Charlamonts who would bitterly disagree with this judicial ruling, and especially the appalling decision to auction his rightful dowry to any old Tom, Dick or Harry.

Simon Charlamont's obsessive love of money was and is (as the newly married Mrs. Courtly would undoubtedly confirm) well known, and he has waited a very long time to get his hands on this particular fortune. The very thought of losing it again would make him turn in his grave — *if he were in it.*

Unfortunately for his legal standing this aristocrat cannot be classed as *living*, and therefore cannot challenge the court ruling.

However, there is one point in his favour.

He does reside locally in an imposing family crypt next to his recently-discovered wife — and incidentally has just acquired a long-lost item of personal jewellery.

Nevertheless, the gentleman has the benefit of unearthly time on his side and no doubt will exercise his aristocratic right to dispute the case whenever he is so inclined.

Bearing in mind the dreadful experiences of a recently married couple, future guests at the Mossley Country Club are warned to beware.

The noble Lord's calling card is easily spotted — copious amounts of dry white dust . . . .

HALSALL

Plain Ghost Trail 46

ASMALL LANE

PRIMROSE HILL

CUT LANE

TO HALSALL

NARROW LN

CLIEVES HILS

TO ORMSKIRK

NOT TO SCALE

46

INSET *Derelict gate posts*

DO NOT DISTURB . . . .

I was browsing through our local Parish magazine the other day when a planning application on the rear page caught my eye. The application in question, "Planning permission for the demolition of barn and adjacent outbuildings granted", reminded me of a cautionary tale which, on reflection, I thought might be of interest to readers.

The unusual story was told to me by an acquaintance whilst travelling to Harrogate for an antiques fair, and was prompted by a break in our journey at one of those quaint coaching inns on the road over the Pennines. We made our choice from the chef's specials of the day and selected a table in a bay window overlooking the yard at the rear of the inn. It was immediately apparent to the most untutored eye that some sort of building extension was in progress. Planks of wood, piles of breeze blocks and bags of cement lay scattered around the yard, adding to the general air of organized chaos associated with this type of activity. This assumption proved correct.

"Yes, the new owners are knocking the old stables down," confirmed the barmaid, "— to extend the restaurant and add a function room, so they tell me."

This piece of information prompted an enigmatic comment from my companion.

"It's sometimes better to leave things as they are," he observed in a serious manner, "— especially when it comes to buildings of this age."

"Now that is an odd remark," I replied in surprise. "Leave things as they are . . . .?"

"I suppose it is," my companion agreed. "But there again Charley Tyson, a friend of mine, would wholeheartedly agree with it, I can assure you — especially after what happened to him."

I was intrigued and decided to press him further about the matter. Eventually my companion went on to reveal the strange circumstances surrounding the case, leading, as they did, to the unfortunate predicament of his friend Charley.

It was indeed a cautionary tale — but you can judge for yourself.

* * *

Charley Tyson was a self-made man, thanks to an upturn in the nation's economy coupled with increased profitability in the quality second-hand car market and a catchy sales promotion "*Charley promises to have you up and running with the minimum of fuss and maximum of choice*". Up till then he had made a precarious living on a small lot at the edge of town, but some shrewd business deals and relocation to higher-class premises with double the amount of display space saw him on the way to his first million. Yes, it could not be denied that Charley Tyson was a self-made man (which he never tired of telling one and all, much to the embarrassment of his wife), but he was the first to admit that he now lacked that vital ingredient so necessary for a man of his financial standing — a suitable residence.

With this suitable residence in mind Charley entered the world of the estate agent and property market, advised by his accountant on matters of finance and guided by his wife on matters of taste. However, as it turned out, the daily routine of Buster, the family Labrador dog, finally settled the location.

Up till then the estate agents had 'failed to come up with the goods' and so, in his search for that elusive (and exclusive) property, Charley had taken to driving into the surrounding countryside,

180

along secluded highways and leafy bye-ways, in the hope of finding something suitable. During one of these lengthy detours he made a fortuitous discovery, thanks to Buster, his amiable Labrador. The dog had become fidgety and restless, a sure sign that it needed to 'make a call of nature' and take some exercise, and Charley decided to pull in at the next convenient place. Moments later he rounded a bend on a lonely country lane and came upon an old stone gatepost standing in the overgrown verge. Beyond this ancient sandstone post a pot-holed farm track skirted a field, wending its way towards a distant rise of land: it was an ideal spot to let the dog out of the car.

Buster barked in anticipation, vigorously wagged his tail and bounded into the long grass at the base the stone post, sniffing around before completing his daily doggy ritual. He then began to amble off along the farm track. Charley, taking this opportunity to stretch his legs, followed the dog at a distance, eventually reaching the end of the track, which finally petered out at the edge of a rough patch of ground. This overgrown area was covered with stunted bushes, brambles and nettles, and here and there assorted debris peeped through the long grass and weeds. At the far side of the plot the earth rose into a small mound topped with dense undergrowth. Charley surveyed the weathered stone and rotten wood and concluded that they were all that remained of a building, possibly a farm dwelling, long demolished. However, the views from this overgrown piece of land were quite superb and Charles contemplated the surrounding countryside with growing admiration.

'I can see why someone would build a house here,' he mused, taking stock of the overgrown patch of land. 'In fact it would be an ideal location for another one.' And so Charley found the perfect site for his future residence, one befitting a self-made man of his financial standing. Granted, it would cost an arm and a leg, but his accountant and business advisor would easily sort that problem out.

Little did Charley realize that the project would also incur another unseen cost, one which fell beyond the domain of accountancy or expensive business advice — one where his financial standing would count for nothing when it came to settling the final bill.

* * *

Charley immediately set about his pet project with enthusiasm. Inquiries locally unearthed some interesting (or "disturbing" in the opinion of his wife, who was rather dubious about the whole affair) details about this isolated plot of land. Charley's assumption that the debris amongst the bushes and brambles was all that remained of a previous building proved to be correct when it came to light that a hall-cum-farmhouse, quaintly named Primrose Lodge, had stood on that spot for some hundreds of years. The old Hall had long since disappeared from the landscape, but had acquired a sinister reputation before its demise. It was said that Primrose Lodge had witnessed some long forgotten tragedy and the aura of this terrible event still pervaded the very foundations of the ancient building. To this day the site is avoided by locals: in other words it is haunted.

However, this superstitious nonsense didn't deter Charley. His mind was made up and he went ahead with the project. The matter of purchasing the site was eventually resolved. It had been a most gruelling and intricate procedure, to say the least, for the difficulty lay in tracing the ownership of this overgrown spot. Land searches revealed that it originally belonged to the Mordants, a wealthy and influential family in the area, but when the last of that line died the property was left vacant.

Then a most unusual, not to say peculiar, fact came to light.

It transpired that when a distant branch of the Mordant family inherited the property, they, for some undisclosed reason, refused to live in the Hall (or, for that matter, have anything to do with the inheritance). Primrose Lodge, untenanted and unwanted, eventually became derelict and fell into total disrepair, finally collapsing into a pile of rubble. Charley and his solicitor persevered with the search for the owners of the site, and eventually traced surviving members of this 'reluctant' branch of the Mordants. The trail ended in Canada, and after brief negotiations and a very reasonable price Charley Tyson became the proud owner of the ancient site of Primrose Lodge, the family seat of the Mordants.

Within days of the purchase work commenced on Charley's "suitable residence". The ground was cleared in preparation for the foundations, and it was during this preliminary stage of construction that an old stone-lined well was discovered beneath the under-growth on the mound. It was presumed to be the original water source for Primrose Lodge and had, for some reason, been sealed up. Charley would eventually turn this part of the garden into a rockery. Soon the new building began to take shape and promised to live up to all expectations, at which point Charley was asked if he had decided on a suitable name for the property.

"My word, it's coming on really well, Mr. Tyson," his head car salesman remarked when he called to see his boss one afternoon. He perused the building with undisguised envy. "Yes, a house fit for a celebrity," he grinned, "— a film star or politician perhaps. What are you going to call it?"

Charley, highly flattered by these remarks, shrugged his shoulders. "I hadn't really thought about it," he replied, pondering the question. "Perhaps I'll stick with the name of its predecessor."

"What was that?"

"Primrose Lodge — that's if my wife agrees to it, of course. What do you think?"

"Well, it's a name that would appeal to a woman."

The salesman was right. The name did appeal to Cynthia Tyson, and an exclusive name plate was duly ordered in readiness for the opening of the new property.

One evening, during this latter stage of construction work, Charley decided to call in at the Lodge on the way home from a business meeting to check on the day's progress — and that's when he first saw the stranger. Looking down on the distant highway from the front of the Lodge he noticed this rather indistinct figure slowly making its way along the lane towards the entrance to the farm track. Considering the lateness of the hour and the onset of darkness he was surprised to see someone travelling this lonely road at that time of night. His surprise swiftly turned to curiosity when he saw the figure stop at the entrance — and turn to contemplate the new building.

It slowly began to move forward — and then suddenly halted beside the gatepost at the threshold of the farm track, as if unwilling or unable to continue further. Here the distant figure remained, stationary and ominous, staring up towards the Lodge. It also had an effect on Buster. The dog, sensing something was amiss, began to growl and bare its teeth, and Charley, in turn, began to feel uneasy. He decided to drive down and confront this unsettling visitor, setting off along the uneven track in the gathering darkness with a reluctant Buster crouching and growling on the back seat of the car. Charley quickly arrived at the entrance, the solitary gatepost starkly illuminated in the car headlights — and to his astonishment found the stranger had vanished into the cold night air. Charley continued his search for the stranger, slowly driving down the solitary lane. To his surprise he found it was empty. He was deeply perplexed by the mystery, and then a conversation with his architect later that week only served to make matters worse.

"By the way, Mr. Tyson," the architect began, "I think this would be a good time to discuss the question of security, now that the property is nearing completion."

"Security?"

"Yes," the architect continued. "I had a rather disturbing experience the other night when I left the Lodge. Do you know I almost hit someone loitering by the gatepost in the lane."

"Really . . . ."

"Yes — and I'm sure it was a woman," the architect went on. "I was certain I'd knocked her down. But, when I got out of the car to investigate, there was no sign of her."

"And you're sure you didn't imagine it?" asked Charley, recalling his own weird experience some nights earlier.

"No, it wasn't my imagination — definitely a woman. And she looked in a bad shape as well."

"What do you mean — bad shape . . . .?"

"Half starved and skin and bone would be a suitable description," the architect replied. "And she made no attempt to get out of the way — just came towards me . . . ." He paused for a moment and gave a slight shudder. "I don't mind admitting the whole experience gave me quite a turn," he concluded. "Although I'd be the first to pooh-hoo the idea, the fact is — I honestly think she could have been a ghost."

On hearing this supposition Charley recalled the local superstition about the place.

"Well — I have to say there was a rumour about the place being haunted," he told the architect, "but I didn't think anything of it at the time — put it all down to a load of superstitious codswallop."

"I would be the first to agree with you on that score," nodded the architect. "But, after what happened to me the other night, I'd be inclined to get a second opinion if I were you."

Charley got his "second opinion" later that year — but by that time it was too late.

Some four months later, on completion of the landscaping (with illuminated fountain, expensive ornamental statuary and lavish rockery) the Tyson family moved into their new residence. Charles now had a property worthy of his financial standing.

However, a certain feature seemed out of place, no longer in keeping with the newly resurrected Primrose Lodge, not to mention its links to ghostly experiences from the recent past and lack of security. It was decided that this questionable feature, the old weathered gate post and last remaining link with the old Lodge, had to go.

"It is rather ugly and spoils the view," declared Charley's wife,

Cynthia, one day soon after they had moved in to their new home. "It lets the place down."

"What do you suggest, darling?"

"Replace it with modern gates, of course," she replied, "something imposing — in fancy wrought iron and electrically operated so you don't have to get out of the car in the wind and rain to open them."

Charley tended to agree, but not for those particular reasons.

"We really could do with something substantial enough to keep out unwanted visitors," he added, recalling his architect's confrontation and his own unsettling experience some months earlier. This observation met with immediate approval.

"I agree," nodded his wife. "In fact I meant to tell you that I thought I saw someone the other night — loitering in the road near the gatepost. As far as I'm concerned the sooner we have the new gates securely in place the better."

Unfortunately it was a misguided opinion. In the case of Primrose Lodge the erection of modern wrought iron gates operated by the latest technology would be no deterrent to that particular visitor.

* * *

A distant cloud of blue smoke and the deep throb of a noisy diesel engine announced the arrival of a grimy JCB digger and two workmen. The machine spluttered to a halt at the Lodge entrance and the men climbed down from the battered vehicle to inspect the old gate post.

"I bet it weighs a bloomin' ton," the first man observed, running his hand over the weathered stone. "Might take some time to pull it out of the ground."

"Naw — no problem, Ken," the other man declared confidently. "Not with this digger anyway."

"Don't be too sure, Les," his companion replied with a sniff. "It has been here a long time, by the look of it, and there's no knowing how deep it is in the ground."

"Well — there's only one way to find out, mate," replied Les, climbing back on the digger and starting the engine. It spluttered and coughed, emitting a cloud of black smoke, and then roared into life. The bucket on the arm bit into the grass verge at the base of the post and delved out the first clod of grass and soil. Within minutes a substantial trench had been excavated around the gatepost, and Ken's hunch proved correct. It had been buried deep in the ground. Nevertheless, the digger proved up to the job and, after a sturdy chain had been attached to the arm and around the stone post, the machine lifted it clear and placed it on the ground beside the gaping hole.

"There — what did I tell you," Les beamed. "No problem!"

At that moment Charley arrived on the scene.

"How are you getting on, lads?" he asked, gazing into the hole. "Any problems with the old gatepost?"

"Naw, dead easy," replied Les confidently.

In the meantime, as Ken began to fill in the hole with his spade, something caught his eye at the bottom of the pit.

"Hang on a minute," he muttered, reaching down and poking about in the cavity. "I think there's something else down there." The others gathered around while Ken proceeded to clear away the soil. He uncovered an irregular slab of stone, nestling in the earth.

"It could be a foundation for the post," Charley suggested. "What do you think, Ken?"

"May be," the sweating workman replied, kneeling down to have closer look at the slab. He scraped away the particles of earth from the surface. "I think there is something scratched on it," he muttered. "Let's get it up and see."

The slab was retrieved from its resting place and the group examined the markings on its uneven surface with growing interest.

"What does it say, Les?" Ken asked his companion.

'It's a bit difficult," Les declared. "Looks as if someone has scored it with a nail. I think it says "this barrier has been set — disturbeth not" — and there's a rough cross underneath the words."

"What does it mean?"

"I dunno, mate," Les replied, puzzled by the strange inscription. "What barrier . . . .?"

Meanwhile Charley took another look at the hole, peering down into its depths. The tip of something embedded there soil glinted in the light. "Hold on a minute, lads!" he cried. "I think you've missed something else. See what it is Ken."

This time, however, Ken seemed reluctant to act. For some reason his initial curiosity had suddenly evaporated. Perhaps it was because of this strange slab of ancient stone with its weird inscription. 'Disturbeth not'. He didn't like the look of it. It seemed like a warning, and he began to have forebodings about the strange discovery.

"It looks a bit fishy to me," he muttered.

On the other hand his mate Les wasn't to be put off by the warning. "I'll see what it is," he volunteered, getting down on his knees to reach down and carefully scrape the earth away. Moments later he retrieved an object from the soil, an object which had lain undisturbed in the ground for centuries and now lay at the feet of the owner of Primrose Lodge. This object, when partially cleaned of its coating of dirt and grime, sparkled in the sunlight.

"Blimey, it's only an old jug," Les snorted with disgust. "I thought we'd found something really important."

"Perhaps you have, mate," Ken muttered half to himself, "— but you don't know it yet. What do you think it is, Mr. Tyson?"

Charley perused the humble piece of earthenware pottery, turning it round and round. The mouth of the jug was quite large and the curve of the lip indicated a pouring rather than a drinking purpose in its design. It was indeed unusual, for it also had a crude scowling, bearded face carved on its surface, the crazing in the lustrous glaze adding to its grim appearance. All in all, considering its time

188

beneath the old gate post, it was in remarkably good condition and still in one piece.

"I think it might be a toby jug," suggested Charley with a shrug, "but may be it is too big for that, judging by the curved top." He then proceeded to clear the earth from inside the vessel, shaking the contents onto the ground.

"There's some old bits of cloth in it," Les observed, prodding the loose remains with toe of his boot, uncovering several soil-encrusted objects from the pile, "— and tiny buttons and a small buckle as well, if I'm not mistaken."

They all stood for a while contemplating the scene, puzzled by the unusual discovery.

"It beats me what it all means," pondered Charley.

"Whatever it is, Mr. Tyson, I'd leave the lot down there," growled Frank. "If I wus you, I'd chuck this slab back in the hole and cover the whole thing up."

"Well, I think I'll keep the old jug," Charley replied. "The wife is interested in this sort of stuff and she might be able to cast some light on it."

"Suit yourself," Ken declared, quickly tossing the slab back into the hole and shovelling the remains on top of it. Within a matter of minutes the work was completed and the nervous man then stamped vigorously on the loose earth. "That's a weight off my mind, I can tell you," he gasped, wiping his brow with his shirt sleeve.

Les started the digger and the two men drove off down the lane. Charley made his way back to the house with the strange jug under his arm. Cynthia came out of the house to meet him.

"What have you got there?" she inquired.

"I was hoping you could tell me," her husband replied. "I found it under the gatepost, would you believe."

They went indoors to the kitchen and Cynthia got to work on the jug, carefully washing away the grime and dirt of centuries. She placed it, sparkling and glistening, on the table, and stood back to admire her handiwork.

"I must say it's in very good condition," she breathed. "You say you actually found it buried under the old post?"

"Yes, that's right. Do you know what sort of jug it is?"

"I'll check my Antiques Catalogues and Directory," Cynthia answered solemnly. "I'm sure there will be something on this style of pottery." And true enough the Directory quickly provided the answer. She handed her husband the book, pointing to the appropriate paragraph beneath a photograph of a similar jug.

'BELLARMINE'

'A large stone beer jug, originally made in Flanders. Rather like the design of toby jugs it has a bearded face on its surface which is supposedly a representation of Cardinal Bellarmine (1542-1621, canonized in 1930), an admirer of Galileo and a noted defender of the Roman Catholic Church of that period. As the leader of the Counter Reformation he was much ridiculed by Flemish Protestants at that time.'

"There — what did I tell you," Cynthia enthused. "It's exactly the same as our one." Charley carefully picked up the ancient piece of pottery and smiled.

"Well, what do you know — a real antique," he mused. "I wonder if it is worth anything?" Cynthia shook her head in disgust.

"Never mind its value," she retorted. "You should be wondering why it came to be buried under that gatepost in the first place."

Even Cynthia's prized Antique Directory wasn't much help on that score. The answer to this disturbing question, it seemed, had been buried with the Bellarmine jug long ago.

* * *

That Autumn evening, as dusk began to fall and a light mist hovered over the land, Cynthia looked out of the bay window to the distant lane. She expected to see her husband's car arrive at the newly installed electric gates at any moment. What she didn't expect to see was a dark figure appear in the lane and linger in front of these imposing wrought iron gates. She had seen this rather disturbing figure before, some months earlier, and her original misgivings returned.

'Who was it? What did it want?'

At least she was now able to console herself with fact the new expensive electronically controlled gates would prevent any intrusion from unwanted visitors, and she also had Buster the Labrador as a back-up. She patted the dog's head, and received a lick and several wags of his tail in response.

She waited for the intercom to buzz, to disclose the identity of the caller before opening the gates.

The device remained silent — and in the next instant her comforting sense of security was totally shattered.

She saw, to her astonishment, that this forbidding figure was now on the inside of this modern electronic barrier — had passed through it without it opening — and was slowly advancing up the drive to the house.

It seemed the expensive gates had proved useless— and so had Buster. The dog became, for some reason, very nervous. Something troubled him, for he shivered and whined, and slunk away, his tail between his legs, to the confines of his basket.

And, as the dark forbidding shape advanced, Cynthia became aware of something distinctly odd and unsettling about the way it moved. After several steps it halted and slowly sank to the ground, seemingly worn out by the effort. Then it began to crawl forward along the drive before painfully rising to its feet to continue for a few more paces. An ominous thought flashed through the mind of the dismayed spectator.

'If it could get past the gates so easily — then my front door would be no problem.'

Cynthia dashed out of the room and down the hall to the front door, slamming the security bolts into place. She drew back, cowering in the darkness, wide eyes focused on the frosted glass, waiting with growing consternation for the silhouette of the dreaded visitor to appear beyond the glass panel. In the meantime Buster the Labrador remained shivering in his basket, growling and baring his teeth.

However, instead of the expected dark shape appearing beyond the door, a flash of bright light illuminated the glass, momentarily blinding the anxious woman. The powerful glare from the headlights of a car pulling up outside the house pierced the darkness, and moments later an extremely agitated housewife and a barking family pet greeted her surprised husband.

"I thought you said those electric gates would stop anyone getting in," Cynthia quivered.

"Of course they will — they're the best on the market," replied Charley, quite taken aback by his wife's tense manner. "Whatever is the matter, darling?"

"Matter!" she retorted. "Well, for one thing — those bloody gates don't work!" She went on to recount the alarming experience to her husband, who was very puzzled by it all.

"I didn't see anyone in the drive, or near the house — that's for certain," he declared. "And the lane was deserted as well," he went on to reassure her, and she eventually calmed down.

But the distressing incident had undermined Cynthia's faith in the latest design in security gates, and there still remained the questions of the identity and intention of that disturbing figure.

The question of identity for the moment remained a mystery — but the intention of the unwelcome trespasser was made perfectly clear to Charley some weeks later.

* * *

Cynthia turned on her laptop and opened her email. Browsing through the various mail shots she came across the following communication from Alberta, Canada. It was in reply to her letter to the Heathcoates, the family who had sold the plot of land to Charley. She had written, on the off chance, for any information on their family history and their time at the old Lodge.

'I am replying to your letter by email (I am now on line). It really is wonderful and the messaging service is so simple to use. Anyway I think this is what you are looking for. Our family emigrated to Alberta in Canada at the beginning of the last century. The Heathcoates had distant marriage ties with the Mordant family and inherited Primrose Lodge when the last of that family, Edward, died. Unfortunately they found it very difficult to settle in the old Lodge (some of the family thought it was possessed) and eventually set out to start a new life in Canada.

The following story, told to me by my Grandmother when I was very young, is unusual and quite scary. She told me that a ghostly figure (she called it the Primrose Lady) haunted the lane by the old stone gatepost near the house and she herself had actually seen this figure. It must have been a terrifying experience for such a young girl. She came face to face with the Primrose Lady one misty night as she cycled back from the village, and I remember her description of the ghost gave me some unpleasant nightmares at the time. My Grandmother went on to tell me that an old lady in the village (she was the housekeeper to Edward Mordant just before his death) told her a most peculiar tale about that family.'

The email went on to relate some revealing details about the last of the Mordants.

Edward Mordant, a devious and rather unsavoury character,

became involved with a girl from the village when he inherited Primrose Lodge. This simple and trusting girl worked as a servant at the Lodge and was unworldly and naive in the extreme. At the time Edward was engaged to the daughter of a wealthy brewer with business interests in Belgium and Germany. She, in contrast, was a lady of substantial means and the union would provide much needed funds for his extravagant lifestyle. The risk of losing this windfall did not deter him from taking advantage of the servant girl. The result of his blatant seduction was an illegitimate child and the baby boy and its mother were swiftly banished from the house.

The whole affair was kept secret.

Edward married and hoped for children, but it wasn't to be. His new wife was barren and Edward was now in a quandary, for he was last in line and needed a son and heir. He came up with a devilish solution to his problem. He decided to abduct his illegitimate son, hoping to pass it off as his wife's child, and put his plan into action. He snatched the boy and, because of his position and influence, got away with the deed. Everything seemed fine at the Lodge, but unfortunately the child became very ill and died some months later. During this time the mother would wait in all weathers at the gates of Primrose Lodge, slowly declining in health and sick with grief, prevented from seeing her ailing child.

She passed away at that very spot one winter's night and from that time on her ghost was said to return to linger by the gates in search of her lost child. Edward's wife died a short time later (it was said the ghost of the Primrose Lady confronted her and frightened her to death) and he remained at the Lodge for the rest of his life, gradually becoming reclusive and withdrawn. The emanations from this tragedy seemed to pervade the very fabric of the house itself and Primrose Lodge virtually became uninhabitable, eventually falling into disrepair. The email ended with a humorous warning.

'Well, I thought it was a pretty wild story, and probably you

will think it superstitious nonsense. Anyway I hope that your new home is free of any side effects from the old Lodge, although I thought that you might have chosen a different name for the place, considering its weird history.
In the meantime watch out for that darned ghost. Believe me — she ain't no Lady.'

'Its a bit late now,' thought Cynthia, wishing she had known about these disturbing facts before Charley bought the property. 'That sort of information doesn't go on deeds, more's the pity.'

* * *

Henry Smith, one of Cynthia's friends and a member of the local antiques fraternity, called in at Primrose Lodge to discuss the next Flea Market and Collectors Fair. Noticing the jug on the window ledge, he picked it up and smiled.

"My goodness, I haven't seen one of these for years. Where did you get hold of it?"

"Charley found it when he installed those new electric gates,"

"Found it?"

"That's right — under the old gate post on the lane."

This remark wiped the smile from Henry's face. His light-hearted demeanour abruptly changed and he looked at Cynthia in astonishment.

"You mean he actually found it buried under the gatepost?"

Cynthia nodded, somewhat taken aback by his solemn manner. Charley came into the room at that moment. "I've been telling Henry about your little discovery, darling."

"I don't know about a little discovery," he laughed. "It was damned hard work shifting that massive post to find it, I can tell you." Les with his JCB would have disagreed with that remark.

Henry turned to Charley and frowned.

"Did you find anything else in the soil?"

195

"Yes, as a matter of fact we did," replied Charley. "The jug was lying under an unusual piece of stone."

"Unusual . . . .?"

"Well I thought it was," Charley sniffed. "A bit of stone slab with words scratched on it . . . ." He paused, recalling the discovery. "What I mean is — that the words were odd — like "don't disturb" and something about a barrier."

Henry drew breath, eyes open wide, and slowly shook his head.

"Now this very important," he spoke quietly. "Was there anything inside the jug?"

"Yes there was," answered Charley, "— bits of cloth, some buttons and a buckle."

"What happened to them?" asked Henry, peering into the jug's interior.

"One of the lads chucked them away, as I recall."

"Oh dear . . . ." Henry shook his head again. "That's another big mistake, I'm afraid."

"What does he mean, Charley?" asked Cynthia, casting an enquiring glance at her husband. "A big mistake . . . .?" Charley shrugged his shoulders.

"Yes — a grave error of judgement," continued Henry, putting the jug back on the table. "Unfortunately you didn't take heed of the warning. Remember those odd words on the stone — a message intended to act as a warning. In other words — under no circumstances remove this jug."

"So if it was removed . . . .?"

"Then the barrier would be broken."

"What sort of barrier?"

"Ah — now the first question you should ask yourself is why the jug was buried there in the first place," replied Henry thoughtfully. "In fact I'd go so far as to say that you have inadvertently stumbled on an old superstitious practice carried out in earlier times."

"You mean witches and broomsticks — that sort of thing?"

196

"Well, not exactly," said Henry, shaking his head. "This was a practice rooted in witchcraft hysteria so prevalent in Europe after the Middle Ages. In those days primitive peasants used what is called a talisman to protect their families from evil and prevent demons and wicked spirits entering their homes. On the Continent a favourite talisman was a large beer jug which sported the face of Count Bellarmine, a prominent Catholic Cardinal, on its surface. Various personal artifacts were placed in the jug and it was concealed in the building, usually under or above the house door."

"So it was supposed to stop ghosts and the like getting in?"

"That was the general idea . . . ." Henry nodded, pausing to let the weird explanation sink in. "The odd thing about your case is — why was the barrier set at the gates at the boundary of the property and not beneath the front door?" He pondered for a moment. "The second question is — who was it intended for . . . . ?"

Charley and Cynthia looked at each other with growing concern. They certainly knew the answer to the second question — and *she* now came and went as she pleased.

When Cynthia showed Henry Smith the email from Canada he read it and then nodded. In his opinion Edward Mordant was the culprit. It would appear that the unscrupulous owner of Primrose Lodge had been plagued by the tormented spirit of the servant girl.

"The unfortunate soul haunted the house and terrified his wife," Henry conjectured. "However, his wife's brewery connections with the Belgium and Germany and her probable knowledge of their superstitious beliefs gave him the idea of using a talisman to keep the vengeful ghost off his property. He got hold of a Bellarmine jug and placed some articles belonging to the dead child in it. The jug was then buried with a warning, not under the threshold of the Lodge, but under the gate post by the lane. This 'barrier' succeeded in preventing the Primrose Lady, as she became known, from entering his property, but not from haunting the lane." As Henry Smith prepared to leave he gave Charley a final piece of advice.

"I don't know what your views on folklore and superstition are," he concluded, "but, in this case, I do think you have unleashed something unnatural. If I were you I'd gather all the stuff together and re-bury it as quickly as possible." Cynthia agreed and Charley set off in search of the strange stone slab and artifacts from the Bellarmine jug.

But it was too late.

The slab, buttons, cloth and buckle had long since disappeared, more than likely carted off with all the other sundry rubbish when work on the erection of the new electric gates was finally completed. Unfortunately, considering the impact it would have on Charley's mental health, the sundry rubbish did not include Henry Smith's "something unnatural".

It would seem that Henry's *something unatural*, the Primrose Lady, was not for moving. *She* stayed put.

* * *

The whole sorry affair came to a head one wintery evening some weeks later, and once again Buster, the family Labrador, had his part to play in the unfolding drama. The responsibility for the dog's nightly ritual fell to his master. Previously Cynthia had always taken Buster down the drive to the lane for his nightly exercise, but, after that disagreeable incident in the Autumn, she now refused point blank to step outside the door after dark. And so from then on Charley was faced with this nocturnal canine task after work.

On the evening in question Charley set out with the dog in tow. The air was crisp, the night was very cold and the pair crunched down the snow-covered drive under a full moon perched high in a cloudless sky. They had progressed for a short distance, Buster ambling on ahead, when the dog suddenly stopped dead in its tracks. It gave a low growl, its fur stood on end, and its gaze fixed on the Lodge gates bathed in the soft light of the moon.

"What's the matter, old chap?" asked Charley, arriving by his side. The dog shivered, uttered a despondent whine and turned tail, dashing back towards the house. Charley's initial astonishment at his dog's strange behaviour swiftly changed to one of dread when he saw the reason for Buster's retreat. In the lane beyond the entrance to the Lodge a dark figure came into view. It shuffled up to — and then passed right through the closed gates.

'Cynthia was right all along,' gasped Charley in mounting panic. 'Those blasted gates are absolutely no use at all.'

The eerie figure lurched forward, tottering unsteadily for several paces before collapsing in a unsightly heap onto the snow-covered ground. After a moment or so it seemed to revive, mustering its strength to crawl painfully forward in the snow. Then, with greater effort, it managed to clamber to its feet and once again continue its ungainly shuffle up the drive. Charley was rooted to the spot, unable to move, held captive by a terrible fascination as this ghastly spectacle unfolded before his eyes. The daunting figure drew near, and the petrified owner of Primrose Lodge, at last, came face to face with the Primrose Lady. The words from Cynthia's e-mail "*in the meantime watch out for that darned ghost. Believe me — she ain't no Lady*" flashed through his mind.

And the email was right on target. She certainly wasn't "*no lady*".

For a start the awesome creature was just a bag of bones covered with a modicum of withered flesh, a thin glutinous coat which more or less held the structure in place. In fact it looked as if she could fall apart at any moment and, in observing this ghastly state of decomposition, Charley realized why the apparition constantly fell to the ground. In life her grim physical condition was indicative of a state at the very point of death — *from starvation.*

Her garments were in a similarly appalling condition, tattered and worn to shreds; they too were on the point of disintegration. And yet the apparition ploughed inexorably on, unhindered by any earthly rules of physics and biology, unlike Charley, who gave a shriek of terror and turned to escape. In his case, however, the earthly rules of extreme weather conditions conspired against him and his feet slipped, skidding on the mantle of ice and snow, and he fell backwards with a dull thud onto the soft white covering, a flailing mass of arms and legs. The Primrose Lady lurched forward, halting at his feet. Bending forward, the spectre fixed him with a hideous glare, her vengeful eyes gleaming through hollow sockets, partially obscured beneath a tangled mass of jet black hair. She meticulously scrutinized his face — but there was no recognition in those searing eyes. It plainly was not the Edward Mordant of her earthly life who now lay defenceless at her feet. And so the spectre moved on, on over the petrified man. In that instant an icy breath of air swirled over him, a piercing chill numbing him to the bone — that cold chill of death.

She headed towards the house.

And as she swayed onwards Charley thought of his unsuspecting wife and the harrowing effect this terrible 'Lady' would have on her: it had happened long ago to Edward Mordant's wife.

He had to warn Cynthia.

The ghastly apparition continued unchecked on its supernatural course — too late for him reach the house ahead of it.

And then Charley gasped with sheer relief.

Instead of continuing along the drive to the front door of the Lodge the spectral Lady suddenly veered to the right and skirted the edge of the building, to cross the snow-covered lawn to the mound where the rockery garden and concealed well lay. There she halted, arms outstretched, and then slowly sank to her knees. There followed a moan of anguish, rising and falling in the frosty air, a dreadful unearthly sound which floated across the lawn, and, as the fearful wail died away, the ephemeral shape of the Primrose Lady began to wane, its ghastly frame becoming indistinct in the moonlight, gradually fading away into the snowy mound.

The shivering man waited for several freezing minutes, wondering why the Primrose Lady had chosen that particular place to vanish.

Would she return?

He waited — and waited in vain. The ghostly figure did not reappear.

However, when Charley recounted those hair-raising events to Cynthia some minutes later, after she had found him collapsed in snow, he was adamant that he witnessed a most extraordinary and moving sight.

For one brief moment, just before the Primrose Lady faded away, a tiny pair of hands, the hands of a small child, appeared from the snow — and reached up to the forlorn ghost.

* * *

A 'For Sale' sign stands beside the imposing wrought iron gates of Primrose Lodge. The sign board, with its peeling paint-work and fading lettering, has a weathered and dilapidated appearance, having stood there for well over a year. The expensive property on the distant rise is currently on the books of several estate agents, both local and national, and, although its description in the brochure is exceedingly charming and asking price highly favourable, the house remains permanently on the market. It had been rented out on a short term basis over this period but tenants up and left well before the expired time.

One would expect in this day and age that this type of property, left untenanted and vacant in such an isolated spot, would attract either squatters or vandals but it seems that, in the case of Primrose Lodge, this fine building has escaped such damaging attentions. In fact the place is shunned by one and all and, if the current situation continues unresolved, the fine new house will gradually deteriorate and eventually crumble and decay as did its predecessor, centuries earlier.

This parlous state of affairs is of no consequence to the current occupant. The Primrose Lady has no intention of ever leaving the home which she claims as her own through her illegitimate son.

Her disconcerting influence began to cast a shadow over the Tysons, and after the traumatic events of that fateful night Charley no longer felt contented and at ease in his 'desirable' residence. His wife was left with an ongoing nervous condition, and he began to have a recurring nightmare.

In this unsettling dream the Primrose Lady roams the house, searching for Edward Mordant, and, since he is long gone, the ghost's vengeful pursuit is directed at the next best thing — the new owner of Primrose Lodge, Charley Tyson.

In spite of the fact that he still had the Bellarmine jug in his possession Charley was not able to restore it as a 'barrier'. That particular talisman needed a dead child's buttons, buckle and cloth from another age, and, since these items were now lost for ever, the Tysons were left with an insurmountable problem.

In the end the unfortunate couple decided to put Primrose Lodge on the market.

Although it does not appear on the dilapidated sale board in the solitary lane, the crude warning, scratched on a rough stone slab and buried for centuries beneath a weathered sandstone gatepost, is an appropriate piece of advice for anyone contemplating the purchase of this 'desirable' residence.

"*Do not disturb*".

At the present time that seems highly unlikely.

DOWNHOLLAND

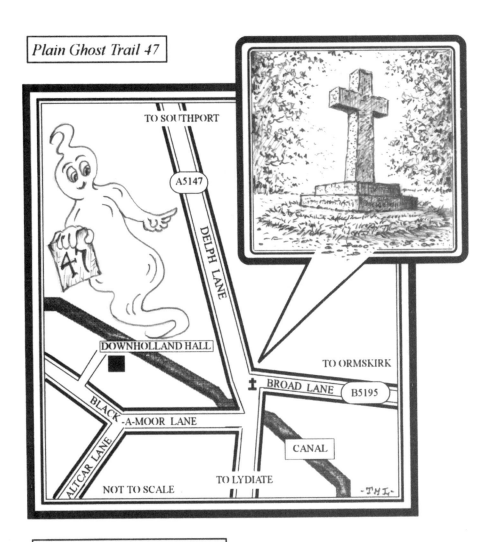

Plain Ghost Trail 47

TO SOUTHPORT

A5147

DELPH LANE

47

DOWNHOLLAND HALL

TO ORMSKIRK

BROAD LANE   B5195

BLACK -A-MOOR LANE

ALTCAR LANE

CANAL

NOT TO SCALE

TO LYDIATE

-THL-

INSET *The Millennium Cross*

THINGS THAT GO BUMP IN THE NIGHT

When I hear the phrase "*things that go bump in the night*" I am reminded of Davina, my first wife, and her two strange fixations — creaking staircases and crown green bowling. As regards the first obsession, Davina stipulated a very unusual matrimonial condition before accepting my proposal of marriage.

She insisted that we live in a bungalow.

The latter obsession manifested itself in a powerful aversion to the game of bowls, crown green or indoor, and even extended to any other form of sport which included a rolling ball.

I eventually found out that this perplexing mental condition could be traced back to her student days, to the time when she enrolled in a College of Further Education in Lancashire. By sheer coincidence a cousin of hers, Ruth Delamaine, enrolled at the very same college, for the very same course, and the two girls soon became inseparable, sharing a room on campus and spending most of their leisure time together. Ruth's mother, Davina's aunt, was delighted with the arrangement, for her daughter was rather shy and reticent when it came to making friends, and Mrs. Delamaine could not help but worry about her daughter's welfare in such a large establishment. Davina's presence and support helped to allay such parental fears and so, in the course of time, Mrs. Delamaine came to regard Davina as a second daughter, inviting her to Downholland Court, the family home, for weekends and holidays.

It was during this period that something happened to my first wife, something so bizarre that it left her with a disturbing mental condition which lasted to her death, and perhaps, on reflection, also contributed to it. It was several years into our marriage before my wife felt able to confide in me about her dreadful experience at Downholland Court.

I set out the details of the affair below, so that you may judge for yourself.

* * *

Davina recalled the day she first saw Downholland Court. Alighting at the bus stop in the village she and Ruth made their way along a secluded country lane to the entrance of a farm track. There in the distance, nestling in the trees at the base of a shallow escarpment, lay an old sandstone house, bathed in late afternoon sunlight, a spiral of blue smoke rising listlessly into the clear air from a weathered stone chimney.

An invitation to spend the October break with her Aunt and Ruth had been gladly accepted and this first sight of the picturesque building served only to strengthen that warm feeling of gratitude. Downholland Court was indeed a charming picture, a veritable haven of tranquillity and peace, a far cry from the hectic daily routine of college life.

"Isn't it lovely," remarked Davina with undisguised admiration, as the pair made their way up the track to the house. "Have you always lived here?"

"Yes, since I was very young," replied Ruth. "We moved here after my grandparents died — when I was about three years old."

"Well, all I can say is — that you were very lucky to grow up in a place like this."

"Yes, I suppose so — but it has its disadvantages as well," Ruth responded. "It can be very quiet and a bit isolated, especially in winter. I wasn't able to play with other children when I was small, and so it could be lonely at times."

They reached the house and were greeted by Mrs. Delamaine.

"I'm so glad you decided to come to stay with us, Davina," she said warmly. "Ruth will show you to your room, and then we'll have tea." Davina followed her cousin up a flight of ornate wooden stairs to a room at the top of the building. This room overlooked the rear of the house, with a fine view of mature trees and sloping land beyond. The room was small but very cosy.

"It is hardly ever used," Ruth explained. "The room is a bit out of the way up in this part of the house, but it is nice and warm on cold nights, and very quiet — so you're sure to have a good night's sleep."

And her cousin's estimation was spot on — except for one thing.

In order to reach her room Davina had to climb part of the ancient staircase in semi-darkness, and the curve of the stairs meant that a section of it remained unlit. At one point her view upwards and downward was severely restricted, provoking a feeling of vulnerability and isolation, not helped by those unsettling creaks and groans associated with a wooden construction of its age. Each time she used the stairs she could not shake off an acute sensation that someone was just round the bend — *waiting for her.* This feeling was most oppressive where the staircase continued upward past her bedroom door, curving away into the darkness. On one occasion she was positive that she heard whispering, soft and breathless, floating down from this gloomy recess, but put it down to those odd noises and occasional draughts linked to houses of extreme age.

However, once inside her room this unsettling impression swiftly evaporated in the warm and cosy atmosphere, and Davina spent a very enjoyable few days at Downholland Court. Weekends and a short pre-Christmas visit followed, ending the year on a happy note.

Unbeknown to her at the time, these halcyon days were the calm before the storm. When she returned the following year it would be a totally different matter.

* * *

In April of the following year the College broke up for the Easter vacation and Davina accepted an invitation from Mrs. Delamaine to spend the holiday at Downholland Court. Recalling fond memories of her previous visits Davina returned to her cosy room at the top of the house in anticipation of an enjoyable Easter break.

It was the Millennium Year, and the nation celebrated accordingly. Throughout the land this special year was commemorated in different ways. Bridges, fountains, gardens and monuments were erected in different parts of the country, and in the village of Downholland the commemoration took the form of a new wayside cross, sited at a nearby crossroads. Davina, accompanied by her Aunt and Ruth, went along to the ceremony, joining the throng of dignitaries and villagers at the roadside, to witness the unveiling of the new cross.

A local newspaper described the occasion.

Members of the District Council and other associated institutions gathered in Downholland on Thursday last to commemorate the Millennium Year. The Council decided to re-establish a stone cross on a central piece of land at the road junction in Downholland. This grassy spot is known to be the site of an ancient cross long disappeared. It was marked on old maps of the area, and was closely connected with other wayside crosses, showing distinct lines converging upon ecclesiastical buildings. In earlier times these crosses were used as resting places on the occasion of funerals by Roman Catholics, a fact which encouraged over zealous Protestants to demolish all within reach. The original wayside cross was lost centuries ago, when records show that it was last used around the time of the Hollands of Downholland Court. However, part of a base stone, uncovered during preliminary ground work, is thought to be part of that original artifact, and has been used in the foundations of the present cross. After the ceremony the assembly withdrew to the Holland Arms for suitable refreshments, and the Chairman of the Council's toast "Let us hope this occasion reawakens the charity and Christian spirit of a bygone age" was celebrated by one and all in the usual fashion.

As far as Davina was concerned the millennium ceremony did reawaken a spirit from a bygone age. However, in her case it was to be neither charitable nor Christian.

After the celebrations she returned to Downholland Court to spend a pleasant evening with her Aunt and Ruth, and then retired for the night. An hour or so later she suddenly awoke — to a most peculiar sound.

She could only describe it as a soft swishing noise, rather like curtains gliding along a curtain rail, slowly dying away and ending in a sharp resounding crack. This sound continued repeatedly for some minutes, and Davina sat upright in her bed, trying to figure out the source of the strange noise. She eventually came to the conclusion that it came from above.

'*Was it something sliding up and down on the roof?*'

Davina climbed out of bed and crossed to the window. Drawing the curtains to one side she opened the window and leaned out, peering up at the eaves of the house, half expecting to see the cause of the strange noise appear in the moonlight. She was to be disappointed. There was nothing out of the ordinary to be seen — at least not in the eaves.

However, as she withdrew her head and prepared to close the window something caught her attention on the distant rise of land. She blinked in astonishment as she observed a horse and rider appear on the crest and canter down the slope towards Downholland Court. Just before the horseman passed out of sight behind the trees and high wall at the rear of the house Davina noticed that his horse was frothing and steaming in the moonlight, a sure sign that it had been worked hard and had travelled far. She was also puzzled by the eccentric appearance of this late night traveller. He wore a long black cloak with a strange emblem emblazoned on the left shoulder, and his head and features were concealed beneath a hood which resembled a medieval monk's cowl: he also carried a cloth bundle which was tied by a length of rope to the pommel of his saddle.

'Who could be out riding at this time of night?' wondered Davina, gazing intently at the trees. She waited patiently for the horseman to reappear, but, as the moon slipped behind a band of cloud and darkness descended upon the scene, she grew tired of waiting and closed the window. And to her relief she found that the peculiar noise from above had also ceased.

The perplexed girl returned to her bed, somewhat troubled by the weird turn of events, and lay awake for ages. At breakfast she asked Ruth if she too had been disturbed by anything the previous night.

"No — I slept like a log," her cousin replied, and when Davina went on to describe the sound Ruth offered an alternative explanation. "Perhaps it was the wind in the trees at the back of the house."

"Oh, I didn't think of that," answered Davina. "Branches hitting the wall could explain the loud knocks as well." She then went on to describe the horseman. "Did anyone call at the house after midnight?"

"At that late hour — certainly not," Ruth declared. "And what's more, I don't know of anyone around here who would be riding a horse at that time of night. From your description he sounds a very suspicious character to me."

Later that morning Davina recalled a disquieting fact. The previous night had been still and calm — with no hint of the slightest breeze. So that put paid to Ruth's "wind in the trees" theory.

The following night Davina was aroused once more by that disconcerting sound. There it was again — a soft swish, slowly dying away to end in a sharp crack. She hurried to the window and peered through the glass pane. She could just discern the branches of the tall trees in the darkness. They were motionless — and on this occasion there was no sign of the mysterious horseman.

Then she heard a different sound — *a soft thud.*

It was followed after a short interval by another thud — and then another. This time the sound came, not from above, but from outside her bedroom. She opened the door and looked out onto the stairs. They were illuminated by a shaft of light from the bedroom — and the next instant something dropped with a soft thud into the light, onto the carpeted step right in front of her. Davina stared in astonishment at the object, spinning and wobbling on the pile carpet — and realized what it was.

A wooden bowl, of the type found on bowling greens across the land, lay before her. Davina watched in amazement as the bowl hovered momentarily on the edge of the stair and then wobbled over to drop onto the next step with a soft thud. It continued in this manner, disappearing from view around the bend in the stairs. She peered anxiously into the dark recess at the top of the stairs, half expecting another bowl to bounce into view, but all was silent. Plucking up courage Davina decided to retrieve the bowl, and set off down the stairs with this in mind. To her dismay, when she reached the ground floor, she could find no trace of the ghostly object. It would seem that the bowl had rolled away into thin air. At that moment Ruth opened the door of her room to see Davina passing by on her hands and knees.

"What are you doing?" she gasped at this unusual sight. Davina stopped and sat there shaking her head.

"I can't find it," the poor girl muttered, half to herself. "I can't find it anywhere. It has just vanished."

"What has — have you lost something?"

Davina looked up at her wide-eyed. "Don't tell me you didn't hear anything — bumping down the stairs?"

"No — I didn't," replied Ruth, helping Davina to her feet. "I suppose you mean things that go bump in the night?"

"Not things, Ruth," she shook her head. "A bowl — a crown

green bowl." She went on to tell a mystified Ruth about her experience.

"Well, I didn't hear anything," said Ruth, "— and there is no sign of a bowl down here, is there?" Davina, casting her eye around the floor, had to agree. "You've had a bad dream, Davina — a horrible nightmare," she consoled the bewildered girl, leading her back up the stairs. "You'll laugh about it in the morning, just you see."

The next morning her Aunt, on hearing about the incident, sought to reassure her guest.

"You must realize, dear," Mrs. Delamaine remarked lightly, "you're bound to hear odd noises in houses of this age."

"But they were definitely bumps — and then I saw a bowl on the stairs," insisted Davina. "I didn't imagine it." She paused. "Do you know what I think . . . .?"

From their blank expressions it was obvious that they had no idea.

"This house has got to be haunted."

"Oh, no — that's not the case with Downholland Court, I can assure you, Davina," retorted her Aunt, shaking her head. "True — the stairs and floorboards creak, and the house is draughty. But in all the time we have lived here we have never been troubled with anything like that — isn't that so, Ruth?"

"That's right," her daughter agreed. "I slept in that room when I was a little girl and everything was fine."

"There you are, Davina," Mrs. Delamaine chuckled. "Ruth wouldn't stay for one second if she thought the house was haunted."

"That's right — I certainly wouldn't," her daughter gasped with a shudder. "The thought of bumping into a ghost on the stairs in the middle of the night would put me off sleep altogether. I'd make sure I left before things got worse."

As matters progressed Davina would be faced with the same dilemma.

Things were about to get worse — much worse.

* * *

'*From where had the bowl come — and where had it gone?*'

Davina turned the problem over and over in her mind. One thing was certain; the bowl had rolled down the stairs from above. Up to that point she had assumed that her room was at the very top of the house, but, since the staircase carried on upwards past her bedroom door, she now reasoned that it must end at another room above her own. Her first course of action was to investigate the staircase itself, to find where it actually ended: and here she came across her first enigma.

She discovered that the staircase went nowhere.

When she climbed to the top she came face to face with a blank wall. The ancient wooden staircase came to a dead end beneath the massive timber beams, and whatever lay beyond had long been sealed off. It was a perplexing dilemma, which left Davina with a disturbing thought. '*The bowl could only have come from the other side of the wall.*'

"Was there another room at the very top of the house?" she asked Mrs. Delamaine later that day. "I see the staircase ends at a blank wall."

"Yes, that's right," Mrs. Delamaine replied. "It has been that way for hundreds of years, so I've been told. It originally went up into the attic, but for some reason the Holland family, who lived here in those days, sealed it off."

"So there is a room on the other side of the wall?"

"Yes," she nodded, "but the entrance to it is now in the kitchen on the far side of the house — through a trap door in the ceiling."

"That's a bit odd, isn't it?" remarked Davina. "I wonder why the staircase was sealed off in the first place?"

"I'm afraid I have no idea, but I suppose the Hollands had their reasons," said Mrs. Delamaine with a shrug. "Anyway, we never use the attic. In fact I have only been up there once."

"Could I go up and see it?"

"Well — if you really want to," replied Mrs. Delamaine with a puzzled frown, "but I can't understand why anyone would want to go up into that dusty old roof space."

"Just to satisfy my curiosity, really," Davina answered with a faint smile. "I'm rather intrigued by a staircase that goes nowhere."

A short time later the inquisitive student climbed a ladder, opened the trap door and entered the "dusty old roof space". Mrs. Delamaine was right. The bright beam of torch light revealed a long room festooned with cobwebs hanging from grime-encrusted beams and a deep layer of dust covering the floor. The room was empty. Davina stepped forward, breaking through the clinging diaphanous barrier, raising clouds of dust at each step, until she eventually arrived, spluttering and sneezing, at the far end of the attic. She was gratified to see the end timbers of the staircase, covered in a thick coat of grime, protruding from the wall. She stood for some time contemplating this blank area, shining her torch over the expanse of rough stone, searching for any sign or clue to explain the mystery of the ghostly bowl. But everywhere had the appearance of overall neglect, undisturbed and untouched by human hand.

'*But why had the staircase been sealed?*'

This strange inconsistency still dominated her thoughts as she withdrew from the attic, covered in dust and cobwebs. Her investigation had proved fruitless and this perplexing question remained unanswered for the time being. Thankfully the next few nights passed without incident. There were no strange sounds from above or bumps on the stairs, and Davina slept soundly in her bed.

By the following Sunday the Easter vacation was over and her holiday at Downholland Court had run its course: her visit had, at last, come to an end. Her suitcase was packed and preparations were put in hand for her departure the next morning. And so, on this night, her last in the room at the top of the house, Davina dropped off to sleep with thoughts of college and the new term foremost in her mind.

In the middle of the night she awoke to that familiar noise. This

214

time, however, the strange swishing was accompanied by additional sounds — muffled voices and the clink of glasses. Raucous laughter and foul oaths bore all the signs of some wild party. Then came the first bump, a soft thud descending one step after the other. Remembering Mrs. Delamaine's disbelief on that previous occasion, Davina resolved to do something about it this time. She overcame her fear and made up her mind to grab that bowl as it passed by her room to prove to her Aunt that it wasn't a bad dream — that the bowl did exist. After all, it was only a harmless round lump of wood. She opened the door and waited for the bowl to appear from the dark recess above.

Thud — thud — thud . . . .

The sound grew louder, and she braced herself, poised to grab the mysterious object. The next instant it rolled into the light, slowly spinning on the stair. She reached down, fingers on both hands outstretched to capture the prize — and gave a gasp of utter dismay.

Lifeless eyes, wide and sombre, stared up at her. Pale lips and bared stained teeth, drawn back in a contorted grimace beneath a matting of blood-stained hair, smiled the smile of death.

The severed head rolled to the edge of the stair, and slowly tipped over.

Bump — bump — bump . . . .

Away down the staircase, out of the light and out of her sight, bounced the gruesome human *bowl*, and the mortified girl could only stand, open-mouthed and speechless, on the stair.

However, she didn't remain speechless for long.

Another sound reached her ear — the sound of heavy stumbling footfalls. They came from the stairs above.

Davina turned — *and gave a shriek of terror*.

Out of the darkness appeared an astounding sight. A terrifying apparition, chest encased in a metal breastplate, staggered feet first into the light. Its arms and legs were clothed in rusty chain mail, torn open in places to expose gaping wounds, and around the ghastly

215

figure's waist hung a belted scabbard lacking its sword. But the most horrifying aspect of this awesome armoured knight was the rivulets of blood which ran down the breast plate and dripped from soiled fingers, to leave a ghastly red trail on the stair carpet. It was plain to see the reason for so much blood.

The body was headless — *the figure had been decapitated.*

The gory spectre lurched forward, descending painfully step by step, in search of its head. This dreadful sight was too much for the trembling girl and she fainted, falling backwards, tumbling down the stairs, bump — bump — bump, to end in a sprawling unconscious heap at the bottom.

It was here that the senseless girl was found by her distraught cousin. Needless to say, Davina, when she eventually came round, didn't make much sense to Ruth and her Aunt, but just kept babbling incoherently about a headless knight and bowls. It was clear she was in no fit state to go back to college, and left Downholland Court to spend the next few weeks recovering from her ordeal at home.

Ruth and her mother, no doubt feeling partly responsible for Davina's condition and wishing to help in her recuperation, begged her to come and stay with them for the Summer holidays. Davina refused the invitation point blank.

She had no wish to be re-acquainted with the headless occupant from the "dusty old roof space" at the very top of the stairs — and never returned to Downholland Court.

* * *

It was some years into our marriage before my wife felt able to confide in me, eventually relating the macabre details of her distressing stay at Downholland Court. Those hair-raising events left a lasting impression. In my opinion, as the years progressed, they were partly responsible for her frequent periods of depression. It culminated in a complete nervous breakdown one October, instigated by that yearly festivity, Hallow'een.

This pagan practice had come to be celebrated in the American style, that of 'Trick or Treat', whereby children would dress up in the most weird and outlandish of costumes. They would then set off in hordes to visit houses in the neighbourhood, demanding 'treats' or threatening practical jokes if you didn't cough up. Gangs of teeny witches, ghouls and ghosties would wander abroad on this witching eve, and all in all it was supposed to be harmless fun.

Unfortunately my wife didn't see it that way.

The door bell rang on that fateful evening, and Davina went to answer it. She opened the front door, and I heard excited cries of "trick or treat". I also heard a harrowing shriek, a dull thud immediately followed by children screaming.

I raced into the hall to see my wife lying in a heap by the door, the figure of a headless corpse outlined in the doorway, and a variety of tiny witches, goblins and ghosties scampering in panic down the path towards the garden gate.

The headless corpse was blubbering.

Trembling hands reached up and parted the tunic of its gory costume to reveal a pale child's tear-stained face beneath.

"I didn't do anything — honest," the child sobbed. "I — I didn't mean to — to frighten her . . . ."

And with that the corpse lost its nerve, turned and raced after its ghoulish companions, scattering assorted 'treats', gathered during the course of the festive evening, in its wake.

I revived my wife with great difficulty. It had been an awful shock and in the end I called our doctor, who prescribed a strong sedative.

"It is a stupid way to behave — that's all I can say," he told me. "I'm often called out because of this nonsense. These kids don't realize how frightening they look in their weird get-ups. They really scare some old people, you know."

I do know — now.

The incident badly affected my wife. A nervous breakdown and a long-standing heart condition took its toll on her health, and Davina passed away a year or so later.

However, in going through my departed wife's personal belongings I came across a folder containing work from her student days. Sifting through various pieces of coursework I discovered newspaper cuttings in a brown envelope, and soon realized that they covered the millennium celebrations during her first year at college. It seems that the District Archive Office and local Historical Society were instrumental in providing background information for the millennium ceremony at Downholland Cross.

These crosses were used as resting places on the occasion of funerals by Roman Catholics, a fact which encouraged over zealous Protestants to demolish all within reach. The original wayside cross was lost centuries ago, when records* show that it was last used around the time of the Hollands of Downholland Court. However, part of a base stone, uncovered during preliminary ground work, is thought to be part of that original artifact, and has been used in the foundations of the present cross.
*Records furnished by the District Archive Office.

The words "*These crosses were used as resting places on the occasion of funerals*" and "*it was last used around the time of the Hollands of Downholland Court*" were underlined in red ink. Davina had also pencilled the words "*and they used it for a diabolical funeral of their own*" in the margin. It seemed an odd comment to make, and I wondered what she meant by it.

I perused the next cutting and read that the Historical Society had provided the District Council with additional information on listed buildings in the area, which included a brief description of Downholland Court and an interesting anecdote concerning a prominent family of the time.

Old Halls of Lancashire
(from the Historical Society's Millennium Revue)

At the beginning of the 20th. Century the county was particularly rich in old halls and manor houses and this district has many specimens of great architectural interest. At the commencement of the 17th century there were about 300 halls and manor houses, but most of those now standing are simply farm houses and so much altered that the original design is followed with difficulty. This applies to Downholland Court, a building dating back to the 15th. Century, altered over the course of time, yet retaining some original features. Massive roof timbers, mullioned windows and fragments of Elizabethan oak in its principal staircase remind us of the medieval pedigree of this once moated hall. The wooden staircase in particular presents an interesting anomaly. It is a staircase which seems to go nowhere, for it stops at a point where a blank wall and a sloping ceiling meet. Other interesting architectural features came to light during renovation work during the last century. A clay floor was discovered in the attic, possibly used by the menfolk in inclement weather for skittles and bowling (games popular at the time), and several hollow recesses, possibly 'priests'' holes', where found in the thick walls behind carved wooden panelling, an indication of the turbulent history of the building.

Holland (de Holande)
This turbulence can also be found in the history of the Hollands, the original owners of Downholland Court. This family, now extinct, had a particularly lurid past. They were prominent in the 'Wars of the Roses' and in the previous

219

century took part in the struggle between the Barons and the ineffectual Plantagenet King, Edward 11. The family supported Thomas, Earl of Lancaster and leader of the Barons' cause (Sir Robert Holland was later to accuse the Earl of Lancaster of treason), while a neighbour, Sir Hugh Bannistre of Brook Hall, Tarlesbank, took the side of the King. Bannistre initially won a victory at Maudlande, near Prestby, but was defeated later that day by the Hollands. He escaped the field of battle and went into hiding in the hilly part of Leyfield, only to be betrayed several days later and handed over to the Hollands. They immediately executed the unfortunate man on the spot, beheading him on Leyfield Moor. The headless body was returned to Brook Hall and interred in the family vault.

I saw that Davina had again underlined certain passages in red ink, with added comments in the margin which revealed her private thoughts on the matter.

"*A clay floor was discovered in the attic of the house, possibly used by the menfolk during inclement weather for skittles and bowling (games popular at the time)*" explained the strange swishing noise followed by a sharp crack, the sound of a bowl rolling along the floor to strike the jack. "*The headless body was returned to Bank Hall and interred in the family vault*" pointed to the identity of her terrifying antagonist, and "*It is a staircase which seems to go nowhere, for it stops at a point where a blank wall and a sloping ceiling meet*" indicated the possibility that the Holland family, plagued by similar visitations, had sealed the entrance to the attic.

I then read the final article in the envelope. It was dated some weeks after the first one.

The Historical Society has disclosed an interesting, not to say gruesome, piece of information bearing on the recent installation of the wayside cross in Downholland. While preparing the ground for the cross several bone fragments were discovered in the soil beneath an original base stone. They were thought to be human and forensic examination later confirmed that they were part of a skull. A possible theory for this unusual burial suggests that it is an example of that ancient practice of burying witches and criminals in unhallowed ground. The bone fragments were sent to the Archeological Department at the University for further analysis and carbon dating has placed them around the 14th. Century. A decision as to their re-interment is awaited, although it has been suggested (since the identity of the skull remains unknown) that they should be returned to the site from whence they came. No decision has been made at present.

Once again Davina had highlighted parts of this article.

"*They were thought to be human and forensic examination later confirmed that they were part of a skull. A possible theory for this unusual burial suggests that it is an example of that ancient practice of burying witches and criminals in unhallowed ground*" gave a clue to the meaning of her odd note about the *diabolical funeral* in the first article.

The words "*since the identity of the skull remains unknown*" were underlined in red ink and "*they used the head as a jack*" and "*the cloth bundle and the horseman*" with a question mark were pencilled in the margin.

Reflecting on her traumatic experience at Downholland Court that fateful Easter Davina had come to certain conclusions. She had guessed the identity of the skull, with all its implications, and in a final pencilled note at the bottom of the article she blamed that initial act of desecration at the wayside cross centuries earlier and the Millennium celebrations in this century for the terrible sequence of events which followed.

"After all those years incarcerated underneath the cross he has been let out like the genie in the bottle to begin his search."

Davina had never been able to free herself from the overwhelming feeling that *he* would search and find her again. The teenage Hallow'een joker had been the last straw.

I have to tell you that the whole sorry business had also left its mark on me. On reading those sinister conclusions in her college notes, I recalled an inexplicable incident at my wife's funeral that misty, rainy day in March. I seem to remember that during the service at the grave side, as Davina was finally laid to rest, I thought I saw a rather indistinct figure loitering amongst the headstones bordering the churchyard.

'Was it a belated mourner, or perhaps a curious passer-by?'

As I said, it was only a brief glimpse, but the vague shape of this figure revived memories of that fateful Hallow'een visit. From the distance involved I could only assume that the figure had a coat over its head to protect it from the heavy rain, giving the impression of being headless. There again, I could also have been mistaken about another disturbing impression.

As the unsettling shape slowly faded from view in the heavy rain, I had the distinct impression that it wore some sort of discoloured metal plate beneath its coat.

I am now left with an inescapable apprehension, especially around the pagan festival of Hallow'een, that somewhere out there is a tormented headless soul searching for something long gone — and, since my first wife is no longer available to answer his plea and point him in the right direction, I am *his* next best shot.

I am also left with two fixations which my second wife (I married again when I found living alone quite unbearable) finds rather incomprehensible, not to say absurd.

For me 'Trick or Treat' lasts the whole year round — *and I don't open my front door to anyone.*

BURSCOUGH

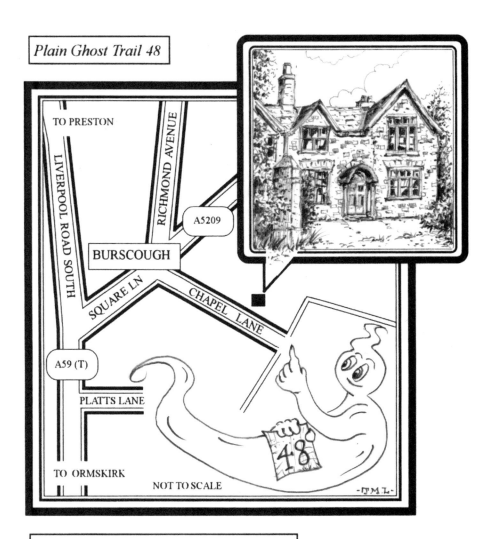

Plain Ghost Trail 48

TO PRESTON

LIVERPOOL ROAD SOUTH

RICHMOND AVENUE

A5209

BURSCOUGH

SQUARE LN

CHAPEL LANE

A59 (T)

PLATTS LANE

TO ORMSKIRK

NOT TO SCALE

48

INSET *Burscough Hall (now demolished)*

"OH YES THERE IS!"

On the first of November last, at precisely eleven o'clock in the morning, I first glimpsed the ghost.

The ghost stood on the stage at the far end of the church hall, deep in contemplation, surveying various articles scattered on a trestle table: it seemed totally engrossed in its examination and didn't notice me.

"Hello there . . . ."

The grey figure of a man turned and stared at me. He had a gaunt bearded face and unkempt appearance, accentuated by a rough frayed shawl draped over his hunched shoulders. He carried a copious canvas bag on his back and could only be described as an old tramp, so common place in these parts in earlier times.

I reached for the light switch to illuminate the stage — and in that brief moment the ghost vanished into thin air.

The stage was empty.

In recalling the incident I have to emphasize that there is absolutely no doubt about the date: that day happened to be my birthday. This also applies to the time: the eleventh chime of the church clock had just sounded the hour.

And as for the ghost . . . .

Well — I must stress, at this point, that I do not believe in such things. As far as I'm concerned ghosts, spirits and all that supernatural nonsense are strictly for the odd and eccentric; for those persons with a vivid imagination and gullible nature.

And yet . . . .

I have to confess, somewhat reluctantly I might add, that this unshakable belief has taken something of a battering recently, and, with hindsight, I can only put it down to an amateur production of that well-beloved pantomime 'Old Mother Goose', and my grand-child, Emily.

And this is how it all began.

* * *

Emily had recently enrolled in a local dancing academy , which in turn had been invited by a local dramatic group to provide the juvenile cast for their forthcoming pantomime. It seems this amateur society, the Stanley Players, had run into financial difficulties. A declining membership, rising production costs and a succession of poorly attended plays had all contributed to a rapidly diminishing bank balance and a much-needed rethink in fund raising. It was all well and good putting on a coffee morning and raffle now and again, but a larger injection of cash was needed if the Players were to keep solvent. And so the committee eventually came up with the idea of a pantomime, a "sure winner" in the opinion of the treasurer.

"Don't you see — lots of children mean lots of doting mums and dads, uncles and aunts and grandparents," she declared enthusiastically.

"And don't forget Uncle Tom Cobleigh," added the secretary rather facetiously. He and the treasurer didn't get on.

"It does means lots and lots of dosh," she continued, ignoring his sarcastic comment.

Nevertheless, it was unanimously hailed as a super fund-saver, and also a great challenge: this pantomime would be a first in the history of the Players.

"As you all know, we haven't put on a panto before," observed the chairman. "Any ideas . . . .?"

The members put forward their favourites and one, in particular, got the largest vote, a decision based on the limited number of actors needed for the main characters and the large number of juveniles needed for the town children. By an overall majority its was decided that the pantomime would be that perennial favourite, 'Old Mother Goose'.

And that's where I came in.

The inclusion of my grandchild in the juvenile cast and her constant and persuasive begging for my participation in this village extravaganza chipped away at my resolve never to have anything to do with that sort of thing. If you have grandchildren you will know exactly what I mean.

"Oh, please, Grandpa — please . . . ." This constant pleading, drip by drip, backed up with tearful eye and soft, gentle hand, slowly eroded my resolve, and I eventually gave way, not, I hasten to add, for a role in the pantomime, but as a helper in the properties department. In other words, I now held the exulted position of tea-maker and general dogsbody in the 'fetch and carry' brigade.

As rehearsals for the show got under way I soon became familiar with members of the cast and their roles in the pantomime. In the main they were a sociable lot, easy to get on with and very helpful to someone who didn't know his 'up stage' from his 'down stage'. However, there was one particular member who did not fall into this friendly category.

George Arrowsmith, who played the part of Sir Penniless Hard-up, the wicked Squire, turned out to be an extremely condescending and, at times, downright rude individual: in the vernacular he would be described as a 'big-head'. I have since been told that you often find this type of person in all amateur groups. However, there was one thing in his favour when it came to "doing the business" on stage. The man was very particular in his interpretation of the role, and went to great lengths to make sure he looked the part in every detail. As Squire Hard-up he managed to portray this character exceedingly well, partly due to the fact that he himself was what is called a hard-nosed businessman, one who would take every opportunity to make a profit, however slight. Stan (Old Mother Goose) Smith told me that George was into property development and had done quite well out of it, so he wasn't short of a bob or two. During the tea break I was singled out for the hard-sell.

"Where do you live?" the pantomime Squire asked me. I told him. "They are rather big houses for someone of your age, don't you find?" I disagreed as politely as I could. "Well you are getting on a bit, aren't you?" he persevered, undeterred by my negative attitude. "You ought to consider looking for something smaller — something more manageable — in fact something like this." The persistent Squire thrust a glossy leaflet into my hand. "One of my little mews flats in Old Hall Court would be just the ticket — but you'll have to be quick if you want one. They're selling like hot cakes." The rehearsal bell rang and put an end to the sales patter.

Later that night I glanced through the glossy document before throwing it in the waste bin. It was a publicity leaflet, intended for interested buyers, which described George Arrowsmith's latest property speculation. Beneath a coloured photograph of a Cotswold Style housetype lay a publicity blurb.

Old Hall Court

Priory Homes welcome you to a better way of living in our new 3 bedroom mews, town houses and 4 bedroom detached homes. Our homes are traditionally crafted, beautifully designed and offer every practicality down to the smallest detail. Situated on the site of Burscowe Hall, partially destroyed by a disastrous fire some years ago, this fine development is the latest in building conception at its most advanced.

Please call in at our sales office. It is open seven days a week and a visit will make you realize why a Priory Home is so desirable.

The developers had included a brief description of the ancient Hall on the reverse of the leaflet.

Burscowe Old Hall

This origins of this venerable building can be traced back to the latter part of the 16th century and later alterations in the half-timbered style added to the size of the Hall. It had strong links with the 'Old Religion' which managed to avoid most of the upheavals of the Reformation and continued to flourish in the county, despite considerable and intermittent persecution. This county was the most catholic in the land, and during this turbulent period the Hall served as a Mass centre, a meeting place for priests and laity. Services were held in a secret chapel in the upper part of the house, and for centuries the Catholic faith was kept alive here, the Hall passing from one Catholic family to another.

Unfortunately my dealings with George Arrowsmith did not end there.

He collared me at the next rehearsal.

"Have you thought about it?"

"Yes — but I'll need a bit more time," I replied, trying to put him off.

"Well don't wait too long," he said, reaching into his pocket.

'Oh, no,' I inwardly groaned. 'Not another of his bloomin' leaflets.'

I was mistaken. He took out a small wooden box and handed it to me.

"I'll leave this with you," he declared. "It's part of my costume for Sir Penniless. You can put it with my wig and sash on the props table."

"What is it?" I inquired, examining the oblong box. It was roughly made and its rather neglected condition clearly reflected its age. A monogram, probably the initials of the owner, was engraved on the lid: the intertwined letters, PLC, were barely legible.

"Its a spectacles case," he replied. "I think a pair of spectacles would be just right for the part of Sir Penniless. I had thought of a monocle but came across these instead. They fit the period and will go well with the Squire's costume. I can put them on when I read the Proclamation and Happiness Ban to the townspeople and the Foreclosure Notice on Mother Goose's old cottage."

I have to admit that George Arrowsmith seemed to relish his heartless pantomime character and made every line and detail count. In fact it could be argued that he upstaged everyone else in his scenes, much to the annoyance of some of the cast.

Then, during one Sunday rehearsal, the spectacles suffered a mishap. Sir Penniless inadvertently placed them on a chair while he adjusted his wig and little Emily accidentally sat on them. Luckily the damage was only slight, but the squire was furious with the poor child, even though it was partly his fault. George calmed down when the society treasurer offered to pay for the damage and suggested that he drop them off at the opticians for repair. It was arranged that I would collect them at a later date.

However, when I called in at the opticians to pick up the Squire's spectacles on the following Wednesday my firm conviction on the non-existence of ghosts received another jolt.

* * *

"I've come to see if George Arrowsmith's spectacles have been repaired," I explained to the receptionist.

"Ah, yes — those spectacles. Could you wait a moment?" she replied, with a hint of curiosity in her voice. "Mr. Fletcher would like to have a word with you about them." It sounded rather mysterious.

She disappeared through a baize curtain into the back of the shop and I heard the sound of muffled voices. She reappeared and ushered me into a small room which I assumed was the work area. Mr. Fletcher, the optician, greeted me and invited me to take a seat. He seemed ill at ease.

"I'm glad you called," he began nervously. "I — I wanted to have a word with you about — about Mr. Arrowsmith's spectacles."

"Oh, don't tell me you couldn't fix them," I retorted, thinking of the fuss the Squire would cause at the next rehearsal.

"Oh, no — no, they have been repaired," the nervous optician quickly reassured me. "You can take the spectacles this instant — yes, this very instant." From his tone of voice I sensed there was something else. "But I wanted to — to ask if you knew anything about them?"

"Anything about them," I replied. "You mean — where did they come from — that sort of thing?"

"Exactly," he nodded. "For instance, take the owner — do you know anything about him?"

"Ah, you mean those letters PLC on the box lid?" I shook my head. "No, I can't say I've ever met him." For some reason this response startled the optician.

"Oh no — you couldn't meet him," he declared nervously. "He has been dead a long time."

"How can you be sure of that?"

Mr. Fletcher opened the wooden box and took the spectacles out. "I'm sure of it, believe me," he answered. "These spectacles were made for someone who lived in the Nineteenth Century. In fact PLC has probably been dead for two hundred years." He went on to explain.

"The metal in the frames is a cheap alloy, unlike more expensive silver metalwork, and the quality of the lenses is poor. The case is just a plain, unvarnished wooden box, with no soft fabric interior for protection. To me these details indicate that the owner had no wealth to speak of, and was getting on in years. Considering the social conditions in the age when these spectacles were manufactured it is more than likely that the owner belonged to the workhouse, that Victorian institution for the poverty stricken."

"So are they worth much?" It was just the sort of question George Arrowsmith would have asked.

"On the face of it — probably not very much," the optician maintained. "However, they are unusual, and if you knew a little more about them — where they came from and who they were made for — then possibly they might fetch a decent sum . . . ."

He paused and I sensed there was something else he wanted to get off his chest. "Tell me," he went on, "— do you believe in ghosts?"

"That is a strange question," I replied with a frown. "If I'm honest about it, I'd have to say I don't. Why do you ask?"

"Until yesterday I was of the same opinion," the optician spoke nervously. He lowered his voice and went on to confide in me what had made him change his mind. It seemed he had arrived early the previous morning to open up the premises. Making his way to the rear of the shop he drew back the baize curtain to enter the work room — and stopped dead in his tracks.

There he saw what he thought to be an old tramp, leaning over the table, examining the open spectacles case. This figure, which the optician described as grey and dishevelled, with a straggling beard and tattered shawl, paid no attention to him, but turned and shuffled across the room to the work bench where the spectacles lay awaiting repair. He gazed down at the spectacles for a moment and then turned to confront the alarmed optician, fixing him with a sorrowful eye.

The old tramp raised his hand and with raised forefinger pointed straight at the optician in a menacing fashion.

He then began to advance and Mr. Fletcher retreated in panic, scattering the baize curtain in disarray. As the optician reached the shop door he looked back, expecting the grey visitor to burst through the flimsy screen in hot pursuit. The baize strips slowly ceased their violent motions and became still. Mr. Fletcher paused, eyes fixed on the curtain. It remained closed, and so, plucking up courage, he cautiously went back to investigate: he found the workshop empty and undisturbed.

The old tramp had gone.

"There was no sign of him — and he couldn't have got out through the back of the shop because that door was securely locked," reasoned Mr. Fletcher. "The only explanation I can think of is — is that old tramp was a ghost."

He seemed genuinely relieved to have got it off his chest, and that I hadn't ridiculed his supernatural theory.

"And another thing struck me as odd," he surmised, "— from the way he behaved I'm sure he was after these spectacles."

As you have already guessed, the description of this disturbing intruder fitted my ghost to a 'T' — and now I knew why the ghost had been contemplating the trestle table on the church hall stage. That is where I kept the pantomime props, which included George Arrowsmith's wig and spectacles.

The optician handed me the case and rose to see me out.

"How much do I owe you for the repair?" I asked.

"Nothing — absolutely nothing," he declared. "If I'm honest about it I'm glad to be rid of them." As he pulled back the baize curtain to let me through, his parting remark mirrored my own thoughts on the matter.

"You wouldn't catch me wearing those spectacles for love or money, I can tell you. Don't forget — I've probably seen the owner."

So had I, but in my opinion, knowing the stage-struck Squire as I did, he wouldn't have given this deeply-felt sentiment a second thought.

I was right.

* * *

I decided to return the spectacles to George Arrowsmith personally, partly to forestall one of his tantrums at the next rehearsal, should he find fault with the repair, and partly to see the site of Burscowe Hall, now Old Hall Mews. I called at the sales office to deliver them and found the receptionist engaged in conversation with a young man in overalls.

"Good morning — can I help you?" she asked, rising from her chair. The workman picked up his hard hat and prepared to leave.

"Could I see Mr. Arrowsmith?" I enquired.

"Unfortunately he is not here at the moment," she informed me. "He's visiting a client in Ormsley."

"Oh, that's a pity," I replied. "I've just collected his spectacles from the opticians and thought I'd drop them off at his office."

The young man, who was on the point of leaving, paused at the door.

"Excuse me — did you say spectacles?" he asked. I nodded. "Are they the ones in an old wooden box — with some initials on the lid?"

"Yes — the very same," I replied. "Do you know where he got them from?"

"I certainly do — from me. I was the one who found them." And with that astonishing disclosure he continued on his way, closing the door behind him. I turned to the receptionist.

"Do you mind if I leave the spectacles with you?" I asked.

"No problem," she smiled. "I'll pass them on to Mr. Arrowsmith when he comes back this afternoon."

I thanked her and hurried from the office in pursuit of the young workman. I caught up with him at the door of a partly completed house.

"Can you spare a minute or two?" I asked, slightly out of breath. "About those spectacles — you say you found them?"

"That's right, I did," he replied.

"Could you tell me where you found them?"

"Under a stone floor in one of the old buildings."

With that reply I knew I was on to something of real importance and decided to press him further on the matter. Perhaps it would lead to the identity of PLC. He went on to tell me about his curious discovery.

When Burscowe Hall burnt down, the site was sold to Priory Properties and he helped to prepare the ground for the new development. The remains of the old hall were demolished, as well as several outbuildings, and it was during this operation that the young builder found the spectacles.

"They were under a floor slab near the fireplace in one of the outbuildings," he said. "I think farm workers lived in them, and they probably hid their gear under the floor for safety."

"Well it worked," I observed. "The spectacles survived the fire."

"And don't forget the other stuff," the young man added. "I found a couple of tankards, some coins and a pipe as well."

"But nothing on the identity of the owner?"

"No — everything above ground had been cleared away by that time."

"So what happened to the rest of the stuff?"

His manner abruptly changed. It seemed this question had touched a raw nerve.

"Don't even ask," he answered grumpily. "Didn't old Arrowsmith come up and swipe the lot."

"Really . . . ."

"Yes — claimed it belonged to Priory Homes, but didn't he go and sell the stuff to an antique dealer," he declared, "Got a tidy sum for it, so I hear."

"And let me guess . . . ." I paused, thinking of Sir Penniless Hard-up's mercurial attitude. "He didn't give you a penny?"

"You're dead right," he replied. "Not a brass farthing."

"But he didn't sell the spectacles?"

"That's right — told me they would be just right for a play or something, and was going to sell them after it had finished. Fancies himself as a actor, so they tell me," he declared caustically. "More like a miserable old skin flint, as far as I'm concerned."

Before I left him to get on with his work he revealed an ominous addition to his story. Whilst engaged in retrieving the objects from beneath the floor he began to feel ill at ease, overwhelmed by a sense of foreboding.

"I was sure there was somebody else there, just behind me," he emphatically declared, "— watching my every move. And when I got the last of the stuff out of the ground I heard a — a sort of mournful groan . . . ." He paused for a moment. "In a way I'm glad old Arrowsmith took the stuff off my hands. He's welcome to it — and whatever comes with it."

Considering the Squire's unpleasant and mercurial persona I hardly thought such a sinister omen would affect Sir Penniless Hard-up's attitude in the slightest.

I was wrong.

* * *

When I arrived home later that day I found Emily waiting at the front door: she ran down the path to greet me. She had some disturbing news.

"Grandpa . . . ."

"Yes . . . .?"

"Someone came to see you."

"Someone came to see me?" I wasn't expecting anyone to call and wondered who it could be.

"Yes — a nice old man."

I began to feel uneasy.

"A nice old man . . . . What did he want?"

"Something to eat."

"He asked you for something to eat!" A stranger begging at the door — asking a child for food. In this day and age it was an alarming state of affairs.

"Well — not really. The nice old man looked very, very hungry," Emily declared. "So I asked him if he wanted something nice to eat, and he smiled and nodded."

I asked Emily to describe the visitor, bearing in mind that anyone over the age of twenty would seem ancient to her.

"Well — he was very, very, very old — with a funny beard," she giggled, "— and a big bag full of pots and pans and stuff."

"Pots and pans . . . .?"

"Yes — and do you know, Grandpa," she continued in a more serious manner. "He needed some new clothes, 'cos the ones he had on weren't very nice."

"Not very nice?"

"Yes — 'cos they had lots and lots of holes in them and they were very, very dirty and very, very smelly. Mummy can put them in our washing machine when he comes back."

"He told you he was coming back?"

"Oh I think so — I went to your cake cupboard to give him one of your special current buns, but when I got back to the front door he had gone," Emily declared sadly.

"So why do you think he is coming back?"

"For your current bun, silly," declared Emily with childish logic. "He's bound to come back for it if he is still hungry, isn't he — and then you can ask him to stay for tea, can't you, Grandpa?"

If the stranger was who I thought he was, he would be the last person I would invite to tea.

Nevertheless, the very thought of Emily meeting my tramp was deeply unsettling, to say the least, even though she seemed totally unaffected by the encounter. It would seem that the ghost was kindly disposed towards young children and meant them no harm. On the other hand he might not feel the same way about me, and I still hadn't a clue why he came to visit me in the first place.

Thankfully Emily's childish logic was misplaced. The "nice old man" didn't return for his special current bun.

* * *

A week later the Stanley Players gathered to reap the fruits of their theatrical labours — the first night of the pantomime. I do not wish to bore you with the story of Old Mother Goose: it is well known and often performed. However, a brief synopsis of the main characters might be appropriate, considering the 'write-up' of the performance in the local newspaper.

The character in the title role is, of course, Old Mother Goose, a large rotund male personage dressed in outrageous female costumes and multicoloured wigs, with the catch-phrase "Does my bum look big in this?" completely summing up the level of humour and wit associated with this type of theatre. Next in order of applause comes Buttons, the gormless knockabout clown who is madly in love with Mother Goose's daughter and utters a high-pitched yell "Hi-ya, kids!" every time he appears on stage. This is spontaneously answered by a screaming mob of adolescents and grown-ups (who should really know better) with a "Hi-ya, Buttons!".

Then there is Rose May (I leave to your imagination the multitude of 'double-entendres' linked to this particular name), the daughter of Old Mother Goose, who always finds her mother in one compromising situation after another and tells her off with a "Oh Mother, stop it! — isn't she silly, kids!" followed by a resounding response "Yes, she is!". Rose May is helped by two comic town bobbies, Dick and Don, with their well known "Evenin' all — 'ello, 'ello — what's a'goin' on 'ere, then?", accompanied by flexing legs and big-booted feet.

And finally we come to the villain of the piece, the wicked Squire, Sir Penniless Hard-up. His "Ah-hah, I've got the silly old moo in my grasp at last — haven't I, kids?" is countered by the stirring,

238

thunderous and high-pitched reply "Oh no you haven't!" immediately followed by loud hissing and booing from an enraged audience. You know the score: it follows the same pattern in all pantomimes.

Traditionally this pattern always has the same interlude just before the finale of the show. It features some of the principal characters in front of tabs (usually a backcloth of a woodland scene), who perform a certain ritual, specifically designed to allow the rest of the cast to prepare for the final scene and to take their bows.

It is, of course, the ghost interlude.

I need not describe it to you in too much detail for it is so well-known. Sufficed to say that when the ghost appears (covered in a copious white sheet creeping menacingly from the wings) and proceeds to billow back and forth behind the unsuspecting actors, there follows that time-honoured 'call and response', a tumultuous clamour designed to mask the backstage clatter of shifting scenery and patter of feet.

It goes something like this.

"What's the matter, kids?"

"It's a ghost!"

"A ghost?"

"Yes — a ghost!"

"Where . . . .?"

"Behind you!"

"Behind me?"

"Yes — behind you!"

At this point all the cast turn and look one way, while the ghost positions itself behind them. The actors fail to see it and turn back to the audience. Then there follows that well-known dialogue.

"Behind us — oh no there isn't!"

"Oh yes there is!"

"Oh no there isn't!" The response becomes louder and louder.

"Oh! — Yes! — There! — Is!"

At which point one of the cast spots the ghost, utters a terrified scream, and scampers off stage in mock fright with the ghost in hot pursuit to howls of delight from the children in the audience.

The routine is repeated until all the characters have fled bar one. The remaining character, in this case Sir Penniless Hard-up, the wicked Squire, stands vulnerable and alone on stage and the children eagerly wait for the ghost to creep out again to claim its final victim.

And don't they love it. At last this horrible bloke is going to get his come-upance for his dastardly behaviour towards the townspeople, little children and dear Old Mother Goose.

Rather than relate the next part of this ghostly ritual to you myself (which I viewed from my position in the wings), let me, instead, present you with an account from one of the audience, the reporter from the Arts Section of the local newspaper. She occupied a reserved seat on the front row.

The first part of her criticism covered the general performance up to the finale, with suitable comments and praise which sought to present a positive and flattering picture of what was, in reality, a basic 'belt and braces' amateur production in a church hall.

Then, at this point, her critical faculties and rather patronizing attitude underwent a decided change.

In all my years of covering pantomimes I have never seen such an imaginative slant on the ghost routine. It began with the proverbial pantomime ghost, a member of the cast under a large white sheet, ducking and weaving behind Dick and Don, Buttons, Mother Goose and Sir Penniless. The audience joined in with gusto, as, one by one, the terrified characters dashed off the stage, leaving Sir Penniless all on his own in the spot light. As he waited for the ghost to return the Squire peered over his spectacles at the audience, nonchalantly taking a large, red-spotted handkerchief from his pocket. He then proceeded to blow his nose in a very noisy manner.

240

In the meantime another spotlight lit the opposite side of the stage where the ghost would soon appear, and the audience waited in anticipation. The actor under the white sheet stepped into the spotlight and paused. The Squire took off his spectacles with an air of feigned indifference and began to polish them with his handkerchief.

And that's when an inspired change in the normal routine took place.

The white sheet fell away to reveal a really frightening figure, and the audience gasped in astonishment. This new ghost had a ghastly pale skeletal face, with sunken eyes glaring beneath a tangled mass of white hair. It fixed the Squire with an expression of hatred, its lips curled back in an angry snarl, revealing yellow rotted teeth. I have to say the make-up was absolutely superb and the acting completely realistic, so much so that the audience were absolutely dumbfounded by this sight. I myself had goose pimples and a cold shiver ran down my spine.

Meanwhile Sir Penniless turned and saw the ghost. He drew back, transfixed by the sight, and his jaw dropped in absolute dismay. Uttering a shriek of mock terror which echoed round the hall, the wicked Squire threw his handkerchief in the air, and fled the stage, hotly pursued by the ghost. It was a superb piece of acting and I can safely say the audience were as frightened as I. It was indeed an acting triumph and lifted the show to a higher level of professionalism than I thought possible. The Stanley Players should be justifiably proud of their latest talented discovery.

The reporter went on to recommend the pantomime, with a proviso that it could frighten some younger members of an audience. That was an understatement, if ever there was one. However, she did have one reservation.

I thought it a great pity that the name of the second ghost did not appear in the programme. I searched for it in vain. Considering the thought and effort he put into playing what was only a minor role, I am of the opinion that this omission should be rectified without delay.

The reporter didn't know the half of it. Had she been standing beside me in the wings and witnessed a petrified George Arrowsmith whiz past with something out of this world hard on his heels, she would not have been so keen to acknowledge the second ghost, never mind include him in the programme.

Acting indeed . . . .

Nevertheless, I have to admit my hitherto firm convictions on the absurdity of the supernatural had received another jolt that night.

Anyway, word soon got around and the review in the newspaper did wonders for attendance figures, although the members of the cast were somewhat perplexed by the critique in the Arts Section. They had not witnessed those events in front of stage, since they were engaged backstage in preparing for the finale. As far as they were concerned the identity of the *new* member was a complete mystery. The company went on to play to packed houses and the 'Full House' sign hung on the door of the church hall for the rest of the week.

However, there was one omission from the cast list. George Arrowsmith was indisposed for the remaining performances. The part of Sir Penniless Hard-up was taken over by Don, the town bobby, who volunteered to stand in for George at short notice.

And what of the second ghost . . . .

Unfortunately, for some undisclosed reason, he failed to turn up on subsequent nights, much to the disappointment of the paying public. On the other hand, the "dosh" rolled in and, when the curtain came down on the final performance, the pantomime was hailed by one and all (with the exception of George Arrowsmith and the second ghost, that is) as a rip-roaring, fund-raising success.

* * *

Once again little Emily was instrumental in providing a most important piece in the ghostly puzzle.

The day her school broke up for the Summer holiday, Emily and her mother, my daughter-in-law, called in to see me on the way home. Emily dashed into the house ahead of her mother. I could see that she was thrilled about something.

"Do you want to see my prize, Grandpa?" she asked excitedly, with one hand behind her back.

"Prize?"

"Yes — guess what it is!"

"Well — now let me see . . . ." I paused for a moment, prolonging the agony. Emily could hardly contain her excitement.

"Is it a football?"

"No, silly old grandpa!" she cried, and withdrew her hand from behind her back. "It's this!" She proudly held out her prize, a children's book, illustrated in colour and entitled "Wild about Animals".

"Well I never — a school prize, would you believe," I replied, warmly congratulating the child. "And what is it for?"

"Because I never, never miss school — and I am never, never late," Emily answered solemnly.

I opened the book and contemplated the official certificate on the inside cover. It read "For full attendance and punctuality" and Emily's name was neatly printed in the blank space provided. The coloured surround on the illuminated document immediately aroused my interest. It had an intricate leaf and floral border branching from

an armorial shield situated in the top left hand corner of the design —
and enclosed within this shield was a monogram. Three intertwined
letters, PLC, sprang out at me — the very same monogram
engraved on the lid of the old spectacles case. I wondered if there
was a connection and turned to my daughter-in-law.

"Do you know what these letters stand for?" I asked her.

"No idea, I'm afraid," she replied, shaking her head. "But I'm
sure Emily's teacher, Miss. Stockbridge, would — she told me that
this prize is awarded each year."

By chance I bumped into Emily's teacher in Ormsley the following
Saturday. I was already acquainted with Miss. Stockbridge, having
worked with her in the pantomime, where she had been involved
backstage with the costumes and scenery. After exchanging views
about the merits of the production, I brought up the subject of
Emily's school prize. I asked about the monogram on the certificate.

"Oh, the letters are the initials of a charity," Miss. Stockbridge
explained, "— the Peter Leytham Charity."

"A charity — you mean like Oxfam?"

"Oh, no — quite the opposite, in fact," Miss. Stockbridge
returned with a smile. "The Peter Leytham Charity is a private concern,
unlike Oxfam, which depends on the public to make money. Each
year the Charity donates money to the school to buy prizes for the
pupils and books for the library."

It looked as if I had come up with a blank: there didn't seem to
be any connection between school prizes and spectacles. That was
about to change.

"A private concern — what type of charity is that, exactly?"

"Well, it is quite a story," Emily's teacher replied, and she went
on to tell me about the origins of the Charity. Her explanation was
indeed fascinating and, considering what had gone on before, very
revealing.

She told me that the Charity was founded at the beginning of the
eighteenth century by a wandering pedlar, who tramped around the

district begging and selling trinkets to survive. It was rumoured that this pedlar, Peter Leytham, came from a wealthy catholic family but had been dispossessed because of the severe penalties imposed on catholics at that time. By law they could not buy or lease land, or bequeath goods and property to other catholics, and so, when Peter the Pedlar, as he became known, acquired land through begging, his earlier taste of dire poverty probably influenced his decision when he made his will. He left everything to the poor, setting up a trust to distribute welfare to those who were desperately in need. Unbeknown to Peter the Pedlar the 'charity' land lay above rich coal seams, and the Leytham Charity became extremely wealthy when coal was discovered over a century later.

"What else does the charity provide for — other than school prizes?" I inquired.

"All sorts of things," Miss. Stockbridge replied. "You have to remember it has been going for over three hundred years, so times have changed. In the old days, before the Welfare State, the trustees would dole out money for coal, food, linen and clothing, medicines and even lectures and evening classes for the poor."

"My word, it is quite a list," I observed. "Do you think spectacles would fit into any of those categories?"

"Well, yes, I suppose so — anything to do with helping the less well-off," she nodded thoughtfully. "In fact that's just the sort of thing people would need, when you think about it. The main thing is that all donations were intended for those on the poverty line, and were strictly monitored. Don't forget in those days, if anyone tried to cheat the system, they would really get into hot water."

"I can believe it," I agreed. "It's a well-known fact that people were transported for life just for stealing a loaf of bread."

And then I thought of George Arrowsmith and his mercurial attitude. It would seem that he had confiscated a pair of Leytham Charity spectacles from an employee who had found them in a poor labourer's home.

Then George had a theatrical brain wave.

It occurred to the vain actor that the old spectacles would compliment his stage image as a money-grasping pantomime character and so he decided to wear them in 'Old Mother Goose', intending to sell them for a substantial sum afterwards. On the other hand it probably would not have occurred to George, had he known about the Charity, that his rather uncharitable behaviour, on stage and off, flew in the face of the beggar's benevolent intentions and would not benefit the poor in any way.

And so Sir Penniless Hard-up provoked the wrath of Peter the Pedlar — and received a courtesy call from an irate ghost bent on putting things right.

It did the trick.

George Arrowsmith was now a changed man, so the treasurer of the Stanley Players informed me several weeks after the show.

"Poor old George hasn't been the same since that first night," she confided in me. "He has decided his role in 'Mother Goose' will be his last. He's giving it all up, you know — a great loss to the Players."

His changed state of mind was confirmed in a telephone call late one evening. George phoned to tell me that he had given his stage collection to the Players, and that included his spectacles. I questioned this, knowing that he had planned to sell them after the show, but George was quite adamant about it. He didn't want anything to do with them and on no account was I to return them to him.

"What changed your mind?" I asked him, somewhat puzzled by this strange request. After a moment's silence he began to speak, disclosing the reason for his change of heart — the ghostly confrontation just before the final scene on that first night.

"That — *that man*, if you could call him that, came after me — and I ran back to my dressing room as fast I could," he began. "When I reached the door I turned to face him, flinging my wig

246

right in his face. It was a waste of time. The wig passed right through him — and I suddenly realized I was up against a ruddy ghost . . . ." He paused for a moment. "Anyway, I followed up with the spectacles — and it did the trick. He pulled up, would you believe. He bent down to pick them up and I shot into the dressing room, slamming the door behind me. I expected *him* to come right through it at any moment . . . ." He broke off.

"What happened next?" I asked.

"Nothing— absolutely nothing. When I eventually opened the door there was no sign of him. He had cleared off," replied George. "That place is haunted, I'm sure of it. I decided there and then that I would never go back onto that stage. So, as far as I'm concerned, you can keep those damned spectacles. Put them back in the box and do what you like with them — but for God's sake don't send them back to me."

Unfortunately I was unable to do that anyway.

After the performance the spectacles couldn't be found. Perhaps a member of the cast picked them up or maybe they vanished along with the ghost. Either way I was left with an empty spectacles case.

So where does that leave me?

With the memory of that first unsettling encounter on a cold November morning still fresh in my mind, and the first anniversary of the event only weeks away, I have taken special precautions to avoid a possible confrontation with a certain *gentleman of the road.*

For a start I have refused to take any part in the forthcoming production of Cinderella, this time firmly resisting the ardent pleading of little Emily and the cajoling of the Chairman of the Stanley Players. For all I know the second ghost might wish to make a stage come-back, repeating his acclaimed dramatic success in 'Old Mother Goose'.

Such is the vanity of the theatre.

So during the week of the show I shall be holidaying in sunny Spain, as far away from the church hall as I can get.

However, there remains one small problem.

When I recall the optician's scary meeting with a sorrowful pedlar intent on reclaiming a charitable gift I am reminded of my own predicament.

I'm all too aware of the fact that there remains one obstacle preventing this persistent ghost from completing his task.

Me . . . .

I know the spectacles are out there somewhere — waiting to be reunited with the monogrammed case.

Unfortunately I still have that particular item in my possession — but does the ghost of the pedlar know that, I wonder?

On the first of November last, at precisely eleven o'clock in the morning, I first glimpsed the ghost.

But, as you already know, I don't believe in such things.

And yet . . . .

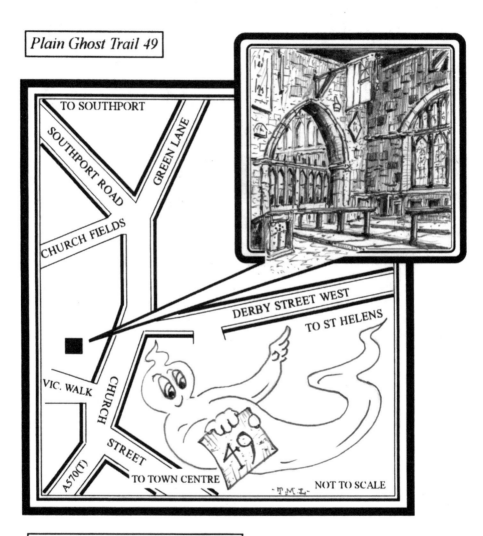

Plain Ghost Trail 49

INSET Ormskirk Parish Church

THE POCKET DAVENPORT

On the face of it one would be hard pressed to find any tangible connection between an alarm clock, a cheese sandwich and a folded newspaper: or, to put it another way — what did the audible, the edible and the readable have in common?

None at all you might reply, and rightly so.

However, in this case (had you been aware of certain facts) the answer would have to be David Thorneton, a financial consultant of independent means.

It so happened that on one fine afternoon in July, these seemingly unrelated elements came together in a town park of all places, and drastically altered the unsuspecting consultant's attitude to life in general and the supernatural in particular.

And it all began with his faulty alarm clock.

* * *

On the day in question the bedside clock stopped in the early hours and the alarm failed to go off, throwing David Thorneton's daily schedule into total disarray, an unmitigated disaster for such a punctilious person. He dashed off to the office without his breakfast and, more to the point, without his lunch box. Consequently, the hungry consultant had to buy a midday snack, in this case a cheese sandwich, from the Light Bite, a fast food bar in the High Street.

The day was pleasantly warm and, rather than spend his lunch hour in the office, David Thorneton decided to munch his sandwich in the park instead, choosing a vacant bench under the shade of a

251

leafy, mature oak to do so.

And this is where the second element made contact with the third.

There, on the bench, he found a neatly folded newspaper. It had been discarded by some recent occupant, who, judging by the number of felt tip circles on the advertisements page, had been busy ringing various items amongst the *Household articles* for sale. The previous owner's domestic taste in second-hand furniture aroused David's curiosity and he casually perused these markings, trying to picture this connoisseur of saleable dispensables. His eye fell upon an item with a question mark beside it. The connoisseur was obviously in two minds about this one and David began to wonder why.

For sale — a small writing desk — offers

This brief advert was accompanied by a local telephone number. David decided on the spur of the moment to phone and enquire about this '*small writing desk*', intrigued, no doubt, by the question mark and the connoisseur's indecision. He took out his mobile and pressed the numbers.

"Hello . . . .?"

The voice sounded faint and frail.

"Oh, hello," answered David. "I'm calling about an article for sale in the paper — a small writing desk . . . ."

"Ah, the writing desk . . . ."

David's imagination came into play and he pictured an infirm old lady on the end of the line, clutching an old fashioned telephone receiver.

"Yes — I wondered what it was exactly — and the price . . . .?"

There followed a short silence.

"Are you an antique dealer?"

"No — definitely not," replied David, wondering how he could describe his profession to this frail old lady. "I'm an accountant —

a financial accountant."

There followed another short silence.

"Well — that seems to be a nice sort of profession," the voice commented. "Yes — a nice, steady job."

There followed yet another short silence.

"Are you married?"

David was taken aback by this strange question.

"No — no, I'm not married," declared David, starting to regret his earlier decision. It began to look like a complete waste of time. "About the writing desk . . . ."

"Ah — that is a difficult one to answer," the frail voice replied. "You would have to come and look at it, I'm afraid."

"Where do you live?"

On hearing the address David immediately realized that the house was situated in the road on the other side of the park. He had half an hour to spare and decided to pop in on the way back to the office to view the small writing desk.

"I'll come round now — if you don't mind," he suggested.

Silence . . . .

"Oh — very well — I'll expect you shortly."

"Who shall I ask for?"

"Miss. Germaine-Smythe — Victoria Germaine-Smythe."

Within minutes David was ringing the doorbell of a weathered and rather dilapidated Victorian property. After a lengthy interval the door opened an inch or two and his 'imaginary' character peered through the gap at the curious consultant. She was indeed a frail old lady and was in as equally a dilapidated state as her house. She scrutinized David from head to foot.

"Miss. Germaine-Smythe?"

The old lady made no reply, but continued to examine the consultant with a penetrating eye. This rather strange behaviour was something of an embarrassment and David began to feel slightly ill at ease.

"I've come to see the writing desk," David explained, breaking the silence.

"Ah — yes — you phoned earlier," she nodded. "You did say you were unmarried?"

"Yes, that's right," replied the puzzled consultant.

"Very good — please come in."

David followed the strange lady along a gloomy passage to a door at the far end.

"The desk is in here," she announced in a reverential tone, opening the door.

The room was in semi-darkness on account of partially closed drapes and thick net curtains, reminding David of that familiar custom associated with a death in the house and funerals. In the middle of the floor stood a large round table. In the subdued light David perceived a small cabinet resting on this table. He had expected to see a desk of a conventional design, an upright cabinet supported by legs.

In this case, however, he was confronted by an unusual piece of furniture. He could only describe it as a bureau cut off at the middle, with the bottom half discarded and the top half now resting on the table.

David contemplated the object.

"I think it could be a portable bureau," he declared, venturing an opinion, "— a sort of travelling writing desk."

"Possibly you are right," nodded Miss. Germaine-Smythe, "but I have to admit I'm not a good judge of these things."

"The same goes for me, as well," admitted David. "Does it have a descriptive label or maker's name — anything on those lines?"

"Oh — a label — no, I don't think so. It is very old."

"Well, it doesn't really matter," David declared, standing back to admire the desk.

He was quite taken with the piece.

It was small enough to fit into the corner of his box room and would be a handy place to store some of his computer paraphernalia.

On the down side it had the look of a valuable antique.

"How much do you want for it?" he tentatively asked, expecting a substantial sum in reply.

"Oh, whatever you think it is worth," the old lady responded, "— as long as it goes to the right person. Yes — the right person. That is very important."

David couldn't believe his luck. Perhaps she thought he was the "right person".

He decided to do a bit a haggling.

"What about five pounds?" he offered, quoting a ridiculously low figure and expecting to be dismissed out of hand.

To his astonishment, this miserly sum was quickly accepted, in his view rather eagerly, as if for some reason the old lady wished to be rid of this unique piece of furniture.

"Are you sure?" he asked her, now somewhat ashamed of his parsimonious attitude.

"Oh, yes — yes, my dear — that will do nicely," she smiled, and nodded her head, "— very nicely indeed."

"You could probably get a lot more for the desk, you know," he advised, not wishing to take advantage of the old lady's trusting nature. "I'm sure an antique dealer would pay a lot for it."

"Oh dear no!" Miss. Germaine-Smythe exclaimed. "Certainly not a dealer! It has to go to the right person — and I have decided that you are the one it is intended for."

It was a mystifying remark.

And so three unconnected elements, the audible, edible and the readable came together that afternoon and provided David Thorneton with a valuable and unique piece of furniture.

The rather bemused financial consultant left the dilapidated house with an antique writing desk worth considerably more than a fiver.

Of course, when he placed the bargain in the boot of his car he had no idea that a fourth element came with the writing desk, a disturbing and tragic element which no one could have foreseen at the time.

* * *

David contemplated his antique bargain with a certain amount of satisfaction and pleasure. Now that he was able to examine it a better light he realized that the desk was much older than he had first thought. Although he was no expert in such antique matters it was plain to him that the design of the drawers and hinged writing lid were beautifully conceived.

However, David had the impression that this piece of furniture had been sadly neglected and, judging by the dust in the grooves around the edges of the desk, hardly used. Over the years numerous coatings of polish and resins had darkened and obscured the wood so that he could only guess at its origin; possibly oak or a similar grained wood.

The hinged writing lid, when in the closed position, concealed a nest of eight compartments, four on top and four below. An oblong receptacle with a plain hinged lid lay above this nest, and a set of drawers on either side of the desk, completed the storage arrangement. Two brass carrying handles, one on either side of the cabinet were fixed above these drawers.

The overall appearance, unlike later period furniture, was one of simplicity, with no hint of veneer or embellishment whatsoever. David came to the conclusion that the unit had been made for someone of a staid nature and conservative outlook, and that it had been designed for ease of movement. The number of storage drawers and brass handles added an extra dimension to its prime purpose as a writing desk.

'It is almost like a davenport,' he mused, 'or a smaller type made for travelling — a pocket version.'

The pocket davenport lived up to all expectations.

Just as David predicted, the storage compartments and drawers were eminently suitable for floppy disks and various other computer accessories, and the unit fitted nicely into the corner of the box room which he had converted into a home office when he first moved into the flat. The davenport proved very useful, serving its purpose extremely well, until, some months later, a niggling problem, possibly a design fault, came to light.

It coincided with the onset of some rather disturbing incidents.

First of all came the whispering in the middle of the night — barely audible but there, nonetheless. David eventually traced these whispers to the box room and he could swear that someone was reciting verses or prayers beyond the door.

The praying immediately ceased when he opened the door.

In the end he resorted to leaving it open — *and the whispering stopped.*

Then David began to sense a presence in the room, especially when he worked late into the night. On these occasions, when the room suddenly became very cold, he glimpsed a dark shape, the vague impression of a figure, out of the corner of his eye, lurking in the shadows beside the davenport.

It was extremely unsettling, and David began to think his flat was haunted. He found he couldn't concentrate and his work suffered accordingly.

He stopped working in the evenings.

And then he noticed the design fault.

One of the drawers on the left hand side of the davenport refused to stay closed.

One morning, as David prepared to leave for work, he found this drawer slightly open. He closed it, but on the following morning there it was again — slightly ajar. It happened on successive mornings, and at first he thought nothing of it, assuming that the davenport was slightly unbalanced or that he had over-packed the contents in the drawer. He tried various methods to overcome the problem, checking with a spirit level and re-packing the drawer — but to no avail.

Each morning he found the same drawer ajar.

He began to wonder if was down to human involvement — that someone had broken in and rummaged through the davenport. However, there was no sign of forced entry into the house, and nothing had been taken or disturbed. It was a mystery.

Then one evening he resorted to wedging the drawer so that it remained firmly closed — and that is when he became really alarmed.

When he entered his office in the morning he found the drawer ajar and the wedge lying on the floor. He repeated the process that same evening and once again he was confronted with the dislodged wedge and an open drawer the next day. It was indeed a worrying situation, especially to the fastidious consultant, who liked everything in its place and where order was the foundation of his daily routine.

Over the next few months this foundation would be severely tested.

* * *

Although the ghostly disturbances seemed to have stopped for the time being, the mysterious behaviour of the drawer still remained unresolved. David began to view the pocket davenport in a different light. It seemed to have a mind of its own.

Maybe there was something special about this unique piece of furniture — something he had missed.

He firmly believed in a rational explanation to account for the strange phenomenon, and he set about proving it in his meticulous way. He began by completely emptying the desk and setting it on the kitchen table. He weighed the antique and then took precise measurements, starting with the overall dimensions of the outer casing, followed by internal measurements of the drawers and recesses. He down-loaded the measurements into his computer and set about analyzing the results, using graphics to visualize external and internal views of the davenport — and at that point the computer programme highlighted a slight anomaly.

The internal graphics indicated an unused space in the rear section of the piece.

'Well, what a turn-up — a secret compartment,' David breathed. 'But why is it there — and how to get to it?'

He took a magnifying glass and began a minute examination, moving over the inner casing in search of any entry point to this secret space. The examination proved disappointing — he found nothing. However, the oblong receptacle on top of the davenport disclosed an unusual feature. When David checked inside this box he found remnants of wax or a similar substance ingrained in the base.

He then turned to the exterior, to the persistent drawer on the side of the cabinet. Using an inspection mirror, a device fastened to the end of a flexible metal rod, he carefully examined the interior with the aid of a powerful flash light. At first he could detect nothing out of the ordinary. There was no sign of a gap in the wood panel or joints.

And then, as he withdrew the mirror, he noticed a slight discoloration in the wood on the upper side of the recess, a spot on the panel where the rough surface had been smoothed out. David reached into the confined space and ran his fingers over this spot.

'Yes,' he thought, 'there is a different texture here.' He pressed the wood surface with his finger.

The next instant there was a loud click — and the casing moved. David quickly withdrew his hand and stood back in astonishment.

The sharp sound had come from beneath the desk lid.

He lifted the lid and saw that the nest of drawers had split down the middle, obviously released by a hidden mechanism.

David reached forward, gently pulling the edges further apart, and the casing opened outwards, accompanied by a harsh, grating screech of reluctant, seized-up hinges.

The astonished man immediately recognized what lay before his eyes.

It was a simple shrine — a portable altar table.

Simple heraldic designs were painted on the side panels or wings (in actual fact the rear of the bank of compartments) and a small, tarnished crucifix was set into the rear panel. A box section, which extended along the length of the rear panel, was obviously the 'unused space' highlighted in the computer graphics.

However, this compartment was sealed, and gave no clue as to its specific purpose other than a small brass plaque, engraved with the words '*omnia vincit amor — dis aliter visum*', fastened to its front surface.

The religious purpose of the furniture also solved the mystery of the wax-like residue in the oblong receptacle on the top of the davenport. This had to be the location for the incense and candles used in a religious service or mass.

David was quite astounded by the discovery.

'I bet I could add a couple of noughts to that fiver,' he thought, recalling the paltry amount he paid for it.

'Even more if it turns out to be very rare,' he mused, trying to estimate the true value of the religious davenport.

At the time David didn't realize just how rare the secret shrine really was — and the exact nature of its rarity factor.

Usually the age of an object has a direct bearing on this 'factor', as well as the status of the owner for whom it was made and the cultural inclinations of society when it was made.

For the time being David couldn't answer these questions, and, even had he been able to do so, he still would not have known that the singular writing desk held another unimaginable factor, a bizarre secret which made it a 'one-off' — in a rarity class all of its own.

* * *

'Perhaps Miss. Germaine-Smythe could throw some light on the subject?'

David resolved to call on the frail lady at the earliest opportunity. First of all he tried to phone to make an appointment but was informed by Directory Inquiries that the line had been disconnected.

'Poor old soul,' he thought. 'Maybe the old dear can't afford to pay her phone bill.'

Some days later he returned to the dilapidated house in the road by the park and rang the bell.

A young woman answered the door.

"Yes . . . .?"

"Could I see Miss. Germaine-Smythe?"

"Yes," the young lady replied. "Have you come about the auction?"

"Well — no, not exactly," answered David. "I have come to see Miss. Germaine-Smythe about a private matter."

The young lady scrutinized him with a puzzled frown.

"I'm Miss. Germaine-Smythe — Alison Germaine-Smythe," she said, "— but I'm afraid I don't know anything about a private matter."

It was now David's turn to look puzzled. Perhaps it was another relation he wished to see.

"I'm sorry," he apologized. "I should have asked to see the other lady who lives here — the very old lady."

The young woman looked even more perplexed.

"Other old lady — living here?" She shook her head. "No-one lives here at the moment."

David couldn't figure it out. There must be some mistake. He went on to explain the circumstances of his previous visit, and the purchase of the writing desk.

261

Alison Germaine-Smythe uttered a surprised gasp.

"So that's where the little desk went," she cried. "I couldn't find it when I made a list of the furniture. I thought it had been stolen."

"Oh no, I paid for it — and the lady who sold it to me was definitely Miss. Germaine-Smythe — Victoria, if I remember correctly."

"Ah — you mean my Aunt Victoria," declared Alison, realizing the mistake. "I'm afraid you can't see her — she has passed away."

"Passed away — you mean she has died?"

"Yes, I'm sorry to say," Alison nodded. "She left this house to me, but it is much too big for a single person — so I have decided to sell it, along with the furniture."

"And that included the writing desk?"

Alison's expression changed.

"No. That wasn't my decision. From what you have just told me it would seem my aunt put that ad in the paper herself."

She seemed very troubled.

"Is anything the matter?" David asked.

"There is — there certainly is," she said quietly. "I can't understand why my aunt decided to sell that particular item just before she passed away. She always told me that she would never part with the desk, not at any price. I was to have it when I married or when she died. It was totally out of character to do a thing like that."

"I see what you mean," said David, thinking of the ridiculous amount he paid for the desk. "I must say your aunt seemed eager to sell it to me — almost as if she chose me to have it."

"Well, if that's the case — it raises another question," Alison replied. "She was very reclusive and didn't like visitors — or answering the telephone. She really must have taken to you in a big way — to part with the desk."

"But why me?"

"We'll never know," said Alison sadly. "The answer to that question died with her, I'm afraid."

Recalling the funereal atmosphere in the old house and its eerie occupant, David reluctantly had to agree with her.

"By the way, I hope you don't mind me asking," inquired David, "— but when did your aunt actually die?"

"On the tenth of July — a Thursday, as I recall."

"But that was the very day I called to see her," gasped David.

Alison looked at him with a startled expression.

"Then you were the last person to see my aunt alive," she declared. "I was told that she passed away peacefully in the afternoon — with a five pound note clutched in her hand."

It would seem that the financial consultant had purchased the rare piece of antique furniture from the old lady just before she died.

Why Aunt Victoria had chosen him remained a mystery, but now that she had departed to a dimension where monetary value counted for nothing, David had a sneaking suspicion that he would have to pay for this rare antique in other ways.

* * *

One surprising development emerged from this unconventional first meeting. To coin that popular teenage expression, Alison Germaine-Smythe and David Thorneton 'clicked'. Although Alison was now fully aware of the possible value of the pocket davenport she didn't dispute the legality of the business transaction and was quite happy for such a rare antique to remain with David.

"For some reason Aunt Victoria never used the desk — kept it in the attic. She told me that it had been in the Germaine family for generations. I have to say I didn't care for it," she confided. "I always had the feeling there was something odd about the desk."

"Whispers . . . .?"

"Why, yes!" Alison cried. "So you heard them as well?"

"I did," nodded David, "— and more."

These two single and rather lonely people, brought together by an unusual piece of furniture, found that they both had a lot in common, so much so that, over the course of time, a caring relationship blossomed. The happy couple became engaged and decided that they would live in the house which Alison had inherited from her aunt. Once the property had been renovated and modernized the marriage could go ahead. In the meantime, Alison and David would continue to live separately, Alison with her family and David in his small flat.

However, during this period of separation a sinister turn of events caused David to reconsider the validity of his bargain — and the advisability of holding on to the antique.

One evening he inadvertently left his laptop computer on top of the davenport.

This was out of keeping with his nightly routine. Before retiring to bed he always made a point of checking the computer and electrical systems, switching the power off and generally making sure everything was tidy and ship shape in the room: to leave his laptop open on the davenport was totally out of character.

When David entered the box room the following morning to check his email he was surprised to see a message scrawled across the screen.

Neither repenteth thee of thy murders, nor of thy sorcery, nor of thy fornication, nor of thy theft

This certainly wasn't a normal email. For a start the words had been written in longhand — and in a most untidy fashion.

'*Who had sent it? What did it mean?*'

And then he realized that the laptop had been switched off.

"That's impossible," he muttered, baffled by this enigma.

He pressed 'Print' and waited for the disturbing message to come through on the printer. When it did he found the machine had printed a blank sheet. In the meantime the message on the screen began to fragment and he could only watch in amazement as the strange words slowly faded away.

David scribbled the email on a jotter. He viewed the word *"murder"* with some alarm, and wondered if it was aimed at him. He didn't know anything about a murder, or even sorcery and theft, for that matter, and found the content and tenor of the email message very intimidating.

Later that day he told Alison about it. She was equally baffled by the whole business.

"Perhaps it is one of those viruses from the internet that ruin computer softwear," Alison suggested. "Or it could be an email hoax from someone on line. There are weird nutters out there, you know." She pondered the problem for a moment. "On the other hand, you could leave the laptop open tonight and see if there are any more strange emails."

It sounded like a good idea. Perhaps Alison was right, and someone was fooling around for a joke. Anyway, David took her advice and left the computer on the davenport that evening. This time he made sure it was definitely switched off.

The next morning David went to check — and found another email waiting for him.

And the devil, that deceived them, was cast into the lake of fire and brimstone, where the beast and the false prophet are, and shall be tormented day and night for ever and ever

Once again the printer came up with a blank sheet but David managed to copy the message before it fragmented and disappeared from the screen. As in the previous message its content was equally distasteful.

Alison emphasized the point.

"Whoever is behind it sounds very bitter and discontented," she noted, "— and a religious fanatic as well. Haven't you noticed that the messages are rather like Bible readings."

David agreed. It could be a religious maniac messing about. But it still didn't explain the switched-off computer. Theoretically the laptop couldn't receive anything in that state. However, it still did.

The following morning a further message appeared.

For without are dogs, and sorcerers, and whoremongers, and murderers, and idolaters, and whosoever loveth and maketh a lie

Once again David made a copy before it faded away. If Alison was right, and the messages were taken from the Bible, he could easily check by using the 'search' facility on his laptop access them.

Alison's hunch was correct.

The computer search disclosed the origin of the emails. They were verses from the Book of Revelations.

A work colleague noticed the texts on David's desk.

"I didn't know you were interested in religious stuff," he remarked.

"I'm not," David replied. "I came across these texts by accident, and wondered where they came from."

'Well, they sound very acrimonious to me," David's colleague observed, "— the wrath of God — that sort of thing. I bet whoever chose them is very vindictive and certainly has an axe to grind."

The thought of someone with that sort of personality coming and going in his flat was very disturbing.

In reality *"terrifying"* would have been a more apt expression.

* * *

David couldn't sleep.

There were two reasons for this bout of insomnia. The first concerned the subject of his impending wedding — and the second concerned the writing desk.

David couldn't take his mind off the unsettling business with the laptop and felt that the problem was in some way connected to the davenport and its unique secret.

To test this theory he left the computer on the table in the box room and found a blank screen the next morning. He concluded that these messages only appeared when the laptop was placed on the writing desk.

And now, once again, the computer lay on the davenport and David lay in bed, wide awake, wondering if a message had been left on the screen. By two o'clock in the morning he could bear the suspense no longer, and decided to go and see for himself.

David got out of bed and stepped into the passage.

There he came to an abrupt halt.

A faint blue light, the soft glow from the laptop screen, filtered into the passage through the open door of the box room.

The intruder had returned.

David tiptoed down the passage. At last he was about to discover the identity of the person who had been messing about with his email. He peered round the edge of the door — and stifled a gasp of astonishment.

There, bathed in the blue light, he saw the culprit responsible for the weird religious texts.

It was the figure of a woman dressed entirely in black. Her long gown was simple, encircled at the waist with a black sash, and her features were hidden beneath a dark veil which fell in folds over her shoulders and upper part of her body.

She stood in front of the davenport, her head bowed and her hands clasped together in an attitude of prayer.

David recalled those early sepia photographs of Victorian funerals. This ghostly figure reminded him of one of the sombre mourners at the graveside.

The lady in black turned her veiled head and the net gauze stretched over her features, accentuating the contours of her nose, cheeks and chin.

It was a frightening sight.

David had the impression of a face contorted by sorrow and grief, but also filled with a deep rage and bitterness. The words of his office colleague flashed through his mind.

"I suppose you could say that whoever has chosen them is very vindictive and certainly has an axe to grind."

The lady in black certainly matched this profile. Her expression fitted perfectly with the acrimonious choice of religious tracts.

Her lips parted, the black gauze drawing against her teeth as she drew a deep breath, and a lamentable wail of sorrow and grief swelled forth, filling the air and echoing through the flat. The restless spirit began to move, gliding across the room towards the door. David was rooted to the spot, transfixed by the funereal spectacle and unable to escape the attentions of this woeful apparition.

The lady in black reached the door — and paused beside him, her veiled face close to his. She leant forward and David felt the icy chill of her breath on his cheek as she whispered in his ear.

"Tell him I curse his works and all his minions — may he burn for eternity in the fires of damnation . . . ."

With these whispered words of hate and loathing the outline of this unearthly figure began to waver, fading away before his eyes. A mournful sigh filled the air, a lingering remnant of her earthly presence and of her passing.

It was some time before David recovered from his trance-like condition. He was left with the searing memory of a vindictive spirit and her whispered curse.

Unfortunately he was also in a bit of a quandary.

"Tell him I curse his works . . . ."

For a start David didn't know of the identity of *"him"*, so he couldn't pass on the message. And that could lead to a return visit from a vengeful ghost — in which case she might not be as amenable a second time around.

* * *

The letter arrived on the Monday, the morning after David and Alison moved into their new home. It came from the editor of County Treasures, a periodical devoted to historical and social matters, and was in reply to David's enquiry regarding the two heraldic designs painted on the wings of the davenport altar.

This letter remained unread for several days, lying on the window ledge in the hall, until the hectic procedure of removals was finally completed, and some semblance of order had descended on the old Victorian house.

Eventually Alison found time to go through this ever increasing mountain of bills, unsolicited mail shots and circulars.

"There are plenty for you," she declared, handing him a pile of correspondence. "Hmmm . . . . This one looks rather interesting." She singled out the letter with a handwritten address.

'Dear Mr. Thorneton,

First of all let me apologize for the delay in replying to your letter, and to thank you for your drawings of the heraldic designs which you kindly sent to me. They are, in fact, the coats of arms of two prominent county families and I have managed to trace their lineage.

The first arms belong to James, the seventh Earl of Harcourte and I have set out the pertinent facts concerning his family, taken from the Notable County Families records.

Harcourte

This ancient line can be traced back to the time of the Conquest, the family holding a minor position of importance in the secular administration of the County. The family was classed as Upper Gentry and had strong ties with the Catholic Establishment. During the Civil War the Earl of Harcourte's strong and fervent support for the Royalist Cause brought him into conflict with Puritan elements in the

269

county, and his fortunes suffered accordingly. Sir James was captured by Cromwell's forces in 1648 and underwent the most extreme privation and torture, which had a lasting and detrimental effect on his devoted wife, Isobel. Betrayed into enemy hands, she was also imprisoned for a while in similar conditions, and never fully recovered from her ordeal and confinement. Sir James was executed in 1651 and became a martyr to the Catholic cause when he was beheaded at Alton. His remains were interred in the family vault in the Harcourte Chapel in the parish church of St. Paul.'

As a matter of interest the editor had added a description of the Harcourte Vault, and it so happened that the church mentioned in the letter was just a stone's throw from David's office.

The Harcourte Vault

The vault was sealed in 1831, by which time the vault lids were ill-fitting, warped by the sun and invariably partly open. The sextant had to chase curious schoolboys from the vault, where he often found them playing with the huge tankards and goblets, or buckling on the swords and pieces armour which lay on several coffins. The vault contained 30 coffins, many very much decayed, with inscriptions on approximately 13 of them which were still legible at that time. The sealing prevented any chance of sacrilegious theft. It had been known for limbs of martyred incumbents to be stolen for private worship, along with other religious relics.

The letter went on to describe the lineage of the other family, and David, on reading it, saw the connection with his fiance, Alison.

'The second coat of arms belongs to the Germaine line, now linked to the Germaine-Smythe family of Dorset.

Germaine

The Germaine family rose to prominence during the Restoration of King Charles, when the estates confiscated from the Harcourte family were reinstated under the ownership of Sir Edmund Germaine, a cousin of Lady Isobel Harcourte, the wife of James, the seventh Earl. This Lady (a Germaine by birth) lived under his protection until her death in 1665. The Germaines flourished as Lesser Gentry during the 18th and 19th centuries, with interests in the East India Company and sugar plantations in the West Indies. The fortunes of the family declined after the First World War, with the loss of Empire, and a disastrous venture into the Stock Market in the 1920's. The family line now rests with a minor branch connected to the Dorsetshire Germaine-Smythes.'

The editor ended his letter with the usual niceties and hoped that the information was helpful and satisfied David's enquiry.

However, he added a postscript which contained certain information of a most alarming nature.

'I ought to mention that in researching my own family history and its links with St. Paul's Church I came across a very singular anecdote concerning the Harcourte Vault which is not included in the official records of the church. I discovered it in the personal papers of a Sextant of the time, which tells of a macabre incident concerning this vault.

It seems that the Sextant's wife had an understanding with a noble Lady (the name was never disclosed) which allowed her to enter the church at any time she thought proper, whether it be day or night. This Lady was always dressed in the black garments and veil associated with deep mourning and during one visit at the dead of night she attracted the interest of an inebriated labourer who was returning home,

271

via the churchyard, after an evening in the local alehouse.

He saw the lady in mourning enter the church and watched her movements from a window in the western aisle. He saw her descend into the Harcourte vault and some time later she reappeared, and the labourer was shocked to see that she carried a withered arm and hand, which she concealed beneath her garments. He staggered to the Sextant's cottage and told him what he had just seen. However, the tale was so garbled and he was so drunk that his story was dismissed out of hand.'

The description of this suspicious night visitor sent a shiver down David's spine. It could well have been that of the woman in his box room. David showed the letter to his wife.

"Did you know you were related to a famous old family?"

"Really — it's news to me," replied Alison, reading the letter. She looked up. "That seems to be an interesting hobby."

"Hobby . . . ?"

"Yes," she answered. "Tracing your ancestors — compiling a family tree."

"Well, in your case it would be a hobby and a half, if this information is anything to go by," David remarked. "I bet it would take years to complete."

"Oh, I wouldn't mind that," declared Alison. "Once the house is sorted out I could make a start on those old books and family journals belonging to Aunt Victoria."

"Well, just as long as you remember there is still a lot to be done around the place," said David.

"Don't worry about that," Alison retorted. "We'll soon have it completed — and then you can help me with research, if you like."

David agreed — and it was fortunate that he did.

* * *

Some months later, while helping his wife to trace the Germaine line he discovered the origin of the pocket davenport and a clue which could explain the supernatural visitations surrounding it.

This important discovery was aided by the ghost of the veiled Lady herself.

Thankfully, since that daunting encounter just before his marriage, David had managed to avoid another face to face confrontation with the mournful apparition, much to his relief and mental well-being. However, there were still times when her spirit returned to pay a ghostly visit. Occasionally David would find the side drawer of the davenport open, and the screen of the laptop illuminated without a power source. She left no email messages, but on these occasions, when the temperature in the room suddenly dropped, he felt her presence in the shadows beside the davenport. Nevertheless it had to be said that the atmosphere was no longer oppressive, almost as if his marriage to Alison had, in some way, placated the embittered spirit.

And then one evening, whilst combing though some of Alison's family documents, he dropped off to sleep in the armchair.

He awoke late in the night, shivering with cold — to see the spectral Lady in black once again, standing beside the table.

She was studying the many books and family papers spread out on the table top, and one book in particular caught her eye. Her hand reached out to touch it, her fingers stroking its cover, and in so doing the apparition sighed and gradually faded away.

David, on recovering his composure, went over to the table and picked up the book in question. It was an old leather-bound tome, worn and dog-eared, and he discerned its ownership from a faded inscription on the inside cover.

'To my beloved Isobel
Omnia vincit amor'

He remembered the christian name of Isobel from the editor's letter — and the Latin inscription on the secret altar in the davenport. Beneath the inscription he perceived some verses from the bible in another hand. He immediately recognized the spiky handwriting and the religious texts. He had seen them before — *on his laptop.*

David was now convinced that he held the personal bible of Lady Isobel Harcourte, the ghost in mourning, in his hand.

Shortly after this development Alison found the final clue to the mystery of the writing desk. In a 1653 Land Commissioner's Inventory of furniture and household items from the Harcourte estates sequestered after the Civil War, she found a brief record of a particular piece which matched the pocket davenport.

The Harcourte Desk

A writing desk, newly constructed in oak, with side drawers for manuscripts, top-mounted box receptacle for candle illumination and internal pocket drawers for inks and sundries. The unique design follows an individual pattern and plan by Isobel, the wife of the seventh Earl, who required a portable device of a compact nature for ease of transport and storage.

"So the davenport was made especially for Lady Harcourte — from her own design," noted David. He thought about it for a moment, and turned to Alison. "But don't you think it is rather odd that there is no mention of the concealed altar?"

"Obviously whoever made the inventory at the time didn't know about its secret purpose," replied Alison. "You have to bear in mind that Lady Isobel was a staunch Catholic, and her husband lost his life for supporting the losing side. No wonder she wanted to keep the altar a closely guarded secret."

Some weeks later Alison found another reason why the Lady in mourning wished to keep the existence of her personal shrine from prying eyes.

She found it in the personal papers belonging to the daughter of Sir Edmund Germaine.

'Lady Isobel has come to live with us and Father instructed us to be kind to her. It is very difficult to do this. She is very troubled and hates Oliver Cromwell and his moralizing Major Generals, for she blames him for her loss and prays secretly for his downfall day and night. The Lady heaps curses upon his head and recites the most grievous verses from her bible as was scarce ever heard of. She is indeed a strange person, with dress and habits to match her pitiful disposition. She is permanently in mourning for her departed husband and has taken to visiting his place of rest in our church at all hours of day and night. It pained Father greatly to witness such unnatural behaviour. Then suddenly Lady Isobel ceased this strange practice and is now content to pass the greater part of her days in her rooms in the West Wing, much to the relief of my dear father. The servants tell me she spends most of her time at her new writing table made to her own pattern by an old Harcourte retainer.'

It all became clear to David.

The macabre incident in the church and the specially designed writing desk, with its sealed compartment, had one thing in common — the tormented and vengeful Lady. Considering this latest evidence David firmly believed he knew the resting place of the sacrilegious theft.

The mummified arm and hand from a long martyred Earl, sacred objects of worship and devotion, now resided in the secret compartment in his pocket davenport, Lady Isobel's "new writing table".

And so this unique piece of furniture had been passed down from one generation of the family to the next, and the hauntings had only begun when this age-old practice was in danger of being curtailed.

However, Aunt Victoria's decision to put an ad in the paper and then sell the Harcourte Desk to David remained a mystery.

"*Why me?*"

Leaving aside the fact that an alarm clock, a cheese sandwich and a discarded newspaper has been instrumental in bringing Alison and David together, there was another incredible explanation to account for Aunt Victoria's uncharacteristic behaviour.

"*Are you married? Are you an antique dealer? You did say you were unmarried?*"

David could now see a reason for these searching questions. Victoria wished her niece to continue the stewardship of the Harcourte altar, and to marry a suitable person, observing "*that seems to be a nice profession — a nice steady job*" when David explained his work to her. Close to death, with her niece and only surviving relative still unmarried, she dreaded the thought of her treasured writing desk falling into the hands of a dealer. So she used the sacred pocket davenport as bait to attract the right partner for this purpose — hence the third degree.

David could only assume that the old lady decided he fitted that bill and acted accordingly. Alison's aunt foresaw the union of her niece and David, and had been happy to part with the writing desk so cheaply. The sum was unimportant, just so long as the Harcourte Desk stayed in the family.

David was convinced that the hauntings would now stop. He was right.

At last the troublesome side drawer remained firmly closed and the laptop screen disclosed no further acrimonious e-mails. As a matter of interest David had the Latin inscriptions in the bible and davenport translated.

"Omnia vincit amor — Love conquers all".

This tender sentiment, expressed by the Earl of Harcourte to his wife centuries earlier, could equally reflect David's present matrimonial situation. The union was a happy one and an atmosphere of tranquillity and contentment pervaded the old house.

However, the same could not be said of the second part of the inscription.

"Dis aliter visum — Heaven thought otherwise"

In this case a small, dark cloud has recently appeared on the supernatural horizon to cast a shadow over his good fortune.

It appeared in second letter from the editor of County Treasures.

'Dear Mr. Thorneton,

I thought you would like to know of an interesting piece of information which I came across during my researches into my own family history.

I discovered that one of my ancestors was distantly related to the Ashursts from Beacon Fell. A certain Colonel Ashurst was a prominent Parliamentarian in the Civil War and also one of the military judges who sanctioned the execution of the seventh Earl of Harcourte at Alton.

You will remember that particular Earl from my previous letter to you last year.

Anyway, I discovered that the Colonel married in 1637, and this is the part which I am sure will interest you. He married a Thorneton — Elizabeth Thorneton — and she could very well be part of your own family line.'

It was shocking disclosure.

If this turned out to be true, then David would be in a right old pickle.

He dreaded the supernatural fury this discovery would unleash if ever the vengeful Harcourte ghost discovered that a member of his ancestral line had been responsible for the death of her beloved husband.

His first course of action was clear.

Alison's hobby was abruptly curtailed, just in case his enthusiastic wife uncovered any similar damaging evidence — and Lady Isobel's writing table was immediately consigned to the attic.

There it now lies, for the moment thankfully dormant under a heavy dust sheet, isolated from the outside world and that 'all-seeing eye', the pervasive internet.

Finally, bearing in mind the well-known adage "if you can't beat them, join them", David Thorneton has prudently decided to change his surname — to Harcourte.

MARSHSIDE

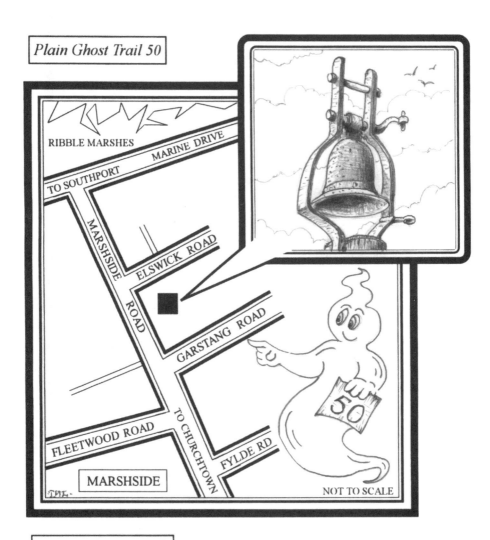

Plain Ghost Trail 50

RIBBLE MARSHES

MARINE DRIVE

TO SOUTHPORT

MARSHSIDE ROAD

ELSWICK ROAD

GARSTANG ROAD

FLEETWOOD ROAD

TO CHURCHTOWN

FYLDE RD

MARSHSIDE

NOT TO SCALE

50

INSET *The Fog Bell*

THE GHOST WALK

A week before the town's annual Flower Show the following poster appeared on the 'Entertainment and Leisure' notice board in the foyer of Sutton's Original Hotel.

WE DARE YOU!

Come along and join the Marshbank Handbell Ringers on a Ghost Walk. This scary event will take place on Friday the 13th (weather permitting) and prospective Ghost Hunters are asked to assemble outside the 'Grand Duke', Marshbank at 8.30 in the evening. Tickets for this daunting experience can be obtained from reception in the hotel or from Mary Bentley, the society secretary (telephone 55623168 evenings). Tickets are £5 for adults and £2.50 for children, and the proceeds will go to the Handbell Refurbishment Fund. Suitable refreshments will be provided for those who remain sane at the end of this unique ghost hunt.

Faye spotted this provocative and colourful poster as she waited for the rest of her family in the hotel foyer. The Marsdens had just arrived, parking in a space reserved for hotel guests, and the excited child had dashed on ahead of her parents, leaving them to struggle with suitcases and all the paraphernalia associated with a seaside holiday. And there in the foyer, as she waited impatiently for her father and mother, she glanced up at this 'daring' poster, and a drawing of a cheeky ghost above the wording caught her eye.

"Can we go and chase ghosts?!" she cried, pointing to the poster.

A perspiring Alan Marsden, struggling with a couple of heavy suitcases, halted at the top the imposing marble steps, breathless and somewhat fatigued.

"Not now, Faye," he replied irritably. It had been a long drive over the Pennines, what with holiday traffic hold-ups on the motorway, and an excited, fidgety child in the back of the car to contend with.

"Don't bother your Daddy now, love," Faye's mother scolded her, ushering Faye through the revolving door. "You'll just have to wait and see. So be a good girl and help mummy with the bags."

However, as usual the little girl did get her way.

On the evening of Friday the 13th Faye set off to "chase ghosts" — but what she eventually saw did not resemble the 'cheeky spook' on the colourful poster in any shape or form.

* * *

The Marsdens had come to the seaside town especially for the prestigious Annual Flower Show. In Jennifer Marsden's case it was the floral displays and wonderful variety of blooms which inspired enthusiasm, while her husband's passion was firmly rooted in vegetables and garden machinery. On the other hand their offspring was devoted to sand, sea water and vigorous activities involving bucket and spade. A conflict of interests inevitably arose over the choice of activities and a compromise was eventually reached to everyone's satisfaction.

Faye got her way, the "dare" was accepted, and the family duly arrived outside the 'Grand Duke' on the evening of Friday the 13th to join a motley bunch of ghost hunters, young and old.

At eight thirty sharp a bearded gentleman dressed in a monk's cowl and large leather sandals stepped from the door of the public bar.

"Is he — is he a ghost?" whispered Faye nervously, tightly clutching her mother's hand.

"No, love," Jennifer Marsden laughed, reassuring her timorous daughter. "But I think he is going to tell you all about ghosts." She was right.

As soon as the monk had collected the tickets from each member of the ghost party, he gave a brief summary of the Walk, explaining that they would follow a prescribed trail, stopping at selected points along the way. He also had an important message for the younger ghost walkers in the party.

"It is particularly important that you stay with your parents at all times," he emphasized, "and on no account stray away from the main party."

He distributed candle lanterns to all the children, a bonus much appreciated by parents and children alike, and then, with a mournful "Come, fellow ghost hunters, let us away — and keep your eyes peeled, kids" the cowled figure set off in the gathering gloom, followed by a line of bobbing, glowing lanterns.

He eventually halted in front of a pair of imposing wrought iron gates, the entrance to a wooded drive which curved away into the darkness. A painted sign on the stone pillar disclosed the name "Bankfield Hall".

At this moment a child screamed and pointed towards the trees. "A ghost — it's a ghost — look, it's a ghost!"

Everyone turned to look and a universal gasp of astonishment arose from the crowd. Out of the darkness there emerged a white, diaphanous shape with arms outstretched, weaving about in truly ghostly fashion. The "ghost" uttered a high-pitched screech.

"Whooo — whooo — eeee . . . ."

It was a spectacular and frightening appearance, and little Faye immediately sheltered behind her mother and grabbed her father's hand, absolutely terrified at the sight and sound of this figure.

The ghost pulled up in front of the group with a final "whooo — eee", and the monk introduced her as "ye White Lady, sorrowful ghost of Bankfield Hall".

There, in the glow of candle lanterns, the sad White Lady began to recount her tale of woe and how she had haunted the Hall for hundreds of years. By this time Faye had regained her courage and composure, peeping out to gaze in awe at the pallid 'apparition' standing before her.

"She must be very hungry after all that time, mustn't she, Mummy?" she whispered. "Would she like a sausage roll and tomato sauce?"

"Oh, I don't think so," chuckled her mother, hugging her concerned daughter. "Ghosts don't eat sausage rolls."

The ghost ended her tale and weaved away, disappearing into the darkness, her parting wail of doom and gloom echoing through the wood.

It had to be said that everyone was impressed by the novel and, in the minds of the younger children, frightening presentation. Each stage of the Ghost Walk followed a similar pattern, with such ghostly characters as "owd Shrimper Sam, ye drowned fisherman" and "ye Smuggler's Wife, yon abandoned woman o'the marshes" eerily appearing from various locations to relate their tales of misfortune.

The Ghost Walk eventually came to an end beside the dilapidated gates of a long disused building, one with a distinctive architectural structure. This rather unusual feature rose some ten feet or more from the apex of the roof, and consisted of a vertical wooden pole and a large bell. The bell hung from a substantial metal bracket fixed to the top of this slender column. A weathered board on the brick wall by the entrance disclosed the purpose of the decaying edifice and the reason for this incongruous structure.

<u>Marshbank Weather Station</u>
(Re-sited and rebuilt in 1896)
This fog bell was erected in 1896 with the object of preventing a similar disaster to that which occurred when 7 fishermen were drowned off the coast while fishing.

The station was especially built to house meteorological instruments designed to record weather conditions along the coast and river estuary. Now it was just an empty shell, landlocked in the middle of a modern housing estate, with its silent fog bell, perched high above missing roof slates and crumbling brickwork, keeping a watchful eye over the bustling neighbourhood.

On another board, nailed to the sealed door, the words "*Closed - out of commission*" disclosed the current status of this old building.

Here, in front of this derelict coastal station, the bell-ringers assembled for an impromptu recital, partly to thank those who had attended the 'scary' fund raising event and partly to showcase their own expertise on the musical complexities of the handbell.

The ringers set to with gusto, bathed in the glow of soft candle light. The chimes of a traditional song floated through the still evening air, as the sonorous bass and the high treble mingled together in harmonious accord. It was indeed a most homely and relaxed atmosphere, one to end a perfect evening of fun and games.

However, this ambience of warmth and pleasure was about to change — *drastically*.

At this precise moment something else floated through the air, stifling these melodious chimes and enveloping ghost hunter and bell-ringer alike in a cold vaporous blanket.

A dense sea fog swirled in from the estuary, swift and silent, cutting visibility to a minimum and causing confusion to all.

And at this point Faye's ghost walk really began in earnest.

* * *

Faye was well and truly lost.

The distressed child sobbed quietly, tired out and shivering with cold — and furthermore, she was standing ankle deep in slowly rising sea water.

When the dense silent fog rolled over the startled ghost walkers, momentarily turning individuals into vague indistinguishable shapes, Faye lost sight of her parents. In those few vital seconds she became completely disorientated — and so the confused little girl joined two other hazy figures by mistake.

"Mummy! — Daddy! — wait for me!" the anxious child cried, as the figures moved off into the dense clinging mass.

They paid no heed to her anxious cries and continued on their way. However hard she tried to catch up with them, they always remained just out of reach.

Faye followed these inconsiderate people, stumbling along with only the faint glow of her lantern to light the way, on and on into the darkness, away from the rest of the party.

Soon the hard surface of the road gave way to a rough, uneven track and then to soft sand and sea grass. Without knowing it the unfortunate girl had strayed out onto the dangerous marshes.

Then, at last, these inconsiderate people halted and Faye finally caught up with them — and at this point she realized her mistake.

The figures in the swirling fog were not her parents.

The soft glow of the lantern revealed two men in thick over-coats, mufflers and caps pulled down over their ears. Their legs were encased in large waders and they carried copious canvas bags and guns slung over their shoulders. They were obviously hunters of some sort — but not of ghosts.

"Where is my Mummy!?" cried Faye.

The hunters ignored her — as if she wasn't there.

"Please — please tell me," she cried again. "Where is my Mummy?"

Again there was no response.

Then Faye noticed something very strange and disturbing about these two men. From their perplexed expressions and gestures it would seem that they too were in the same boat — totally lost. Faye could plainly see the despair on their faces.

She tried again.

"Please — oh please tell me where . . . .?"

But even as she spoke, the ghostly figures began to melt away before her eyes, fading into the swirls of vaporous mist. This was a Ghost Walk for real, and the itinerary, so carefully planned by the Marshbank Bell-ringers, certainly did not include anything like this.

From this moment on, Faye's walk went from bad to worse. The horrified girl found herself ankle-deep in freezing water.

The tide was rising, and soon the fogbound marshes would be totally immersed in another of Nature's destructive elements — cold, numbing sea water.

Her ghost walk had now entered a dangerous and frightening phase, and it was most unlikely that she would ever see her 'mummy' and 'daddy' again.

The candle in her lantern spluttered, a sure indication that her one and only comfort in this dismal place would soon be gone.

And at that moment a dark shape emerged from the dense wall of mist — to stumble and fall with a huge splash at her feet.

Little Faye uttered a shocked gasp at this sudden and terrifying manifestation.

The shape lay in the water, motionless — and then it slowly and painfully rose to its feet.

Faye screamed and recoiled from the dripping figure now towering over her.

She beheld a bearded man in yellow oilskins, his face and straggling hair caked in sea salt, and his body entwined in long strands of seaweed. Around his chest he wore a battered, cork life-jacket, of the type used by sailors in earlier times, and his water-proofed garments were ripped and torn. This seafaring man had also lost one of his sea boots — and now seemed on the verge of total collapse.

"Have you seen my Mummy and Daddy?" Faye sobbed. "I can't find them anywhere."

The swaying figure looked down on the little girl with a mixture of sadness and pity.

"Please can you take me to them?" she begged.

The seaman slowly nodded and held out his hand.

"Oh thank you," she cried out in gratitude, reaching up to grasp it, "— thank you . . . ."

Her tiny hand passed right through his.

The sobbing child was left clutching thin air as the apparition faded away into the overpowering fog, leaving her shaking with fear and consternation.

The rising water had now reached Faye's knees and she was filled with panic and despair.

"Mummy — Daddy," she whimpered. "Oh, Mummy, where are you?"

And at that very moment, somewhere out there in the silent fog, a distant bell tolled in answer to her pathetic plea, a faint but gratifying reply.

It also heralded another welcoming sound — the splish, splash, splish of someone approaching through the rising tide, drawing ever closer to the distressed girl.

Rescue was on hand.

"Is that you, Mummy?" Faye cried out, her spirits rising. "Is that you . . . .?"

Out of the darkness, splashing through the water into the flickering candle light, there appeared the very last thing she expected to see.

Into view trotted a black labrador dog. It halted before her, sniffed the air and wagged its tail. This friendly creature, its coat streaked with mud and sand, examined the child with curious eyes.

"Hello, doggy," Faye greeted this unexpected traveller. "Are you lost as well?"

The labrador dog barked and shook its coat, showering droplets of sea water and particles of mud in every direction. It barked again and wagged its tail, and then proceeded to amble off into the fog, leaving the despondent child alone.

"Come back," she sobbed. "Please don't leave me — please don't leave . . . ."

And then Faye breathed a sigh of relief — and wiped the tears from her eyes.

Out of the darkness and back into the light ambled the labrador. *The friendly wanderer had returned.*

It uttered a sharp bark and wagged its tail. The dog paused for a moment and then backed away, wagging its tail and barking furiously, waiting for Faye's response. She interpreted these actions as a canine "come with me", and sensed that the dog wanted her to follow it. The trusting child set off through the deepening water, trailing behind her new-found companion, her lantern lighting its wagging, mud-caked tail.

The labrador patiently ambled on, travelling at her pace, and before long Faye found the water becoming shallower at each step and the muffled sound of the distant bell growing louder by the minute. Soon she felt dry land and soft sand underfoot.

Faye had escaped the cold embrace of the incoming tide and treacherous grasp of the marshes, thanks to her canine Samaritan and the bell. But her ordeal was not over yet. The tired child was now on the point of collapse and still had not escaped the clutches of the fog.

Moments later the lantern candle flickered and spluttered and the comforting glow was extinguished in an instant, leaving her in total darkness.

The light deserted her — but not her faithful companion.

In the darkness she felt a wet nose touch her hand and a soggy tail brush against her leg — and all the while the distant bell tolled its message of hope.

* * *

In the meantime Faye's mother and father were frantic with worry.

In the confusion immediately following the onslaught of the

dense sea fog Jennifer Marsden had buttoned up her coat — and, in doing so, inadvertently let go Faye's hand.

When she reached down to Faye she found her daughter gone. *There was no sign of the child.*

"Faye — Faye, where are you!?" she called out, her anxious cries stifled by the oppressive fog. "Faye . . . ."

However, it soon became apparent that the little girl had wandered off into the fog, and the situation was looking quite serious. By this time most of the ghost walkers had dispersed, heading for the warmth and refreshments in the village hall, but a few remaining bell-ringers and friends quickly organized search parties which spread out through the fogbound streets.

This search proved futile.

After an hour of patiently combing the area Faye still had not been found. By now it was well after midnight, and fear and panic had set in.

Had she been abducted or had a serious accident?

It all looked very black indeed.

Suddenly the thick fog began to clear, melting away as silently and swiftly as it had arrived, and soon the insidious vapour had completely vanished, leaving a rising moon and starry sky in its wake.

Then came the breakthrough.

The heartwarming message crackled on the police radio.

"Mrs. Marsden," the officer shouted from the patrol car. "Good news — your daughter has been found."

"Oh, thank heavens," Jennifer cried with relief. "Is Faye alright — where is she?"

"She's fine — and at the local station," he replied. "A motorist has just brought her in."

Jennifer greeted her husband with the glad tidings.

"Faye has been found, Alan," she told him. "She's at the police station."

The search was immediately called off and the Marsdens were taken to be reunited with their daughter. Tearful scenes followed, and the relief and delight on seeing Faye safe and sound can be imagined — but one aspect of this emotional reunion surprised her parents.

The little girl seemed remarkably unfazed by her ordeal. She wasn't in a state of shock or nervous exhaustion, as one would normally expect in such cases.

It was immediately apparent that Faye's main concern was "my muddy friend", as she describe the labrador dog. That was all she could talk about, and she refused to answer any questions on the subject of her ghost walk-about and her experience on the fogbound marshes. The welfare of the labrador was uppermost in her mind.

"Where is he, Mummy," she constantly inquired, "— where is my dog — is he still lost — can Daddy find him for me?"

Her parents were totally bemused by Faye's behaviour, and put it down to her over-active imagination and the strain of her ordeal. A policewoman came over with tea and biscuits.

"She is a very lucky girl," the officer remarked. "The driver nearly ran over her on the coast road."

"How did she get to the coast road?"

"Well, it's something of a mystery at the moment," answered the policewoman. "But that's where the driver said he picked her up. Unfortunately he wasn't able to catch your dog. It went off into the fog."

Alan and Jennifer looked at the policeman in amazement.

"There must be some mistake," gasped Jennifer. "We haven't got a dog."

Faye, of course, was in complete disagreement.

* * *

The next morning the secretary of the Marshbank Bell-ringers called at the hotel to see the little girl and her family. Mary Bentley was worried that the initial success of the unique fund-raising event could be marred by adverse publicity surrounding Faye's unfortunate experience.

Happily everything had turned out extremely well, and she found the family happy and relaxed. However, Faye immediately began to ask after her muddy companion.

Had the secretary found her dog — where was it — was it very hungry — when could she see it — and so forth.

The ghostly figures she encountered on the tide-covered marshes were completely forgotten for the moment, and she made no mention of them, concentrating on finding her good Samaritan.

"I'm sorry I can't help you, dear," she told the disappointed child. She turned to Faye's mother.

"It was so unfortunate the way the walk ended. The forecast was excellent for the weekend, so we had no idea the weather would turn out like that," she told Jennifer. "Until that moment it had been absolutely perfect, and the walk had gone better than we thought. Well — you know the rest."

"Yes, it was a bit uncanny," replied Alan Marsden, "the way that dense fog came in so quickly. It surprised us all."

"Yes, as I mentioned, it was completely unexpected," answered Mary Bentley.

"Does it happen often?"

"Oh dear no — well — not that type of fog, anyway. But when it does . . . ." She paused. Something was obviously playing on her mind. "When it does — then some would say that would be the best time to see ghosts."

"Ah, you mean the real White Lady and Shrimper Sam?" Jennifer laughed.

"Oh no," replied Mary Bentley in a serious tone. "Those ghosts come from local folklore and are well known. We based our Ghost Walk on them and our actors told their stories. But in recent times there have been other incidents — or may be sightings would be a better word — which do not appear in local folklore . . . ."

She paused again, deep in thought. "By any chance did Faye hear a bell — a fog bell — last night?"

"A fog bell?" the Marsden's replied. "No, I don't think so — and we didn't either."

"Anyway, the bell on that old weather station no longer works," added Alan Marsden. "It said so on a notice on the door."

They called Faye and asked her about the bell.

"Oh, yes — I did," the little girl answered. "Yes, there was a nice bell in that nasty fog." Then she added another observation which visibly shook the concerned secretary. "Yes — it was much nicer than those horrible men. They didn't take any notice of me — just left me alone without my Mummy and Daddy."

It was indeed a shocking revelation.

This was the first time her parents had heard of it. They asked Faye to describe the "horrible men" and then the true nature of her ordeal became clear. They sent her out to play and turned to Mary Bentley.

"Well — can you make any sense of all that?" they asked.

Mary Bentley nodded. "Yes, I think I can," she murmured.

"So — do you think she is making it all up?"

"Oh, no — no — certainly not."

"What makes you so sure?" asked Jennifer, knowing her daughter's fertile and vivid imagination.

"The dog . . . ."

"You mean that imaginary dog she keeps going on about?"

"I know she didn't imagine it," replied the secretary, "and neither did the driver who picked her up. The dog he saw in the fog is the proof of her experience — and I'll tell you why."

She began her explanation with a story her grandfather told to her when she was about Faye's age.

"My grandfather was a crusty old beggar, and he loved fishing," she began. "Sometimes he would fish off the end of the pier, and at other times he would go out onto the sands with his net to catch shrimps or gather cockles."

"Like Shrimper Sam?" Alan remarked, recalling the Ghost Walk.

"Yes, you could say that — but I can assure you my grandfather doesn't come back to haunt me," chuckled Mary Bentley. "Anyway, he would shrimp in the season, setting off early to catch the tide — and it was on one of these trips that something happened which had a lasting effect on him. Like little Faye, he too met a ghost."

She went on to retell his story.

Her grandfather had spent a fruitful morning with his shrimping net, and set out across the sands, heading for his home in Marshbank with a full basket of shrimps. Then suddenly and swiftly a dense fog rolled in from the sea, blanking out the sun and enveloping him in a cold, impenetrable mist. He could see no further than the end of his arm and he totally lost his bearings. It was a very dangerous position to be in, especially with a rising tide and treacherous marsh close by. He could easily fall into one of the numerous deep gullies which criss-crossed this area of the estuary, or stumble into quicksands, which had been known to swallow up people and horses.

The authority responsible for coastal navigation safety had realized that this type of freak weather condition was bad news for fishermen out on the marshes or shrimping boats in the estuary. When several fishermen were drowned they decided to erect a fog bell on the roof of a small weather station in nearby Marshbank. Time and again its comforting tones, cutting through these dense and oppressive fogs, had guided stranded fishermen to safety and warned shrimping boats of shallow waters ahead.

Now this bell came to his rescue.

He was about to set off towards its welcoming sound when he came face to face with a terrifying figure, stumbling unsteadily out of the dense mist. Being a local fisherman himself, and from an old established family in the area, her grandfather knew who this man was — and how he came to be there.

He also knew for a fact that this man was a ghost.

Before him swayed the coxswain of the Eliza Jane, the town lifeboat wrecked on these sands some fifty or so years ago. As the ghostly coxswain reached out to him the fog closed in, swirling round this ghastly figure, and in an instant the apparition was gone.

"The Eliza Jane sank with the loss of all her crew bar one — the coxswain," Mary explained. "He was washed ashore near Marshbank, but later died from his ordeal. As you can imagine, this tragedy left a terrible mark on the local community. Most of the lifeboat crew came from the village, and many families were left destitute. You can read about it in the Botanical Museum in the town. There's a special exhibition devoted to the tragedy in one of the rooms."

"So Faye didn't make it up after all — she actually saw the coxswain's ghost?"

"I believe so," Mary answered. "He is only seen when certain freak weather conditions occur, in this case a rising tide and dense sea fog — and that is when those lost on the marshes hear the bell on the disused weather station."

The Marsdens were silent for a minute or so, taking in this unusual story.

Eventually Jennifer spoke.

"But what about the two men our daughter followed in the fog — and the dog. Don't tell me you think they were ghosts as well?"

"Hmmm — that is a difficult one to answer," Mary Bentley nodded thoughtfully. "As far as I know, there has never been a sighting of anyone like that up to now — but . . . ."

She pondered for a moment.

"In answer to your question all I can say is that — that some years ago two hunters foolishly went out onto the marshes to shoot wild duck without properly checking tide and weather conditions. The fog came down — and unfortunately they didn't make it back. They were drowned. Their bodies were found in the deep gullies out on the estuary . . . ."

She paused. "And this is where I believe Faye's story . . . . ."

The secretary of the Marshbank Bell-ringers picked up her coat and stood up to leave.

"They had a dog with them — a black labrador — and this dog managed to find its way back to dry land," she added. "It came ashore at the very place where Faye was picked up by the motorist."

"What happened to the labrador?"

"Unfortunately, like the coxswain, the dog died some weeks later. Its body was found by the gate of the weather station and some say it just pined away for its master."

*　*　*

The Marsdens set off for home after breakfast the next morning. The Botanical Museum lay on their route out of town and so Alan Marsden, recalling Mary Bentley's tale of her grandfather's encounter and the Marshbank lifeboat tragedy, decided to call in and see the exhibition. As usual Faye raced on ahead of her parents, running and skipping up the steps into the museum.

The next instant she came racing out again.

"Mummy, mummy!" she cried in excitement. "Come quick. He's inside — that man is inside."

The Marsdens hurried into the building, followed reluctantly by their anxious daughter.

The main staircase ran directly from the museum entrance up to the first floor, and there, in pride of place at the top of the stairs, hung a large oil painting in a heavy ornate gilt frame.

The family gazed up at a life-size portrait of a bearded man dressed in oilskins and sou'wester. Although the details in the canvas were somewhat obscured by many coatings of varnish which had darkened over the years, it was just possible to make out that the seaman also wore a cork life-jacket and held a large oar in one hand and a circular life belt, bearing the name "Eliza Jane", in the other.

A brass plate fixed to the heavy gilt frame gave his name and nautical standing.

Richard Albert Mayhew
Coxswain of the Lifeboat Eliza Jane
lost in the great storm of 1886
'No greater love hath he than to lay down his life for his
fellow man'

"Are you sure he is the one you saw in the fog?" Jennifer asked her wide-eyed daughter.

"Yes, he is — he is," Faye declared, vigorously nodding her head, "but — but he wasn't wearing that funny hat and — and one of his big boots was missing." She took her mother's hand. "Can we go home now, Mummy. I don't like him — and he might come down and get me if we stay here much longer."

Her father laughed.

"Oh no he won't," he told his timid daughter, "— not while your Daddy is here."

"And he was a very brave and kind man, love," added her mother. "I'm sure he wanted to help you."

They all left the museum, Faye leading the way, and resumed their homeward journey.

However, the sombre portrait of the coxswain had unsettled the little girl, bringing back memories of her ghost walk on the marshes, and as soon as she got back into the car she began pestering her parents.

She went on and on all the way home, until they finally gave in, and a couple of days later the Marsdens had a new addition to the family — a black labrador puppy, which Faye immediately named "Muddy".

Considering her "*daunting*" ghost walk one would have expected Faye to be absolutely terrified of the dark and fearful of being left alone. But happily this was not the case, much to the relief of her parents.

"Oh no, I'm not frightened, Mummy," the little girl would declare. "Don't forget I have Muddy now — and he isn't afraid of silly old ghosts."

To reinforce this feeling of security Faye pestered her parents for another addition to the household. It was rather an unusual request from a child of her age, and it took the form of a beautiful carriage clock which struck the hour and quarters by means of soft bell chimes.

Faye calls it her "foggy clock".

It stands on the small dressing table in her bedroom, and is a great source of comfort to the child on stormy, window-rattling nights, when the wind howls round the chimneys and ghosts walk abroad.

However, Faye insists that Muddy, her devoted Labrador, sleeps in a basket at the bottom of her bed — *just in case* . . . .

APPENDIX

A brief note on the locations and area in which the *Tales* series of ghost stories are set, and the sources of inspiration from which these fictional tales are derived.

The boundaries of the West Lancashire Plain lie in that part of the county between Preston in the north, Ormskirk in the east and Liverpool in the south, with the Ribble Estuary and Mersey Bay limiting its western border and the Harrock, Ashurst and Parbold hills defining the eastern edge of the plain.

The area is, for the most part, very flat and fertile, a substantial portion of the land having been reclaimed from the sea and inland lakes in earlier times by means of earth embankments or sea walls, drainage levels and pumping stations.

This fertile plain has a rich historical and architectural heritage dating back to pre-Roman times, with discoveries of artifacts from Early Briton (eg. a primitive wooden dug-out canoe from Martin Mere, now in the Botanic Gardens Museum, Churchtown) and Viking settlements (eg. the God Stone in a wall in Little Crosby), while later periods in our history have left us with many fine churches (eg. Ormskirk Parish Church) and halls (eg. Rufford Old Hall).

The Black Death (eg. the Aughton angels), centuries of religious turmoil (eg. the secret chapel in Bickerstaffe Hall barn and the attic in Martin Hall) and the Civil War (eg. the celebrated siege of Lathom House) have also left their marks on the landscape, providing a valuable source of inspiration for many of the stories.

Sadly in recent years many of the locations which feature in the stories are now either derelict through neglect (eg. Bank Hall near Bretherton) or totally ruined (eg. Lydiate Hall), while others have disappeared from the landscape because of unfortunate accidents (eg. Walshe Hall and Burscough Hall destroyed by fire in1885 and 1998 respectively) or reclaimed for agriculture purposes (eg. Martin Mere, now a celebrated bird sanctuary).

Many other features have also disappeared from the area over the years. Peat's Light, the wooden 'lighthouse' erected at the mouth of the River Ribble (eg. the support piles finally destroyed around 1952) as a navigation aid for shipping using Preston docks, and railway tracks (eg. the defunct Cheshire Lines track bed near Altcar is now a popular cycle path and the Barton Branch a nature walk), sand dunes (eg. now vast housing estates in Ainsdale and Formby) and woodland have gone for ever.

Hopefully, in this fast and ever-changing world of ours, the stories in the *Tales* series will go some way to preserving the memory of this 'lost' heritage for those generations of readers to come.

ABOUT THE AUTHOR

T.M.Lally was educated at Hutton Grammar School, near Preston, and, on leaving school, joined the Audit Section of the Borough Treasurer's Department in Southport. On entering the Armoured Corps in 1956 he spent his National Service with the 9th Lancers Regiment in Germany and then went on to study at Didsbury Training College for Teachers, Manchester.

In 1962 he married and moved from Banks on the Ribble coast near Southport to Shirdley Hill (the old coastline in earlier times), near Ormskirk, and taught in Primary and Secondary schools in Tarleton, Formby and Southport, the area of West Lancashire in which many of the stories in the *Tales* series are set.

Besides his writing commitments and book research his other hobbies include painting, drawing and book illustration, camping and caravanning. His many musical interests include composition and arranging, and he is a member of a variety of musical organizations in the area, playing several musical instruments and possessing a wide musical experience ranging from jazz to orchestral, concert and brass band work.

He is a member of the Society of Authors and is currently retired.